Lynn accompanied Emily down to the blue deck. When they reached the bottom of the second staircase, they rounded the corner into the hallway and were surprised to find the door to number 8 ajar.

"Becky must've forgotten to close it," Lynn said.

Emily glanced at her, then went over to the door and pushed it open. Marcella Hemsley lay sprawled on the bed, her face bloated and purplish, and her arms and legs splayed. Her macramé belt was twisted tightly around her neck, and the compass lamp was lying beside her head, a smear of blood on its base. She looked like a huge rag doll that had been carelessly tossed on the bed.

Emily proceeded into the room and laid two fingers on Marcella's wrist.

"Oh, my God, is she—?" Lynn asked.

Emily released the wrist. "Yes. She's dead."

Lynn sputtered. "But—that's impossible! Becky said she just looked in here!"

"I know."

RANSOM AT SEA

FRED HUNTER

WORLDWIDE®

TORONTO • NEW YORK • LONDON
AMSTERDAM • PARIS • SYDNEY • HAMBURG
STOCKHOLM • ATHENS • TOKYO • MILAN
MADRID • WARSAW • BUDAPEST • AUCKLAND

RANSOM AT SEA

A Worldwide Mystery/April 2005

First published by St. Martin's Press LLC.

ISBN 0-373-26524-7

Printed in U.S.A.

For Tony

ONE

"CAN YOU TELL ME how to get to the sea?"

The startled shopper came to an abrupt halt, the red-and-white paper bag she had tucked under her left arm nearly slipping away. The stranger who had approached her so brusquely in the middle of her Michigan Avenue spree was young and wiry. His face was pale and glistening with sweat, and tiny pupils quivered slightly in his anxious, bloodshot eyes. His hands were clutched around a disreputable-looking brown paper parcel tied with a length of twine.

"The sea?" the shopper asked blankly as she clumsily tried to rearrange the errant bag, a difficult proposition since she was grasping shopping bags with both hands.

"The lake, I mean," the stranger said. "The lake. I'm supposed to be at the lake."

"Oh. Well, if you go that way," she replied, swinging the bag in her right hand toward the east, "you'll run right into it."

He glanced uncertainly in the direction indicated. "And... and from there, I'll be able to get to the pier?"

"Navy Pier? Yes. Once you reach Lake Shore Drive—which is two or three blocks away—you'll be able to see the pier and where to cross over to it."

"Okay...okay..."

He hurried away without so much as a thank-you. The woman secured the red-and-white bag under her arm to her satisfaction, hoisted her shopping bags, then started down the street. She clucked her tongue noisily, thinking of a time when Chicago was cleaner, safer, and not quite so overrun with tourists.

FROM HER VANTAGE POINT on a low slatted wooden bench, Emily Charters could take in a great deal of the activity going on around her. The structure at the heart of Navy Pier was basically a long hallway enclosed behind garagelike doors with neat rows of windows. The doors had been thrown open to admit the unexpectedly fine weather, and most of the souvenir carts had been rolled out onto the promenade so that the owners could enjoy the sunshine. Some of the booths were still closed, their proprietors preferring to put off the daily grind until the noon hour brought heavier traffic.

Emily mentally noted that the late risers were surely losing money. Though it was not quite eleven o'clock on Monday morning, the cement promenade that makes up the pier was already bustling with activity: young women, all clad in pastel shirts and shorts, aimlessly pushing strollers; youngsters (as Emily thought of them) with pierced body parts and frantic hairdos Rollerblading in clothes so baggy Emily wondered that they didn't catch in the wheels and send the skaters sprawling. A group of impossibly young sailors clad in white bell-bottomed uniforms noisily made their way past a booth selling paste trinkets and stopped at another boasting elephant ears and funnel cakes, apparently drawn there by the heavy scent of deep-fried batter. Once they'd made their purchases, they continued down the promenade, blocked from Emily's view by a long, rectangular kiosk whose front advertised events on the pier, and whose back was blank.

On the water to the left of Emily's bench was the *Ophelia,* a soaring white ship with lines of portholes that stared out like perfectly round, black pupils. The ship was so vast it looked more suited for a transatlantic crossing than the simple dinner cruises it maintained. To Emily's right was *Ophelia*'s sister ship, the *Orrington*. It was the former's equal in both size and purpose.

Directly in front of Emily, dwarfed by the twin titans, was the boat on which she would be traveling for the next four days: the *Genessee*. It was shaped like a garden trowel, broad in the aft with its forward tapering to a point. It had three levels: the top was devoted to the wheelhouse and a spacious observation/sundeck; the second was a dining room and lounge, and on the third were the staterooms. The decks were reached by twin staircases on the port and starboard sides, about two-thirds of the way to the aft. The boat had recently received a fresh coat of patriotic colors, the top level painted white, the second red, and on the third, resting in the water, a deep blue spotted with stars.

It's rather like an oversized toy boat, Emily thought.

In the elderly woman's eyes the *Genessee* was a much friendlier vessel than its bloated betters. It looked large enough to be comfortable but not so large as to be imposing. Unlike the ships that surrounded it, the *Genessee* seemed like a proper boat.

"You aren't too hot sitting in the sun, are you?" asked Lynn Francis.

"Not at all," she replied. "At my age the sun can only be a benefit."

Lynn pushed a stray strand of damp, tawny hair back from her forehead and laughed. "I don't know why I ask! You never complain about anything."

"There seems so little point," Emily said.

"Still, it's awfully hot for this early in June."

A man came out of the wheelhouse and onto the deck of the *Genessee*. He was tall and exceptionally straight backed, had dark brown hair with a rime of frost, and was dressed in a white shirt and white pants. He strode purposefully around the wheelhouse to the front of the boat and rested his hands lightly on the railing.

"From his bearing I would say he is the captain," Emily said. "Captain Farraday, I believe the brochure said."

Emily's attention was drawn by movement on the second

deck. At the foot of the stairs was a small nook with a window looking into the dining room, and a door beside it. A woman emerged from the door and lit lightly up the stairs to the top deck. She had long, dark hair gathered at the nape of her neck with a gold clip. She wore a white sundress cinched about her slender waist with a thin belt of black patent leather. Her face and arms were deeply bronzed by the sun and heavily freckled.

She paused at the top of the stairs and quickly scanned the deck, then crossed to the captain with an easy, fluid gait. When she reached him, she slipped her left arm through his right and rested her other hand on his forearm.

"I assume that's Mrs. Farraday," said Emily.

"She's at least ten years younger than him," Lynn said without inflection.

"At least." There was a twinkle in Emily's eye.

Lynn looked down at her seated friend and grinned. "I was making an observation, not a judgment."

"Oh, I know, my dear, I was thinking something quite different."

"What?"

"Look at them."

Lynn turned back to the couple. The captain remained as stiff as a mast, while his wife rested her head against his shoulder.

"What about them?" Lynn asked.

"They look so completely different, and yet…they look as if they belong together, don't you think?"

Lynn drew her lips to one side. "Yes, I do." Her attention was caught by an approaching figure. "Is that one of your friends?"

"I wouldn't say any of these people were my friends," Emily replied, craning her neck to the west. "They are acquaintances from church. I've rarely seen any of them outside of there, and even that has only been at church functions."

The lady in question was walking down the center of the promenade. She was thin and rather tall, but it was her bearing more than her height that made her seem statuesque. As she neared the two ladies, Lynn noticed that although the woman's face was narrow, with prominent cheekbones, the lower part of her face was running to jowls, so that she resembled a well-appointed, underfed basset hound. Her hair was conspicuously tinted ash blond and atop it was a sunhat with a broad brim decorated with a wide band the same color as her suit.

"Good morning, Claudia," Emily said.

"Emily," Claudia Trenton replied with a slight dip of her head. She continued past them and stopped three benches down. She had been followed closely by a teenaged boy with long, greasy blond hair with dark roots. He carried a large suitcase and a shoulder bag that she instructed him to place beside the bench. She dipped her hand into the jacket pocket of her beige jacket, extracted a five-dollar bill, and handed it to the boy.

"Thank you, young man," she said dismissively.

He took the bill, murmured something unintelligible, and stuffed it in the pocket of his tattered jeans as he ambled away. Miss Trenton lightly touched each of her bags, much in the way a diffident trainer would give a steadying pat to an animal that has had a potentially jarring experience, as if counting them to make sure they were both there, then arranged herself on the bench with elaborate care.

Emily and Lynn had watched the proceedings dispassionately. When Claudia had finally posed herself, Lynn shot Emily an amused glance.

"Do you know who all is coming on the cruise?" the young woman asked.

Emily shook her head. "No. The church arranged it for seniors. It was mentioned in the church program. All we had to do was call Miss Warren—she's the church secretary—to express an interest. I haven't really spoken with anyone else about it, so I have no idea who's coming. I suppose if I'd asked Miss Warren she would've told me, but it really didn't make a difference to me, and I think that would've been rather like being invited to a dinner and not accepting until you know who the rest of the guests will be.''

Lynn laughed. ''Always faultlessly polite.''

''Not faultlessly,'' Emily said with a broad smile.

Next to arrive was a gentleman with a high forehead and sharply receding hairline. What was left of his hair was light gray. He walked slowly, keeping his back erect, which seemed to take an effort. He looked quite out of place in a bright blue Hawaiian shirt that had huge white flowers printed on it. He wore this over a pair of navy blue dress pants. In his right hand he carried a large brown suitcase.

The man slowed to a stop about three yards from Emily and Lynn, who noticed for the first time that his dull blue eyes had the blank, confused look of the perpetually disoriented. His gaze traveled uncertainly from the women to the *Genessee* and back again. Then he hesitantly came up to them.

''Excuse me. Is this the ship for the seniors' cruise?''

''Yes,'' Emily replied.

''Oh. Thank you. I just wanted to make sure.'' He started to walk away, then stopped and turned back to her. ''I'm…my name is Jackson Brock. I believe I've seen you at church.''

''Yes. I'm Emily Charters.''

There was an awkward silence during which Brock appeared to be trying to think of something else to say. His mouth opened and closed once or twice, then finally he said, ''Yes. Well, thank you.'' He crossed to the bench between Emily and Claudia, laid down his case, and sat beside it.

''Shipboard romances never last,'' Lynn said quietly.

Emily smiled, absently straightening the white lace trim on her collar and muttering something that sounded like ''tut.''

''Don't fuss me, Becky!'' a voice rang out crossly. Emily and Lynn turned to see two women approaching. The elder was a large woman in a shapeless floral print dress in various shades of tan, brown, and yellow. Her face was puffed from exertion and her cheeks flushed. Although her dark gray hair was cut fairly short, it fanned out from her head in an alarming fashion. She looked the way Lynn had always imagined a Valkyrie would, lacking only a horned helmet and spear to complete the picture.

The other woman looked to be in her late thirties. She had long auburn hair that framed an oval face. Her eyes were brown and noticeably sad, and there were anxious lines at the corners of her mouth.

"I'm not fussing," the young woman said lightly. "I didn't want you to trip. There was a crack in the walk. I didn't think you saw it."

"Nothing wrong with my eyes!" the old woman replied. There was an edge to her tone, as if she had sensed an implied accusation.

When they reached Emily and Lynn, the young woman said, "Excuse me. Would you mind if my aunt sat with you?"

"Not at all," Emily said. She shifted farther to one side of the bench, though there was already plenty of room.

"Thank you," the old woman said as she lowered herself onto the seat.

"You are Marcella Hemsley, aren't you?" Emily asked.

"That's me."

"And who is this nice young woman?"

Miss Hemsley started to reply, then stopped and looked up at her companion.

"I'm Rebecca Bremmer," she said hurriedly. "Her niece."

"Let me introduce Lynn Francis," Emily said. "She's being kind enough to accompany me on the cruise."

"Oh," said Rebecca, shooting a glance at Lynn that looked almost relieved.

"Will you be accompanying your aunt?" Emily asked.

"Yes. Yes, I thought it best."

Miss Hemsley sat staring straight ahead. Her mouth had hardened into a thin line, her lips all but disappearing, but she said nothing. It was apparent that she either didn't relish the company or didn't appreciate the implication that it was needed.

Lynn was at a loss as to how to bridge the awkward gap in the conversation that followed, but the moment was rescued by Emily.

"Ah! Here come the Millers."

Lynn turned and saw the approaching pair. The Millers were one of those couples who, after decades of living together, had come to resemble each other to the point of blood relations. The man's head was the shape of a pie plate and crested with hair so thin that from a distance it couldn't be seen at all. He was stocky but not fat, and his nose skewed very slightly to the left. An expensive-looking camera dangled from a large black strap around his neck. The wife was the same size, shape, and coloring as the husband, and though she had shoulder-length hair, it too was thinning markedly. Their incautious bearing was identical, making them appear as if they might at any moment make contact in the area of the hips and be sent careening way from each other like human bumper cars. They each carried matching suitcases and shoulder bags.

"Good morning, Emily," the man said amiably. "Looks like a good day for it, doesn't it?"

"Good morning. Lynn, this is Martin and Laura Miller. Martin, Laura, my friend Lynn Francis."

"How do you do?" said Martin, jutting a paw at the young woman.

"I'm pleased to meet you," Lynn said, shaking his hand and then his wife's.

"Take a seat over there, why don't you, Laura?" He gestured toward the bench where Brock was sitting.

"Okay, sweetie," Laura replied. The two of them crossed to the middle bench, dropped their bags to the ground and sat heavily on the bench. They noisily greeted Mr. Brock, whom they appeared to know in passing. Brock visibly stiffened at the voluble recognition.

The next to arrive was a very thin gentleman with powder white hair and a florid complexion. He wore a dark gray suit and tie and a smile that twitched as if its owner were putting a brave face on oral surgery. His head hung down and his shoulders were slightly raised, which gave him a predatory look. He muttered greetings as he passed the three benches, choosing to stand off to the side by the kiosk. In one hand he held a leather briefcase, in his other was an olive green vinyl suitcase.

"That," Emily whispered to Lynn, "is Stuart Holmes. He was once a lawyer, I believe."

Lynn peered over Emily's head at the old man. "Of the type that could be found in one of your friend Ransom's favorite books."

Emily laughed in a quiet, ladylike fashion.

Holmes's arrival was followed closely by that of another man, this one the antithesis of the lawyer. He was thick around the middle and had damp black hair streaked with gray. His face was heavy, his cheeks sagging so much they appeared to be losing the war with the law of gravity. He wore a canary yellow shirt, lime green checkered pants, and white shoes. He made straight for the first bench.

"Why, hello, Miss Charters!" he said expansively. "So glad to see you this fine morning! Didn't know you'd be coming on this little trip!"

"Good morning, Mr. Driscoll," Emily replied primly. "Lynn, this is Bertram Driscoll. Mr. Driscoll, my friend Lynn Francis."

"Glad to know you. And what's all this Mr. Driscoll and Bertram stuff? Just call me Bertie!"

Emily made a doubtful noise.

He continued. "I really am glad to see you here. I can't tell you! 'Least I know there'll be some good company on the trip!" This statement was aimed over Emily's head in the general direction of Claudia Trenton, who ignored it. He looked back down at Emily. "Yes, I'm certainly glad to see you here."

"Thank you," she replied. "The trip is a birthday present from a dear friend."

"Well, that's nice! That's very, very nice. This everybody, here?"

Emily did a quick survey of the assembly. "I seem to remember the church bulletin saying there would be space for twelve. We're a couple short."

"That's always assuming they actually got twelve people to join in this shindig."

"Quite."

"Didn't have all that much notice." He aimed the explanation at Lynn. "This here boat doesn't usually go out this early—preseason, they call it. But the weather's been so good that our preacher—"

"Reverend Hurley," Emily interjected.

"—struck up the deal with the owner. I'd still be surprised if they filled up the tour. Most people our age are dead!" He laughed loudly at his own joke.

Nobody spoke for a short time. Driscoll seemed rather uncomfortable with the silence.

"Boy, she does look to be a regular tub, doesn't she?"

"Hmm?" Emily said.

"The boat! The S.S. *Genessee!* Our home away from home for the next four days!"

Emily glanced up at the deck and noted with dismay that the captain's wife had turned in their direction, apparently unable to miss Driscoll's booming comment.

"I wouldn't say that at all, Mr. Driscoll," Emily said with surprising volume. "The boat looks rather charming to me."

Driscoll laughed loudly, and Emily feared that he was about to be even more embarrassing on the subject, but he was stopped by the sudden arrival of a small vehicle resembling a golf cart. It was driven by a youth who looked too young to have a license of any kind, and in the passenger seat was a tiny woman with windblown white hair, who looked a trifle startled, presumably because she hadn't expected the conveyance to move at such a speed.

The young man brought the cart to a stop behind the passengers, and Emily swiveled around on the bench so that she could see.

"Good morning, Lily," she said.

The woman turned to her and blinked, then her lips moved. Lynn was unsure of whether or not a sound had emanated from them.

"I beg your pardon, dear?" said Emily, leaning forward.

Lily attempted a bit more volume. "I said, is this it? Am I in the right place?"

"Of course you are!" Driscoll said with a hearty laugh. "Unless you think we're all in the wrong place!"

"You said you wanted the *Genessee,* ma'am," said the driver. "This is it." He climbed out of his seat and lifted her suitcase off the back of the cart. Then he came around to the passenger side and helped the old woman to step down from it with a measure of patience that was beyond his years.

While they were doing this, Emily noticed movement beyond them. In the dark hallway of the main building, a man appeared to be hovering near one of the rolled-up doors. Emily supposed it wouldn't be odd for a visitor to the pier to loiter in this fashion, but this man seemed to be paying particular attention to the members of their party. In his hand was a parcel wrapped in brown paper.

Lily managed to struggle from her seat with difficulty while clutching the driver's hand with her tiny claw. When the old woman was finally standing on solid ground, Lynn thought for a moment that she had dropped something for which she was searching the pavement. When she didn't straighten after half a minute, Lynn realized that she was stooped with osteoporosis. The driver led Lily to Emily's bench and dropped her bag carelessly beside it.

"May I?" Lily asked in her barely audible whisper.

"Certainly," Emily replied, shifting a little closer to Marcella Hemsley.

Lily began to lower herself onto the corner of the bench, pausing at the halfway point as if uncertain whether or not she was going to hit the mark. Then she proceeded until she had touched down.

Lynn smiled to herself as she watched this. The phrase "suspended between heaven and earth" came to mind. She exchanged a glance with Rebecca, who was also smiling as if the same thought had occurred to her.

Emily introduced the woman to Lynn as Lily DuPree.

"I'm so excited," Miss DuPree said so softly it seemed to belie her words. "I've never been on a ship before. It will be a new experience for me."

"I'd hardly call it a ship," Driscoll boomed with a snort, miraculously having heard the faint voice.

"You've never been on a boat before?" Emily prompted, ignoring him.

"No! And I've been looking forward to it ever since it was announced in the bulletin. I've brought some of my favorite books along to read on the trip."

Emily produced a perceptive smile. "I see." She turned to Lynn. "Lily was once the secretary to our former minister, Reverend Dawson. For...how many years was it?"

"Close to thirty!" Lily said glowingly. "Oh, Theodore Dawson! Now, *there* was a holy man. A true man of God. He was one of those ministers from whom goodness just shines! When he retired...well, I just thought it was time for me to retire as well. There'll never be another like him." Her face clouded over. "I don't know about this new minister at all...Reverend Hurley...."

"How long has he been your minister?" Lynn asked.

"Seven years," Emily replied with a twinkle.

"Well, there's eleven of us so far," Driscoll piped up. "Always assuming that the two young 'uns are going along with us!"

Lynn and Rebecca exchanged a quick, embarrassed glance.

"Yes, we are going along," said Lynn.

"Lot of fun you're going have with a boatload of old cats!" Lynn's cheeks reddened on Emily's behalf, but she was stopped from replying when she noticed the amused look on Emily's face.

"So I guess we're waitin' here for one more," said Driscoll, oblivious to the effect he had caused.

"Oh, no, Mr. Driscoll," said Miss DuPree. "There's to be only eleven. I called up Miss Warner yesterday and asked specifically." She turned to Emily. "I only wanted to know—just for my own peace of mind—who would be coming on the trip. It will be four days, after all, in a small space, and one does want to be sure of one's company."

On the deck of the *Genessee,* the slight flush that had appeared on Samantha Farraday's cheeks at Driscoll's words had faded. She sighed heavily and gave her husband's arm a squeeze.

"Look at them," she said, though they had their backs turned to the passengers on the pier. Her husband patted her hand. She continued without animosity. "A bunch of doddering old folks. Do you mind too much?"

The captain laughed lightly. "I don't mind at all."

"You must! This has to feel like a comedown after the navy."

He looked at her out of the corner of his eye. "Is that how it seems to you? That I've come down?"

"No!" Samantha exclaimed with distress. "No! I didn't mean that. I love what we're doing. I love the business. I love being on the lake. It's just, when I look at the caliber of our passengers sometimes, I worry about what *you* think of our life."

"I don't miss being in the navy. And I love our life as much as you do." He said this in what Samantha called his textbook tone, which always left her wondering what he really thought.

A man appeared through a door on the second level. He was tall with short blond hair he kept combed back. He was dressed in black denim pants and a tight white nylon shirt that showed off a well-chiseled torso. He sprinted up the steps to the first deck, gave a wave in the direction of the captain, then headed down the boarding plank.

"Good morning, ladies and gentlemen," the man proclaimed jauntily as he reached the promenade. "My name is David Douglas—you can call me David. I'm the head steward on the *Genessee,* which means that I pretty much do everything." He laughed self-effacingly. "I guess we've reached that time in the world when everything's reversed—used to be if you were the head of something, that meant you got to sit back and delegate. Now it means just the opposite. I'm the one that makes sure all the work gets done, that each and every one of you is happy, and that everything's shipshape and Bristol fashion—whatever that means. And usually I do it myself. I'm just telling you so's you know that if you want anything at all while you're on board, anything at all, you just say the word to me, and if it can be done I'll do it!"

The passengers all seemed to be a bit taken aback by this sudden, lengthy introduction. They stared at Douglas with bewilderment.

He broke the silence with a clap of his hands. "So! Anybody feel the need for help getting up the boarding plank?"

"Oh, yes, yes," Miss DuPree said eagerly. "I think I would like some help!"

"Okey-doke, ma'am! Just leave your bag there."

A small young man had come down the plank and joined Douglas. The new arrival had black hair and skin the color of a football.

"Oh!" said Douglas. "This is Hoke, the other steward, which makes up my whole staff. He'll be helping out as well."

Hoke smiled uncertainly.

"Get the bags together first, out of the way so they don't trip over them, then help some up." Douglas instructed Hoke quietly. Then he held out a hand to Miss DuPree. "Now, ma'am, if you will, I'll help you up the ramp."

DuPree placed her hand in his and rose unsteadily. Douglas

bent slightly and put a hand on the old woman's thin wrist in an attempt to steady her.

"There you go, ma'am. You're all right now."

"Thank you...David." She said his name as if she were trying it on for size.

He allowed her to slip an arm through his and then began the slow process of walking her up the ramp. The captain's wife appeared at the top with a clipboard in hand, ready to check in the passengers.

Claudia Trenton emitted a not-so-muffled "*hmpf!*" from the third bench. Emily glanced in her direction. From the displeased downturn of Claudia's mouth, she apparently found fault with something of the proceedings. She walked away from her suitcase without giving it a backward glance, her regal bearing showing her confidence that a vassal would see to her luggage. Lynn crouched beside Emily, and said, "She looks like she thinks we should've been admitted in order of arrival."

"That would never do for Claudia Trenton," Emily said with a quiet chuckle. "She didn't arrive first."

Claudia was stopped temporarily at the top of the ramp by Douglas and Lily, the latter of whom teetered in the entrance as the captain's wife greeted her and gave her her cabin number. Once Lily had cleared the entrance, Claudia swept onto the boat.

Lynn glanced over at Hoke, who was just finishing lining up their bags. "I've never seen so much Samsonite in one place." She paused, then added with a grin, "Do the elderly always gravitate to that type of luggage?"

"Sturdy and reliable." Emily nodded. "Which is usually best, given how they're generally handled."

"Yes," Lynn said after an appreciative glance.

"Well, that young man seems to be taking good care of them."

Still carrying the briefcase, Stuart Holmes crossed to the ramp and went up. Hoke had finished with the suitcases, and without being asked followed Holmes up the ramp, contriving to look as if he'd forgotten something on board while keeping a watchful eye on the stringy old man. The Millers then got up from their seat, adjusted their shoulder bags and headed for the ramp.

Douglas hurried back down the ramp and came directly to Emily. "How about you, ma'am?" he asked.

Emily was a bit surprised at what she saw: with his youthful demeanor, from a distance she had taken Douglas to be in his late twenties or early thirties, but at close proximity she could see the deep crow's feet, the small lines around the mouth, and several strands of silver in his blond hair. She placed him somewhere in his midforties.

"No, thank you, young man," she said cordially. "I'm quite all right."

"Could you use some help?" Douglas said to Marcella Hemsley.

Instead of replying to him, she looked at Rebecca. The deep furrow in her brow took a sharp dip in the center, which made her appear not just confused but angry. "Are we boarding now?"

"Yes, Auntie," the niece replied.

Marcella began to struggle up to her feet. "Well, what are we waiting for?"

"Are you…are you absolutely sure you want to go on this trip?" Rebecca asked.

She hesitated with both palms flat on the bench. "'Course I am! Did I talk about anything else for the past six months but how I wanted to go on this tour with my friends?"

Lynn glanced at Emily and mouthed, "Six months?"

Marcella continued. "'Course I want to go. But listen, you don't have to come along if you don't want to. I always told you that. I don't need anybody to take care of me. I can take care of myself."

Rebecca slipped a hand under Marcella's arm and helped her up. "I know you can, Auntie. But I want to come along. I need a vacation. We've already had this discussion."

She led her aunt toward the boarding plank, and Marcella continued to profess her independence as they went arm in arm up it. David Douglas had stood to the side during this exchange, not wanting to interrupt or offer assistance for fear of further antagonizing the old woman. But he followed them up the ramp at a discreet distance to ensure Marcella's safety.

"Poor thing," Emily said softly.

"The aunt or the niece?" Lynn asked.

"Both of them."

"Well, Miss Charters," Driscoll said broadly. "I reckon you turned your nose up at that young fella because you wanted to be escorted onto the boat by someone a bit more mature, am I right?"

"Not at all, Mr. Driscoll," she replied pleasantly but firmly. "I declined the young man's offer because I don't require assistance. Thank you just the same."

"Oh!" Driscoll said blankly, some of the wind going out of his sails. Then he shrugged and laughed. "Oh, well, all aboard!"

He went to the plank and ascended, followed closely by Jackson Brock.

Lynn held out a hand to Emily, who took it lightly and rose from the bench.

"Thank you, dear," she said.

Hoke had came rather noisily down the plank and stopped before them. "I can help, if you want."

"Thank you, young man, but there's no need," said Emily. "Did Mr. Douglas say that your name is Hoke?"

His dark skin flushed. "Yes."

"That's a most unusual name. Is it short for something?"

He nodded. "My name is Joaquin. They call me Hoke for short." He said this with the colorless resignation of someone who knows it would be futile to protest.

"I think Joaquin is a lovely name. If you don't mind, I'll call you by that."

He blushed again, this time appreciatively. "No, no, I don't mind. I like it! You go onto the boat now."

Emily and Lynn started for the plank, and Hoke followed them up it, apparently anxious lest Emily should topple back down the incline.

"I don't know how you do it," Lynn said quietly.

"What?" Emily asked innocently.

"Don't be coy with me," she replied with a sly smile. "I suspect you were quite the little siren when you were young."

Emily laughed. At the top they were greeted by the captain's wife.

"Welcome aboard," she said brightly. "I'm Samantha Farraday. I take it you are…" She consulted the clipboard. "Emily Charters and Lynn Francis."

"That's right," said Lynn.

"Miss Charters, we've put you in cabin ten and Miss Francis is in cabin eleven. You can go down to your cabins now if you like, but you may want to stay on deck for a little while—we'll be getting under way as soon as the last passenger arrives, and most people like to be on deck for that."

"The last passenger?" Emily said. "I thought we were the last."

"No, there's one more."

"I see." Emily glanced at the deck. All of the female passengers appeared to have chosen to remain topside, while the males had gone below. "Thank you."

As Emily and Lynn moved away from Samantha onto the deck, David Douglas came up from below and went to the boarding plank. He stopped beside Samantha and scanned the promenade.

"That's all of them. Now I'll get the other bags," he said with a wink as he went down the ramp.

Samantha gave him an indulgent smile. "Careful, David!"

Hoke followed him down to the pier to help.

"Do you want to stay up here?" Lynn asked Emily.

"Oh, yes. I don't want to go downstairs and have to come right back up again."

Deck chairs were arranged haphazardly around the perimeter of the deck. Laura Miller sat facing the water. She'd placed her purse on the chair next to hers as if saving it for her husband was still necessary despite the small company. Marcella Hemsley was on a chair facing the pier, her face lit with delight. Her niece was in the chair beside her, sitting forward, her forehead creased.

Lily DuPree was seated near the aft railing, her chair skewed around toward the deck. Emily noted with an inward smile that Lily was already engulfed in a book, oblivious to what was going on around her. Claudia Trenton sat near the boarding plank, her chair in a characteristically rigid upright position. There were two empty chairs nearby her, and Emily and Lynn sat down in them.

Emily had no sooner adjusted the hem of her light blue cotton frock when a billowing cry came soaring up from the pier, accompanied by the clatter of a pair of wooden soles, the sound of which resembled the confused clop of an agitated horse.

"Yoo-hoo!" cried the voice. "Yoo-hoo! Don't leave without me! I'm here!"

At the sound of the voice, the passengers on deck, with the exception of Emily and Lynn, tensed so noticeably they sent ripples through the air.

"I'm coming, I'm coming!" The voice had neared and the wooden soles resounded on the boarding plank.

"Oh, dear God!" Claudia exclaimed in an undisguised whisper.

The source of the voice came into view. She wore a green knit dress with a thin brown cord tied around her waist so tightly it made the bulk above and below it shift like the contents of a lava lamp. Her hair was raven black, which couldn't have been natural given her sixty-plus years, and the whiteness of her doughy face was interrupted by a beauty mark on her right cheek. From a distance it looked as if she'd neglected to swat away a small insect. In her right hand she carried a large, dark red suitcase, heavy enough that it caused her to list to one side.

"Who's that?" Lynn asked, not unaware of the sensation the arrival had caused among the other passengers.

"That is Muriel Langstrom," Emily replied.

"A loudmouthed, tiresome boor of a woman," Claudia added unbidden.

"I'm so sorry I'm late!" Muriel said loudly. "I couldn't get a taxi, and when I did the traffic was just unbelievable! It took twice the time to get here as I thought it would! And don't you know, Navy Pier is farther away than I thought it was!"

"Yes, Miss Langstrom," Samantha said patiently. "You're in cabin twelve. If you want to leave your bag here, one of the stewards will bring it down for you. We're about to set off, so if you like you can stay up here with the rest of the passengers. The captain usually says a few words before we leave."

"About to set off?" Muriel said with anxious brown eyes. "You haven't been waiting for me, have you? Not just for me? I'd hate to think that I held everyone up."

"No, she wouldn't," Claudia said under her breath.

"That's certainly no way to begin a trip. That would really be starting off on the wrong foot!"

"No," Samantha said quickly when Muriel paused for a breath. "You're the last to arrive, but you're not late."

"Thank God for that!"

Claudia emitted a "*huh!*" "I'll bet she's the last to arrive with good reason!"

Muriel moved onto the deck, continuing her monologue to no one in particular. "Do you know what I mean? About it being farther away than I thought it was? A lot of things are like that. Like Orchestra Hall, for instance. Or…they've changed its name, haven't they? It's not called Orchestra Hall anymore, is it? No…I can't remember what it's called now. I suppose it doesn't matter. Anyway, as many times as I've gone to hear the symphony, you'd think I could remember exactly where the hall is. But it's always farther away than I remember it. Just like Navy Pier. Of course, I never come here, so it's understandable that I'd be confused about it."

"Ladies and gentleman!" The captain's voice boomed out over the loudspeaker so suddenly and loudly that Muriel cut herself off with a cry, and Lily DuPree's book was startled out of her hands. She struggled to retrieve it from the deck as the announcement continued.

"Ladies and gentlemen, this is Captain Farraday. If those of you who are on the lower decks would like to come up top, I'd like to welcome you personally to your Lake Michigan cruise aboard the *Genessee*. Thank you."

The loudspeaker crackled and went mute.

Bertram Driscoll and Martin Miller came up the stairs from belowdecks almost simultaneously, none the worse for their fairly rapid ascent up the two flights. Then Jackson Brock emerged, a little more slowly than the others. Stuart Holmes was last, managing the stairs with evident difficulty. He came onto the deck cautiously. Emily noticed this and suspected it was not so much from fear of losing his footing as an attempt to not appear winded.

"Well, here we are again!" Driscoll exclaimed, apparently from an inbred determination to state the obvious. His eye caught sight of the late arrival, who had seated herself at the rear of the deck near Lily DuPree. "And lookee who we have here! Miss Muriel Langstrom! I didn't know you'd booked onto our little cruise!"

Immediately upon being addressed directly, Muriel began to flutter. "Yes! It was a last-minute decision, really! I don't know why I couldn't make up my mind about—"

Driscoll cut her off amiably. "Well, glad to see ya!" He went briskly to the other end of the deck and sat not too far from Emily and Lynn. The other men had found seats during this exchange.

Once they were all situated, as if on cue, the captain came out of the wheelhouse with his wife at his side. They stood at the center of the rear wall of the wheelhouse, from which they could see the entire company. David and Hoke appeared from below, having just completed stowing the last of the luggage. They were accompanied by a plump, pleasant-faced woman in a pale gray dress and white apron.

"Good morning, ladies and gentlemen, and welcome to the *Genessee*. I'm Captain Neil Farraday, and just in case you're wondering, you can call me Captain. You've met my wife, Samantha...." Here he gave a nod of acknowledgment in her direction. "Samantha is our cruise director. If you have any questions about any of our ports of call, recreation on board or what-have-you, she will be glad to answer them. You've also met David and Hoke, our ship's stewards. They are here to see that you're kept happy, so anything you need, just ask them. One last member of the crew is Mrs. Margaret O'Malley...." He extended a hand toward the plump woman, who beamed at the passengers. "She's the ship's cook. Not just the ship's, she's one of the best cooks I've ever run across." Mrs. O'Malley's face reddened and she dipped her head toward the passengers.

"To those of you who haven't been to your cabins yet, you will find a complete itinerary and tentative time schedule on your nightstand. If there are any problems during the trip, please feel free to come to me directly. I'm always at your disposal. Now, I think it's time we got under way. I thank you for choosing a *Genessee* tour, and I sincerely hope you enjoy your trip, our maiden voyage for the summer. Now I'll turn things over to my wife."

He touched two fingers to his forehead in an abbreviated salute, rounded the wheelhouse, then disappeared inside of it. Mrs. O'Malley quietly went down the stairs, and Hoke and David crossed to the boarding plank.

"In the words of your generation," Lynn said to Emily, "he cuts a rather fine figure, doesn't he?"

Emily laughed. "I'm not sure I would assign that phrase to

my generation, but you're right, he does. And so does his wife.''

The lady in question cleared her throat. "Just a few words about the boat. I'm sure you noticed the color of the boat when you arrived, patriotic red, white, and blue. The level we are now on we call the white deck, directly below us is the red deck, which is where the dining room and lounge are located. Last but not least is the blue deck, which is where your cabins are. Snacks are always available in the lounge, and drinks upon request. In about an hour we'll be serving a light lunch in the dining room. Now, as you know, this is a preseason trip specially arranged by your church. Despite the warm weather, you'll find a little less activity along the lakefront than we would later in the month when the season really begins, but there will still be plenty to do and see. As the captain said, we hope you'll enjoy your trip. And please, please let us know if you require anything at all. Thank you.''

Samantha disappeared around the corner and into the wheelhouse.

During this speech, Hoke and David hoisted the boarding plank up, swiveled it into position on the outer rim of the deck, and locked it securely into place.

When the engine started up, Emily was surprised by how quietly the machinery worked, though she'd had no reason to believe it would be otherwise. Slowly the boat began to move away from the dock and out from between its two enormous neighbors, into the wide channel alongside the pier.

"Isn't it exciting!" Muriel gushed.

"Good God," Claudia said under her breath.

Emily's attention was caught by something on the pier. The young man she'd seen lurking in the darkness of the main building watched as the ship slid away. He then stepped out of the darkness and hurried toward the entrance of the pier. Emily noted with interest that he no longer carried his parcel.

Once the *Genessee* was clear of its larger sisters, it surveyed a slow 180-degree turn and headed out toward the breakwater.

The water was calm and the sun very hot as it shone down on the deck, but the humidity was low, and a pleasant breeze tickled the few strands of gray hair that had come loose from the large bun at the back of Emily's head.

"It's peaceful, isn't it?" Lynn asked as the noise of the pier receded into the distance.

"Yes," Emily replied. "It's been a very long time since I've been on a boat. I thought I should like to do it again. It was very nice of Jeremy to make a present of it to me."

The Jeremy in question was Jeremy Ransom, the Chicago police detective who had become an adoptive grandson to Emily. They had met on one of Ransom's cases, and over the years had formed a bond more secure than any the detective, a confirmed lone wolf, had known before. Though the friendship between the elderly woman and the fortyish detective might've seemed a curious one to the casual onlooker, it was a relationship born of mutual trust, respect, and a sort of familial affection.

Lynn smiled. "He knew you wanted to go. Did you expect any less of him?"

"I make it a point never to expect anything," the old woman replied. "So my life is full of pleasant surprises."

Lynn raised her eyebrows. "As many times as you've gotten involved in murder investigations, I would think that life had enough surprises!"

Emily produced an enigmatic smile. "Yes, but consider how much more time I spend *not* involved in murder cases."

Lynn laughed. "Emily! You make it sound like you enjoy murder!"

"Not murder, my dear," she replied, her tone one of mild rebuke, "but I do enjoy puzzles."

"Isn't it exciting!" Muriel exclaimed again, ostensibly to Lily DuPree but loud enough to take in the rest of the company.

Claudia Trenton sighed with exaggerated weariness from beneath the sunhat she had tilted forward. She mimicked Muriel under her breath. "Exciting."

"Now, Claudia," Emily said lightly.

"I wish I had your patience, Emily. But..." She hesitated before continuing with slightly less vigor. "I've never been able to suffer fools gladly." She fished in her purse and pulled out a pair of large violet-tinted sunglasses. She put them on, laid the purse to one side, and lowered the back of her chair to the halfway mark. She then lay back with another sigh and closed her eyes.

Muriel continued to chatter happily to Lily, whose responses, if there were any, were completely inaudible to the others.

"Looks just like one of those picture postcards, doesn't it?" Martin Miller said to his wife, indicating the skyline with a sweeping gesture. Laura Miller nodded in agreement. "Just like all the postcards you see at the drugstore: the city seen from the water."

"Yes, it does," Laura replied. She narrowed her eyes at the scene as if trying to envision it framed in a small rectangle. Martin lifted his camera and took a picture. Then he slued toward his wife and snapped one of her. They both laughed.

"Just beautiful!" he said, turning his lens back toward the shore. "I wish...I wish our grandkids could be here. They'd love this."

His wife's expression darkened and her chin quivered. "Marty, please..."

He instantly put an arm over her shoulder and said soothingly, "Now, honey, don't. It's all right. You wait and see."

Driscoll's head had dropped to his chest. Having divested himself of some bluster and settled into the chair, he had quickly succumbed to the gentle movement of the boat on the water. But he wasn't completely asleep. The steady chatter from Muriel kept him from that.

"My late husband and I—did I tell you this?" She was addressing Lily DuPree, whose expression was one of baffled interest. "My late husband and I often talked about going on a cruise. Of course, that wouldn't have been on the lake, it was a world cruise that we talked about—a big one...the Orient

and such. But we never got the chance to do it. He died right
after he retired. That happens so often, doesn't it? You work
hard and save for your retirement, and the minute you finally
have the time and the means to enjoy yourself, bang! You die!
And what was it all for?'' Before Lily could offer an opinion,
Muriel continued. ''Well, I'll tell you…''

''The minute he retired and had all that time to spend with
her, he died. Doesn't surprise me in the least,'' Claudia murmured.

Driscoll, his head still lowered, looked over at Emily and
winked rakishly. ''Muriel prattles on,'' he said quietly, ''but
she's a good-hearted soul.''

With these few words, he rose a bit in Emily's estimation.
She favored him with a smile, and he let his eyes close sleepily.

Martin Miller had gotten up to take pictures of the lighthouse
as the boat passed through the opening in the breakwater. The
rest of the passengers looked on in a kind of confused awe,
not knowing whether or not they should be impressed by the
structure.

Miller's jockeying for a particular angle brought him near
the foot of Emily's deck chair.

''You're a photographer, I see, Mr. Miller.''

''Sure am,'' he said brightly. Like all enthusiasts he was
happy to talk about his hobby. ''Me and Laura, both. Have a
darkroom at home and everything—don't want any cheap lab
ruining my pictures! I want to get one of those digital cameras
one of these days, but I'm waiting for the price to come down
on the good ones first.''

''I see.''

Even though the boat was still well within sight of the shore,
once they'd passed the breakwater the passengers experienced
a noticeable sense of release, as if the low-lying wall that barely
broke the surface of the water separated them from all of their
problems. They felt as if they were now well out to sea, and
that their vacation had finally begun in earnest.

"I think I'd like to go down and see our cabins now," said Emily.

"Sure thing," said Lynn, rising from her chair.

Emily got up and the two of them went to the staircase and started down. On the red deck, through the window to the dining room, they could see Mrs. O'Malley supervising the stewards in laying out a buffet. Emily and Lynn continued down to the blue deck and into the vestibule at the bottom of the stairs. To their left was a doorway covered by a curtain separating the crew's lodgings from those of the passengers. To the right was a narrow hallway lined on both sides with cabins, the odd numbers on the left and even on the right.

Lynn's room, number 11, was the last on the left, and Emily's room was kitty-corner to it.

"I'm afraid you're going to have Miss Langstrom for a neighbor," Lynn said.

Emily smiled. "That's quite all right. I'll trust that she doesn't talk in her sleep."

"If she doesn't, it's only because she doesn't have anything left to say."

Lynn opened the door to number 10 and stood aside as Emily entered. Despite the attempt to evoke a certain amount of old-world charm in the rest of the *Genessee*, the cabins were a marvel of modern, if cramped, convenience. Directly to the right of the door was a closet, to the left a bathroom, barely large enough to turn around in, with a shower stall constructed of heavy plastic. The sink was located in the room itself, next to the closet. A twin bed was hard against the left corner of the room, and beside it was tiny chest on which a small brass lamp stood, its base designed to look like a ship's compass and weighted to keep it in place. Above the chest was a high porthole. The room was so immaculately clean it looked as if it had never before been occupied.

"Well!" Emily said appreciatively. "Even Mr. Driscoll must approve of the rooms."

Emily's suitcase had been laid on the bed. Lynn popped it open. "Have a seat. I'll just unpack your things."

"You don't have to do that, I can take care of it," Emily protested mildly.

"I know you can. But I want to."

She pulled out the first dress, a lightweight beige, held it up, shook it out, then slipped it onto one of the stationary hangers in the closet. She did the same with the rest. As she worked, she said, "Emily...I was just wondering...." She hesitated, narrowing her eyes at a small wrinkle in one of the garments.

"Yes?" said Emily.

"You did want me to come along with you on this trip, didn't you?"

"Of course I did! Why would you ask that?"

"Well..."

Emily smiled knowingly. "You heard the way Miss Hemsley spoke to her niece."

Lynn nodded. "She certainly seemed to resent the idea of being...accompanied."

Emily shook her head slowly. "That's not what she resents."

"It's not?"

"She resents the fact that she *needs* company. You came along with me as a friend, and I'm very glad you did. Surely you knew it was safe for me to travel on my own."

Lynn paused for a split second as she stowed some of Emily's linens in the top drawer of the chest. It was a slight but telling gesture. "You want me to be honest?"

"Yes?" Emily said with some surprise.

"Well, Emily, I know you're a perfectly capable woman, but that doesn't stop me from worrying about you." She looked down as if a bit ashamed of herself. "I mean, I know you can take care of yourself, but when you first brought up the subject of this cruise, I was...concerned."

"Yes," said Emily.

"I knew you'd be fine on your own, but I...felt better about it knowing that I was coming with you." She looked into Emily's eyes again, her cheeks an attractive red, and shrugged. "Besides, I thought it might be fun. As Miss DuPree would say, I've never been on a ship before." She added this in such a perfect imitation of the other woman's breathless speech that Emily couldn't help but laugh.

"Are you angry with me?" Lynn asked after a pause.

"Good heavens, no! You wanted to come even though you knew I'd be fine. Rebecca Bremmer came with her aunt because she knew she wouldn't be."

TWO

AT TWELVE-THIRTY the captain announced over the loud-speaker that lunch was being served in the dining room. The passengers assembled quickly, more from curiosity than from hunger, each eager for a first glimpse of what the cuisine and service would be like for the next few days. They were not disappointed. There were plates piled with a variety of fruit and perfectly rounded scoops of fresh melon, a platter of cold meats and cheeses, three different kinds of salads, stacks of bread, and pats of butter in small bowls of ice. It was simple fare, but admirably abundant.

Emily and Lynn were the last to enter the dining room. The rest of the passengers were ranged in front of the long buffet table gabbling approvingly over the spread. Hoke stood at attention at the left end of the table beside a pile of plates, ready to hand them out. The captain's wife moved back and forth behind the table making slight, unnecessary last-minute adjustments to the layout of the food.

"If you'd like to begin down there," Samantha said with a casual wave toward Hoke, "you can take a plate and help yourselves. We like to be very informal for lunch. Once you have your seats, David will be around to take your beverage requests."

A line quickly formed by the young steward, led by the Millers. Hoke handed the husband and wife their plates, and they made their way down the table, snatching up food like ravenous hawks. Claudia Trenton was next. She gave a slight sniff at the plain white dinner plate, then made a slow survey of the buffet with her nose tilted up and her eyes tilted down.

Marcella Hemsley gazed uncertainly at the items on the table, unable to make a choice.

"That's turkey," her niece said as she deftly forked a couple of slices onto her aunt's plate. "You like turkey."

"Oh, yes!" Marcella replied.

"And there are strawberries. You like them." She made this a statement rather than a question as she scooped some of the fruit onto their plates.

"I have a friend named Bonnie," Muriel chattered to no one in particular as she followed the aunt and niece down the line, "who took one of those big ocean cruises. It was a singles cruise…at her age! You would think she would know better! But—what was I saying? Oh, yes! She went on one of those big liners and she said the food was incredible! Not just the quantity but the quality! Food, food, everywhere! Every time she turned around there was something else to eat. When the cruise was over, she'd gained ten pounds."

Samantha Farraday, who had remained behind the table as they helped themselves, nodded at Muriel with a vacant smile.

Next in line was Lily DuPree, who hesitated from taking the plate that Hoke proffered, eyeing it doubtfully. When she finally accepted it, the muscles in her rail thin arms tightened, and she moved slowly toward the food. David Douglas appeared at her side, seemingly out of nowhere.

"Can I be of any assistance, Miss DuPree?"

She looked up at him with a grateful smile, then turned back to the buffet as her cheeks turned pink. "I…there are so many things I just don't know which to choose."

He smoothly took the plate from her, to her evident relief. "I'll tell you what you do. You let me decide for you. You go over and have yourself a seat, and I'll get you a little bit of everything and bring it to you. How would that be?"

"Oh, I couldn't ask it," she said, tilting shining eyes up at him. There was a peculiar note in her voice: not so much appreciative as a sort of girlish delight.

"It's what I'm here for, ma'am."

"Well…yes…that would be very nice. Thank you."

Lily faded out of the line and wandered away through the tables. Lynn thought she looked rather like a Ping-Pong ball that had been caught in a very slow eddy on the lake. Lily finally came to a table near the door, pulled out one of the heavy wooden chairs with some difficulty, then sat down.

Emily and Lynn followed David.

"That was very nice of you, young man," said Emily. "And very observant."

"She was a little teetery when she came on board," he replied with a smile that tried to be winning but to Emily looked more like pride. "I noticed that right off, so I made up my mind to keep an eye on her."

"Very astute. It makes me wonder if you've worked with the elderly before."

"Oh, yes, ma'am! I worked at the Hide-Away Nursing Home. That wasn't its real name, you understand, it was just what we called it 'cause that's what the residents' relatives were using it for, to hide them away. Shameful, if you ask me. Most of the residents were sweethearts, and I couldn't imagine them just getting dumped there the way they did, so I was extra nice to them."

"That was very considerate," Emily said as she transferred a pickle onto the side of her plate. "And where was this?"

David's attention seemed to wander uncertainly over the contents of the table.

"Mr. Douglas?"

"Hmm?"

"Where was this nursing home?"

"Oh…in Wisconsin. Do you think Miss DuPree would like some macaroni salad?"

"Perhaps," Emily replied with an curious smile. "So you're from Wisconsin?"

"Uh, no, but I lived there for a while." He appeared to be concentrating very intently on placing a spoonful of the salad on the plate.

"And then you moved to Chicago?" Emily said, contriving to sound like an inquisitive old lady.

"Yeah," he said, staring down at the plate now piled with food. "I think I might've overdid it a little. What do you think?"

"Just a little," Emily replied without looking at the plate.

"Well, I'll just tell her she can pick at what she wants and leave the rest for the fish!"

With this he headed for the table.

"Emily," Lynn said softly, "what are you up to?"

"Hmm?" The old woman turned a twinkling eye at her. "Just making conversation."

The three single male passengers had waited in a gentlemanly fashion for the ladies to get their food before taking up their own plates and serving themselves. When Emily and Lynn were halfway down the table, the men started.

Emily and Lynn finished their selections with a spoonful of cole slaw each, then turned away from the buffet and looked for a place to sit. There were more tables than necessary so that the passengers had managed to spread out. The Millers were at the table nearest the lounge, and Muriel Langstrom had buttonholed Lily at the one by the starboard door. Apparently Lily's natural reticence made her destined to be Muriel's sounding board for the length of the voyage.

Claudia Trenton was seated alone at a table beneath a porthole, but Emily suspected she wouldn't be for long: the three empty seats would prove most inviting if the single men decided to sit together.

Marcella and Rebecca were seated at a table in the center of the room, and Emily and Lynn joined them.

"I must say, everything looks very good," Emily said as she unfolded a paper napkin and placed it on her lap.

Marcella nodded and took a bite of the sandwich she held

with both hands. "It is, except...I can't figure out what this is...this meat. It tastes like turkey."

"It is turkey, Aunt Marci," Rebecca said with a weary smile.

David came over to their table carrying a pitcher of ice water, its exterior covered with condensation.

"What would you beautiful ladies like to drink?" he asked as he filled their glasses.

"Just water," said Emily, which was echoed by the other women.

"How about you, little lady?" he asked Rebecca rather suggestively. "Are you sure you wouldn't like something special? I mean from the bar."

"No," she said firmly.

David scurried to the next table.

"He's a very personable young man," Emily said. "And very attractive, don't you think?"

She had addressed this to Rebecca, whose eyes widened with surprise. "What? Oh, do you think so? I don't know."

"He's a tart," Marcella said a little too loudly.

Rebecca shot a guilty glance over her shoulder in David's direction. He was busy talking to Muriel and Lily, and didn't appear to have heard.

"I've seen his type before," Marcella continued.

"Please, keep your voice down!" Rebecca said in an anxious whisper.

Marcella shoved a forkful of potato salad into her mouth. "I know his type. I've seen 'em before!"

Emily, who was seated across the table from Rebecca, saw David turn his head a fraction of an inch in their direction. Lily reached out and patted his hand.

"Auntie, please!" Rebecca pleaded quickly.

Marcella's color deepened, and her niece braced herself for the expected explosion. But Marcella's expression suddenly altered, as if a cloud was passing before her eyes, and try as she might she couldn't penetrate it. When it cleared, she continued eating. "Did you say this was turkey?"

"Yes, Auntie," Rebecca said, breathing a sigh of relief.

The captain entered through the port door and made his way around the tables, stopping briefly at each one to greet the passengers. When he reached Emily's, he said, "So, how is everyone doing?"

"Just fine," Marcella said happily, the momentary distress apparently now forgotten. "Very nice boat you got here."

"Thank you, miss," he replied with a salute.

"Yes, it is very nice," Emily agreed. At close proximity she found the captain quite attractive. Aside from his piercing eyes, he had a smooth, flat forehead across which were three symmetrical, evenly spaced age lines that looked as if they'd been penciled in very faintly. Emily added, "And the rooms are quite comfortable."

"Don't know about that," said Marcella. "We haven't made it downstairs yet."

"They are nice," Lynn assured her.

"Captain…," Rebecca started, but let her voice trail off with an unsure glance at her aunt.

"Yes, Miss…Bremmer, isn't it?"

"Yes. I was just wondering…what happens if there is an emergency?"

The lines on his forehead deepened. "An emergency?"

"Well, I mean, like if one of the passengers became ill, or something like that."

"You always worry too much!" her aunt said.

The captain looked from the aunt back to the niece. "You don't have to worry about anything like that, Miss Bremmer. Throughout the trip, we'll never be all that far from shore. We keep a list of all the hospitals along the way and the fastest way to them. There won't be any problem. I hope that allays any fears you might have." He touched his cap again and went on to the next table.

"Honestly, Becky!" Marcella exclaimed, scooping up another forkful of potato salad. "You're always worried about your health!"

Rebecca looked down at her plate disconsolately, absently moving the food around with her fork.

"Well, it's reassuring to *me*," Lynn said with unexpected vigor. "I mean, to know that we won't be that far from help if we need it. Even though I don't have any fears about being on the water, it's still comforting to know that. Don't you think so, Emily?"

Lynn had turned to her friend, who had one brow upraised and an odd gleam in her eye.

"Oh, yes!" said Emily. "I do agree."

Marcella dropped the fork on her plate. Her eyes glowed, and her mouth formed a broad grin.

"Aunt Marci? What is it?" Rebecca asked.

"I can't wait! I just can't wait to see the island again."

"The island? Which one?"

Marcella blinked. "The island. It's in Michigan....It's on the tour...."

"You've been to this island before?" Emily asked. She noticed the pained look that crossed Rebecca's face.

"Yes...I...don't remember offhand who it was I went with, but I do remember what a beautiful place it was. We stayed in a lovely home off the lake. A bed-and-breakfast."

Marcella kept her head uptilted as she said this, as if picturing the scene somewhere above and behind Emily's head. Emily had been watching Marcella's eyes as she'd spoken: they were sparked with energy that seemed to flicker as if not properly connected to the source of their power. This continued through the rest of the meal, with Marcella getting more vague as time went on. Rebecca prompted her from time to time, always receiving an irritable rebuke for her efforts.

When Marcella had finished eating, Rebecca turned to her, and said, "Maybe we should go down and see our cabins now."

"What?" Marcella said blankly.

"Our cabins. Wouldn't you like to lie down?"

The aunt's face turned red. "No! Why would I want to lie down?"

"You usually do after lunch."

The redness drained from her aunt's face, then suddenly surged back again. "Well, I don't want to now! I'm not tired!"

"That's all right, that's all right," Rebecca said quickly, with an embarrassed glance at the other two women. "But we haven't been down there yet, and we really should get unpacked or everything will get wrinkled."

"I'm too old to care about that sort of thing!" She turned to Emily. "Long time ago I started wearing this kind of stuff." She pinched the side of her roomy peasant dress. "I wouldn't travel with anything else. They look the same whether they're wrinkled or not."

"Very wise," said Emily with a single nod.

"After all, I've got enough wrinkles of my own that I'm not going to get rid of. You know what I mean."

"Aunt Marci—"

"All right, all right!" Marcella replied testily. She struggled to her feet with difficulty. Rebecca tried to help her but Marcella swatted her hand away. "I can do it!"

Emily and Lynn watched as the two women, so different in temperament it hardly seemed they could be related, made their way past the tables to the port side door and left the dining room.

Emily turned to her young friend. "You're very quiet."

"Hmm." Lynn resumed eating.

MARCELLA KEPT both hands on the railings going down the steep metal stairs to the blue deck. Rebecca followed one step at a time, as if she were a bride reluctantly descending a sharply slanting aisle on her way to the altar.

Marcella paused at the foot of the stairs, blocking the way. Rebecca said, "To the right." When her aunt didn't immediately move, she gently dislodged one of the old woman's hands and shifted around her. "This way."

Marcella followed her down the hallway to cabin number 8. Inside they found her suitcase lying on the bed.

"Here," Rebecca said with all the cheerfulness she could muster. "Why don't you sit on the edge of the bed while I unpack."

"I can do that!" Marcella said, though she sat down immediately and made no move to help.

Rebecca popped the latches on the case, flipped the top up, and took out the first garment.

Marcella smiled. "I brought you up right, didn't I?"

"Hmm?"

She lowered herself on the bed. "I used to like doing things, when I was younger. Remember? Baking bread. Whole wheat. Long, long before it was fashionable to do it, and they started selling those...those machines...the bread makers. Pies with crust made by hand, and fillings that had real fruit and were naturally sweetened. Remember?"

"Yes," Rebecca said as she continued working. As far as she was concerned, sugar was a natural substance. "I remember."

"And coconut cream pies—the ones that made their own crust?"

Her niece smiled. She remembered them. They were dreadful. But at the time her aunt had been able to convince her they were ambrosia, and she'd been fascinated by the fact that you put a bowl full of a thick liquid mixture into a hot oven, and when it came out it had formed a crust along the bottom— albeit a gloppy, gummy crust.

"And this!" Marcella said. Around her waist was a macramé belt wound from white cord, which she wore tied loosely. She lifted its dangling ends toward Rebecca. "This. Remember this? I taught you how to do this...."

"Macramé, yes, I remember." She could also remember when she'd considered the art of knotting cord into a useful article to be magical. She could see her own childish face filled with wonder as her aunt showed her how to form the simple knots, and her aunt's delight as Rebecca was able to do it for herself.

Rebecca hung the dress in the closet, came back to the case and pulled out another, then registered surprise.

"Aunt Marci, what is this?"

Marcella craned her neck and peered into the suitcase. Nestled in the center of her underclothes was a brown paper parcel that looked very much the worse for wear. Marcella's eyes traveled up to her niece, who was staring down at her with a puzzled frown.

After a moment, Marcella said, "It's mine!"

"I figured that," Rebecca replied, inwardly rolling her eyes. "But what is it?"

Marcella snatched the parcel up by the twine that bound it and shoved it under the bed.

"It's mine! It's none of your business."

Rebecca sighed. "I just wondered."

"I HAZARD TO ASK," Lynn said with a sly smile, "but do you want to take a nap?"

She and Emily had finished their lunch, and Emily folded her napkin and laid it beside her plate. "Not in my cabin. I'm going back up to the top deck to enjoy the view and the sunshine. Whether or not that ends in a nap is purely up to the laws of nature."

Lynn laughed. "Well, if you'll excuse me, I think it's about time I got my own things unpacked. Do you need any help getting upstairs?"

"I'll be fine."

They parted, Lynn going down one staircase while Emily went up the other at a much more measured pace. She paused at the top of the stairs. The white deck was empty except for Claudia Trenton, who was occupying one of the lounge chairs on the port side, the sunhat—which Emily found faintly ridiculous—once again perched on her head. Emily was not antisocial by nature, but she had no wish to have her quiet enjoy-

ment of the afternoon punctuated by the inevitable sotto voce
criticisms. After calling a cheerful greeting to Claudia, which
was met with a slight nod of the hat, Emily went to a seat on
the starboard side.

After adjusting the back of the chair to a comfortable angle,
she lay back and enjoyed the gentle movement of the boat and
the purr of the engine. As the captain had promised, although
they were a fair distance out in the lake they were not out of
view of the shoreline, and it wasn't long before it developed a
dreamy sameness. That, along with the quiet of the nearly deserted deck, soon lulled Emily to sleep.

She wasn't sure how long it had been when something broke
in on her sleep. Through half-opened eyes she looked out
across the water at the shoreline, which seemed closer than it
had been. She had the disquieting, illusory sense that the shoreline itself was moving slowly to the right while the boat sped
to the left, as if they were not parallel, but rather turning on
the same axis.

Into this image came a woman's voice.

"It wasn't there," the voice said in a whisper. Emily
couldn't decide whether or not the voice was anxious or angry.
"I'm telling you it wasn't there! Of course I looked!"

Another voice seemed to say something, and in her half-
waking state Emily strained to hear it, but couldn't.

"You've lied to me before!" said the woman.

Emily couldn't make out to whom either of the voices belonged. She tried to turn around to see who it was, but found
herself riveted in place, unable to command her head to turn
or her limbs to move. She struggled against herself, exerting a
monumental effort, but couldn't budge. Knowledge of her pa-
ralysis caused a momentary and highly uncharacteristic shock
of fear to race through her heart. But the panic brought with it
the sudden awareness that she was dreaming, the knowledge
of which caused her to quiet down. A feeling of peace over-
came her, and she began to drift out of the dream. As the scene

dimmed, she heard the woman's voice say, "All right! I know I have to find it…but if you're lying—Wait!"

Footsteps could be heard coming up the metal stairs.

"Emily?"

The old woman opened her eyes and found herself shielded from the sun by the bulky shadow of Bertram Driscoll.

She cleared her throat gently. "Yes?"

"Sorry. I didn't like to wake you, but you were all frowny. You looked like you were having a troubled sleep, there."

Emily twisted around in her seat and looked over its back. Claudia Trenton was still seated on the opposite side of the deck, as she had been when Emily dozed off, and was now apparently asleep herself. She was also quite alone.

Emily turned back to Driscoll. "Mr. Driscoll, may I ask…did you just come up onto the deck?"

"Yes, ma'am."

"Did you see anyone else here?"

"Nope. Just you. And the Trenton woman."

Emily's brows knit closely together, and her mouth pursed into a tiny O.

"Is something wrong?"

She relaxed and smiled at him. "No. Not at all. Thank you for waking me. I was having a rather bad dream."

"I can't imagine a fine woman like you having anything to cause you nightmares."

"On the contrary. At my age I've seen enough of life to have very bad dreams. Fortunately, I don't usually."

Driscoll straightened a chair beside her and carelessly lowered himself onto it. "Must be being out on the water that makes people so sleepy. I dropped off myself, earlier on, before lunch."

"Yes, I know."

"Or boredom," he added incomprehensibly.

"I beg your pardon?"

"Boredom. That makes you drop off, you know. I do that

at home—fall asleep in front of the TV set more often than not, right in the middle of the day, now that I'm retired.''

His face was turned toward her, and out of the corner of her eye she could see the eagerness in his florid features. She sought to deflect him.

''You were a salesman, weren't you?''

He nodded. ''Medical supplies. Don't get me started on sales! You get me talking about business, and I swear to God I'll end up sounding just like Muriel Langstrom!''

Emily laughed despite herself. ''Now, Mr. Driscoll! You were the one who said she was a good soul.''

''Caught by my own words! But you know what I mean. If I start talking about work, I'll never stop.''

Again there was an eagerness in his expression that Emily recognized: the slightest encouragement on her part would allow him to proceed onto his favorite topic, despite the polite objection.

''Isn't the lake peaceful?'' she said. ''I don't know why, but I always expect that when you're out on the water, it will be rougher than it is.''

''I don't know about that. You know, I wouldn't mind if it was a bit rougher. That would be exciting, at least. I get all the peace I need at home. Near drives me crazy, sometimes. Don't you find it like that? I mean, you live alone, just like I do.''

''Oh, no, not at all,'' Emily replied brightly. ''There is so much in life in which to be interested. Tending the garden, going to theaters and films, reading the newspapers. And of course, friends. Visiting with them, having lunches and dinners together. Yes, I would say that my life is very, very full.''

''Yes…well…,'' Driscoll began falteringly, his usual bluster somewhat daunted. ''That's just the way it should be, a woman such as yourself.''

A period followed during which Driscoll clumsily tried to regain his conversational footing, but his attempts were so awkward that Emily, though more than capable of holding her own in any social situation, was relieved when Lynn emerged from the stairwell. She pulled one of the chairs to Emily's side and sat down.

"All unpacked?" the old woman asked.

"Yes. Rebecca and her aunt were down there doing the same. Good grief, you should hear how that woman complains."

"You sound upset."

"Oh, I'm not really. I guess I…well, I know how some people get as they get older, and I can understand it…." Her voice trailed off and she noticed Emily's kindly smile. "What is it?"

"I've a feeling that you wonder why Rebecca puts up with it, and you know why at the same time."

The young woman sighed deeply. "You're right, as always."

Emily patted her hand gently, then lay back in her seat.

As the afternoon wore on, one by one the rest of the passengers made their way up to the deck and relaxed in the sun. Lynn could hear Marcella Hemsley coming up the stairs long before she came into view. Apparently Rebecca's aunt had fallen asleep in her cabin not long after Lynn had finished unpacking and left the blue deck, and Marcella was chastising her niece for allowing her to sleep so long.

"We paid good money for this cruise," she said as her mop of gray hair rose into view, "and I don't want you to let me sleep the trip away!"

"Yes, Aunt Marci," Rebecca said patiently.

Driscoll grunted from behind closed eyes.

Marcella and Rebecca came onto the deck and seated themselves off the starboard quarter, where Marcella promptly fell asleep again. Rebecca stared off toward the shoreline.

David Douglas came by making one of his rounds of the passengers to see if anyone required him. He made a special point of stopping by Rebecca. "Can I get you anything?"

"No, thank you," she said in a pleasant but dismissive tone.

"Are you sure? It would be no trouble to run down to the bar and bring you up something. Whatever you like."

"That's very nice, but no."

He crouched down beside her and whispered. "I can see how things are for you, with your aunt....If you want a break"—he paused and a broad smile spread across his face—"when we get to town I could have Hoke look after the old girl, and maybe I could show you around. There's a nice English pub the Red Lion...we could have a few drinks...."

She eyed him frostily. "I guarantee that you don't know how things are for me."

With this she lay back and closed her eyes.

Douglas rose with a complacent shrug and moved on.

The *Genessee* continued its leisurely pace along the coast. After another half an hour, Driscoll roused himself with a snort, smacked his lips a couple of times, then rolled his eyes over in Emily's direction.

"Sorry to doze off like that, Miss Charters. Guess it's the sea air."

"That's quite all right," Emily said, her face implying that he was not expected to keep her entertained.

"Anyone look at the itinerary?"

"I did," said Lynn. "We'll arrive at Sangamore in a little while. We'll be anchored there—if that's the right term for it—overnight."

"What's there to do there?"

"I suppose we shall see," said Emily.

"LADIES AND GENTLEMEN, we will be docking soon at our first stop, Sangamore, Michigan, where we'll stay for the night," the captain announced over the loudspeaker. "You may like to have dinner at any of the fine restaurants in town, or if you want you can have dinner on the boat. Just let one of the crew know if that's the case and Mrs. O'Malley will be glad to prepare something for you."

The loudspeaker emitted a loud metallic pop as it was switched off.

The *Genessee* continued to cruise north for several minutes before the passengers noticed a break in the endless shoreline. It was the entrance to a small branch of the Kalamazoo River. The boat veered to the right and headed for it.

They followed the river southeast for a short distance before navigating a corner that took them into a short stretch that went straight south. To their left was the town. The street along the river—appropriately named River Street—was lined with small galleries and shops, most of which looked as if they'd been converted from private residences. After a few more minutes, the *Genessee* reached a small harbor, and Captain Farraday maneuvered the boat up to a long, weather-worn pier.

David and Hoke had come up to the deck, and as soon as the boat was beside the pier, David leaped over the side onto the dock in an ostentatious display of athletics that stole the breath of some of the elderly passengers. Hoke threw him the lines and he tied off the boat. Then Hoke swung the boarding plank into position.

David secured the plank, then sprinted up it and called out, "All ashore that's goin' ashore!"

The passengers moved to the top of the plank en masse, then went down it, progressing slowly due to the fact that by some quirk of fate, Lily DuPree had managed to be in the lead. She was followed by Muriel Langstrom. When the two ladies reached the bottom, Muriel gave her arm to Lilly.

"I'll stay with you," said Muriel, "so you have somebody to hold on to. It's been years since I've been to this town, but I remember it well! The main street and all the shops are just over that way. Come on, now!"

She went charging up the pier with Lily nearly running to keep up.

"I feel sorry for Miss DuPree," Lynn said to Emily as they went down the plank.

"Do you?" Emily replied with surprise.

"You mean you don't?"

Emily's gaze followed the retreating forms of the two old women. "No, I would think one's sympathy might be better spared for Muriel."

Lynn laughed. "You know, sometimes I think you work at being an enigma!"

"Me? Oh, no. I'm sure I'm an open book."

The passengers more or less fell naturally into the groups they had formed at lunch: the Millers were arm in arm, Martin's expensive camera bouncing rather alarmingly against his sternum as they went along; the three unattached gentlemen talked amicably as they followed Claudia Trenton, whose hand braced the back of the sunhat, which was threatened with flight by a soft breeze; and Rebecca and her aunt stayed close beside Emily and Lynn. At a glance from Rebecca, she and Lynn fell slightly behind the two older women.

"Do you think you and Emily will be having dinner in town?" Rebecca asked.

"We haven't talked about it, but I imagine so. Emily loves an adventure."

"Do you think…would it be all right if my aunt and I had it with you? She seems to do a little better when there's other people around, and she likes Emily. And Emily doesn't—"

"You don't have to explain," Lynn replied, cutting her off sympathetically. "It's really fine. We'd enjoy the company."

"That's very kind of you," Rebecca said with barely masked relief.

"I'm not being kind. It's true. Why don't you come along with us and look at the shops?"

"Oh…no. It would be better for Aunt Marci and I to be on our own. She has a tendency to get…distracted."

In her mind Lynn formed a protest along the lines of the fact that she and Emily would not exactly be blazing any trails through the town, but she didn't say it because she thought it likely that Rebecca was using the term "distracted" diplomatically. "Anyway, where should we meet?"

"Well…David told me that there's an English pub that might be fun. It's called the Red Lion."

Lynn raised her eyebrows and grinned. "David told you that, did he?"

She sighed. "He's been kind of a pest. A little bit. Hovering around me."

The grin faded. "He has? Maybe you should do something about that."

"He hovers around everyone. He doesn't mean anything. I know the type."

"Now you sound like your aunt," Lynn said without thinking. The anguished look that crossed Rebecca's face caused Lynn to inwardly kick herself. She would've apologized, but she thought acknowledging that she'd seen Rebecca's pain would've made it worse.

"I mean," Rebecca continued as if nothing had happened, "if it got any worse, I would do something. But I think he's harmless."

"Well, if you say so. Anyway, the pub sounds like fun to me. Emily?"

The two older women paused and turned around. "Yes?"

"Rebecca was just telling me that there's an English pub here that's supposed to be good. Do you think that would be all right for dinner?"

"That sounds great!" Marcella exclaimed. "An English pub! Don't think I've ever been to anything like that!"

"That would be fine," Emily said.

"Where should we meet you?" Lynn asked Rebecca.

"Why don't we meet at the pub? It's a small town, I'm sure anyone can direct us to it. Six o'clock?"

"Fine."

Once the passengers arrived at the end of the dock, they dispersed like a mist spreading in the general direction of Main Street. As Rebecca had predicted, her aunt's attention was distracted almost immediately by a pair of very young, unsupervised little girls who were playing on the grass between the pier and a riverside motel. Both girls were wearing faded plaid jumpers, and giggled with delight as they tossed an underinflated beach ball back and forth.

Marcella stood on the grass, tilted to the same degree as its slope, gazing at the girls with rapt attention, an envious grin on her face. She looked very much as if she'd like to join in with them. Lynn exchanged a hasty glance with Rebecca, then she and Emily left the two women behind.

It was a short walk to River Street, where they found themselves beside a small white, cottagelike building that housed a shop selling Christmas ornaments.

"Well, that's unseasonal," said Lynn. "Would you like to go in?"

"It looks charming," Emily replied, peering through the window in the door.

They spent some time inside the shop, which Emily felt was like being spirited to the inside of a Christmas tree. The overall ambiance was rather dark, while miniature lights and painted glass ornaments glittered on artificial trees. When they'd finished making a circuit of the store, they continued on to Main Street. Just before reaching it, they passed a sort of wide, bright alleyway. Near the opening was a door over which hung an old-fashioned wooden shingle that said Red Lion.

"Ah. There's our pub," said Lynn.

They turned the corner onto Main and felt as if they had stepped back in time. The street was lined on both sides with shops fronted by small, evenly spaced trees in full foliage. There were also occasional public benches for the benefit of tourists. There didn't appear to be very many people shopping at the moment, though there were a few.

"My, my, this is a lovely place," Emily said, her arm through Lynn's as they strolled down the street.

"It's very quiet," said Lynn.

"Just as the captain's wife said, it's not quite the season yet, and it is Monday. Do you mind the quiet?"

"Not at all. It's a welcome change from Chicago. Everything moves so fast there, and everything is so noisy."

There was a weariness in the young woman's tone that caught Emily's attention. She couldn't remember hearing it before.

"I don't think you've ever told me," said Emily. "Have you lived in Chicago all of your life?"

"Yes, I have." They paused in front of a small wood-framed store that was painted a muted mustard yellow. In the window were shelves lined with tiny glass fantasy figures, including a unicorn whose horn was tinted purple, and a gargoyle with glimmering green eyes.

"Would you like to go in?" Lynn asked.

"No," Emily replied with a chuckle. "They're very pretty, but there are enough things collecting dust in my house. I don't need any more."

"I beg your pardon!" Lynn exclaimed with mock distress. "I do your dusting!"

Emily laughed. "It's just a figure of speech."

A little farther down the street they came to a shop with white lattice windows. A sign painted in plain script boasted an array of cutlery, cookware, and comestibles. They stopped and looked in the windows.

"I'd like to go in, if you don't mind," said Lynn.

"Not at all," Emily replied. "But I think I'll wait out here and enjoy the sunshine." She gave a nod toward a bench by the curb that faced the shop.

"I won't be long."

"Take your time."

Lynn hesitated in the doorway for a split second, then entered the shop.

Emily took a seat. It was a typical wooden bench with the back curved to fit the general shape of a man's back—which made it out of proportion for most women—and the whole seat was tilted back a little too far. But exposure to the elements had left the wood soft, and Emily found it surprisingly comfortable.

She sat for a while listening to the wind rustling through the trees. The air smelled deliciously damp, with the kind of freshness that signals the presence of a nearby body of water, rather than the cloying heaviness of Chicago's humid climate.

Three young women came out of a small shop that specialized in handmade jewelry that Emily and Lynn had already passed.

"Yeah, but do you like it?" said one of the girls, a petite brunette, as she held her right hand up for the others to inspect.

"I *like* it," said the tall blonde. "It's right for *you*. It's just not my kind of ring."

The brunette *tsk*ed noisily, then turned to the third girl. "What do you think?"

"I love it! I just love it!" she replied with the intensity of youth that betrays a desperate desire to please.

As they passed Emily, the first girl lowered her hand with her fingers splayed out and looked down at the glittering trinket. "Well, I like it," she said with finality.

Emily smiled to herself at their youthful innocence. She was an eminently practical woman, and wouldn't have wanted to be young again for all the tea in China, if such a thing were possible. But the brief exchange reminded her of a time of life when problems were small and only *seemed* big.

Emily watched as they continued down the street, then stopped and looked in the window of another store. After a hurried conversation, they went in. Emily was just about to turn away when she noticed something at the end of the block: a man was standing by the building at the corner. At that distance she couldn't clearly make out his face, but from the color of his hair and the clothes he was wearing she took it to be Stuart Holmes. She became certain when he gestured in Holmes's tentative manner. Whomever he was speaking with was out of sight, behind the building.

She thought nothing of this at first, since she assumed that the three single men had stayed together and presumably it was one of them with whom he was in conversation. But then his companion stepped into view, and Emily was startled to realize that she'd never seen him before. He was wearing a pair of black pants and a white shirt over which he sported a red jacket. After two or three more minutes, they disappeared, either into the building or around the corner.

Emily sat staring after them for a moment, then shook her head.

Well, after all, she thought, *we're not that far from Chicago, and many people from there come here. He could easily have run into someone he knows. For that matter, he could've simply become involved in a conversation with one of the local people. But...there was something in their posture and the way they were gesturing that indicated familiarity....*

"You have the funniest look on your face," said Lynn, who had come out of the store without Emily noticing.

Emily started and put a hand to her chest. "Oh! I didn't hear you!"

"I'm sorry. What were you thinking about so intently?"

The old woman sighed. "I was just thinking that I must stop making a mystery out of everything."

"I knew this cruise was getting to be too peaceful," Lynn replied with a wry smile as she helped Emily off the bench. "What have you seen in this sleepy little village that's so mysterious?"

"Nothing at all. That's just the point." As they started down the street, she added, "I see you're empty-handed."

"Yes. I don't really need anything for the kitchen at the moment, but...they do have some lemon curd I might pick up on the way back."

"What ho!" cried Bertram Driscoll as he emerged from the shop they were passing. "Hey, there, ladies. Nice little town, isn't it?"

"It's generally very quiet," Emily replied primly.

Driscoll cleared his throat and lowered his voice somewhat.

"I've been looking around. Haven't found anything I want but they got a lot of nice stuff here."

"What has become of your companions?"

He wrinkled his nose questioningly, then allowed it to relax. "My—Oh, yeah. Well, Dismal Jack—otherwise known as Stuart Holmes—the minute we reached River Street, he said he was going off on his own."

"How odd," Emily said lightly. "Of course, some people do like to be on their own." *But he isn't on his own.*

"He turned down the street before this one, I guess to get away from us. Truth to tell, I don't think he wanted to be seen with us, more's the pity for him!" This was said in Driscoll's usual, jovial manner, but Emily sensed a degree of hurt behind the words: a lifelong hurt.

"Not-So-Dismal Jack," he continued, "otherwise known as Jackson Brock, is still in this little hidey-hole of a store. Sells scented soaps and things. The stink started to get to me. I had to come up for air."

It was at that moment that Brock emerged from the store carrying a small red shopping bag.

"Sorry I took so long, Driscoll, but they had a very big selection," he said in the wide-eyed manner that was peculiar to him. It seemed to Emily that Jackson Brock always looked as if he'd just heard something that had seriously thrown him for a loop.

"Oh!" he exclaimed when he noticed the two women. "Hello. I didn't mean to ignore you."

"So you've found something already?" Emily said with a glance at his bag.

He spread the handles wide and showed the contents to her. "Yes. Soap. They have many flavors—er, aromas—of them in there."

"And a bottle of lavender," she said, peering into the bag.

Brock closed it, his cheeks flushing a deep crimson. "Yes. I've been having trouble sleeping, and...of course now, in a strange bed. I thought it might help. It's supposed to be very good for that...spraying it on the pillow."

"Yes, it is," Emily said kindly. "And it does work."

"I have a friend who is an aromatherapist," Lynn interjected. "She recommends it to everyone who's having trouble sleeping. She says the scent is very relaxing, and you find yourself dropping right off."

Brock's cheeks had returned to their natural color. "I'm glad to hear that."

"Well, that's all interesting," Driscoll said. "Now, how about the two of you coming on with us?"

"I'm afraid we can't," said Emily. "We have quite a bit of shopping to do, and some of it is for—" She lowered her voice. "Personal items."

Driscoll recoiled slightly, and he silently worked his jaw as if bracing for the unwelcome eventuality of a further explanation.

"So you will excuse us?"

"Oh, yes, yes!" he blustered, stepping to the side so they could easily pass. "Enjoy yourselves!"

"We'll see you back at the boat," Brock added.

The two pairs headed in different directions. When there was some distance between them, Lynn chuckled. "Personal items?"

"Well...anything we'd be buying for ourselves could be considered personal items, couldn't they?"

"I've always said, you're a very sly woman!"

"Tell me something, Lynn. Do you really know an aromatherapist?"

She laughed. "I know a lot of people. There must be one among them somewhere."

When they reached the corner where Emily had seen Stuart Holmes, she stopped and looked up the side street. The corner building was an old-fashioned drugstore with a row of apartments on the second floor. The entrance to the shop opened onto Main, while the door to the apartments was on the side of the building. Behind the building was a parking lot, after which the street ran into the residential district, where homes were surrounded by trees and shrubs.

"Emily? What are you looking for?" Lynn asked.

"Hm? Oh! Nothing. I was just wondering what was in this direction."

"Well, there doesn't appear to be any shops that way. There are some in down that way." Lynn gave a nod in the opposite direction of the side street, which led down to the harbor. "Why don't we go that way?"

Emily agreed, and they crossed Main and headed down the side street. They went past a store selling party supplies, and another whose theme neither of them could make out, since its window displayed a variety of hand-knitted afghans and homemade fudge. They found a place called the Corner Kitchen: a clean, glass-framed sandwich shop, where they decided to stop for a cup of tea. The shop was on the corner of River Street, which had followed the natural curve of the river and at that point was separated from the water by a brief expanse of park.

"Look, there're the Millers," said Lynn as she raised the cup to her lips.

Emily had to twist in her seat to see them. Martin and Laura Miller were at the far end of the park, pressing a passerby into the role of photographer while they posed against the background of the water.

"Oh, dear," she said lightly.

"What?"

"I have a feeling that the Millers are the type of people who make nuisances of themselves wherever they go."

"The Millers? I'd plump for Muriel Langstrom, or Marcella Hemsley."

"Marcella, I think, can't help herself," Emily said, still watching the Millers. "And Muriel is the type of person who one instinctively tunes out. But you'll observe that the Millers are the type of people who draw others in."

They fell silent and watched the distant couple, each with

FRED HUNTER 61

an arm around the other's waist. Laura laughed as Martin waved at the cameraman to take more pictures.

When Emily turned back to Lynn she was met by a pair of very amused eyes.

"What is it?" she asked with an upraised brow.

Lynn lowered her cup onto its saucer. "Nothing. I was just wondering where you'd like to go next?"

Emily elevated her shoulders a fraction of an inch. "I suppose we should go back to Main and finish our tour of the shops."

"You make it sound as if that's what's expected of us!"

On the short stretch back to the town's main street, they passed a large Victorian-style house with a broad, inviting front porch on which there was a pair of unoccupied wicker rockers. In the center of the lawn that fronted the house was a sign announcing the Evergreen Bed-and-Breakfast. Next to this was a small recessed building, once a bungalow, that had been converted into a shop selling ceramic masks.

On Main they continued to wander to the end of the business district. They stopped in at a store that sold homemade candies where Emily bought a box of peppermint-striped saltwater taffy, and Lynn succumbed to the allure of some hand-dipped strawberries.

Farther down the block they went into the Southwest Trading Company. The air inside was tinged with a hypnotic, salty incense, and from unexposed speakers a gentle, soothing Indian melody played on wooden flutes.

The two women spent nearly an hour in the store, examining the jewelry and other wares. Emily at last purchased a hand-woven blanket with brown, white, and muted pink stripes.

"I want to bring something back for Jeremy, you see," she said when they finally left the shop.

"Do you think when he picks us up at the dock he's going to say 'Did you bring me anything?'" Lynn said, obviously amused at the mental image.

The touch of red that flowed into Emily's cheeks was accompanied by a somewhat coy smile. "It's only proper that I should bring my host a gift."

They spent the remainder of the afternoon making their way in and out of the shops on the opposite side of Main Street, stopping twice to rest on one of the benches and enjoy some of the proceeds from their visit to the candy store.

"You're right," Lynn said out of the blue as she finished off her second strawberry. "It is very nice here. Very peaceful."

"Yes," Emily agreed, pleased to find that Lynn had lost the anxiousness that had been evident earlier.

"This might be a nice place to—" Lynn had begun this wistfully, then broke off. After a moment, she continued. "It would be a nice place to come with someone for a weekend."

"I quite agree."

By the time they'd reached the end of Main Street, it was nearly six o'clock, so they headed down River Street and into the paved alley that served as the entrance for the Red Lion Pub.

After passing through the heavy, dark wooden door they found themselves in a well-lit room with a small fireplace at its center. The entire wall directly across from the front door was the bar, shaped like an inverted J. In front of it was a row of stools with wooden seats and backs, each of which was occupied.

The wall behind the bar was lined with glass shelves that ran almost all the way up to the ceiling. These held an array of bottles in all shapes and sizes. A small slate at a break in the center of the shelves boasted in blue chalk a selection of one hundred brands of imported beer.

A fresh-faced young woman was working behind the bar. She had a ready smile and sparkling eyes, and dark, wavy neck-length hair. She was wearing a crisp white shirt and leather vest. Emily wondered with an inward smile if the woman's name might be Colleen.

"Hello, Lynn," Rebecca said.

Lynn and Emily had been so taken by the environs and the general noise and bustle that they hadn't noticed the long, high-backed bench just to the right of the door. Rebecca and her aunt were seated there. Rebecca stood up as she greeted them.

"Hi," Lynn replied. "I'm sorry, I didn't see you."

"It's a beautiful place, isn't it?"

"It looks like a proper British pub, only in the wrong country."

"Good evening, Ms. Charters," Rebecca said.

"Good evening. And please, call me Emily."

"When are we going to eat?" Marcella asked peremptorily.

"In just a few minutes," Rebecca replied. She turned back to Emily and Lynn. "When we got here I told the host we'd need a table for four. He said it would be about twenty minutes. That was ten minutes ago."

"Ah," said Emily.

"Why don't we sit down?" Lynn suggested as she guided Emily over to a place on the bench next to Marcella. Rebecca and Lynn sat beside their respective charges.

"I'm hungry!" Marcella said.

"It will only be a few more minutes," Emily said soothingly as she gave a gentle pat to Marcella's hand.

There were booths along the wall to the left of the door, and about twenty tables arranged around the room in a way that looked very haphazard, but given the dexterity with which the staff was navigating the room, Emily thought there might be a design at work that simply escaped her. All of the tables and booths were occupied by parties of various numbers, boisterously drinking and dining.

After Emily had surveyed the room for some time, something caught her attention.

"Now, there's something that surprises me," she said to Lynn, keeping her voice rather low.

"I don't believe anything surprises you," said Lynn. "What are you looking at?"

"At the table for two, all the way at the back of the room by the kitchen."

Lynn looked toward the back and emitted a "hmm." At the table, facing front, was Claudia Trenton, eating with mechanical intensity and occasionally stopping to say a word or two to her companion. The surprise was that her companion, whose back was toward the women, wore the unmistakable clothing of Bertram Driscoll.

"I would say that was a very unlikely couple," said Emily.

"I've always heard that shipboard romances could be very odd," said Lynn with a grin.

"It doesn't quite look like a romance."

Lynn observed them for a moment. "No, it doesn't."

The corners of Claudia's mouth were turned down in something nearing a scowl, and at the rare moments that she spoke to Driscoll, she seldom actually looked at him. After a few minutes, apparently sensing that she was being watched, Claudia raised her eyes directly at Lynn and Emily. The two women nodded greetings toward her. Claudia pursed her lips, inclined her head slightly, and looked back down at her plate.

Several more people arrived, and their names were added to the waiting list by a young man wearing the uniform of the Red Lion: a pair of casual, light tan pants, a spotlessly clean white shirt, opened at the neck, and leather vest. Before going back to the kitchen, he spoke to Rebecca.

"I'm sorry, I know it's been a little longer than twenty minutes, but we do have a party that's almost done, so it'll only be a little longer."

"That's all right. Thank you," Rebecca replied, though she was getting anxious on her aunt's behalf. It really hadn't been that long a wait, but Marcella could be quite irritable if her needs, real or imagined, were not met.

The waiter hurried away, and true to his word it was only a few minutes before a group of four rose from their table and left. Another waiter set about clearing it as the departing patrons filed past the hungry people waiting by the door.

It was during this bit of confusion that Claudia Trenton got up from her table. With little more than a glance at her dinner partner, who remained seated, she headed for the door.

"Ladies," she said stiffly when she passed the bench on which her four fellow passengers were seated. She didn't wait for any sort of reply before exiting the pub.

"Never could stand that Trenton woman," said Marcella loudly. "She was always an uppity bitch!"

Rebecca cast an apologetic glance toward Emily and Lynn. The latter smiled in return.

"She doesn't have any reason to think she's better than anyone else," Marcella continued. She turned to Emily, "You ever hear about her grandson?"

"No." Emily replied with a quizzical tilt of her head.

"Everybody around the church knows about it! You know how gossip goes around."

Emily wore an unreadable smile. "Yes, I do."

"He's been arrested...more than once!"

"What was his crime?"

As Emily expected, once faced with a direct question, she faltered, leaving Emily to wonder if the matter was another of Marcella's fancies. Her expression became distraught as the specifics failed her. "It was...it was..." Frustrated, she sliced the air with her palm. "It doesn't matter! He's been in jail, and she raised him! She has no call to think she's better than anyone else."

"Every family has its black sheep," Emily said lightly. "Entirely too much emphasis is placed on blaming the ones who raised them. There are so many outside influences these days."

"It's not like you to excuse something like that," said Lynn.

"Oh, I'm not excusing it, my dear. But families have become more splintered for any number of reasons, and I just don't think it's quite fair to blame the parents...or grandparents...anymore. I mean, of course, when one hears of a young person committing a crime, one naturally thinks 'Where were the parents?" But there is only so much any parent can do against all of the influences in the world."

"Well, hello there, ladies!" Bertram Driscoll appeared before them, having finished his meal and settled the check. He seemed genuinely surprised to see them.

"Good evening, Mr. Driscoll," Emily said. "I trust you had a nice dinner?"

"The food's great here." He patted his stomach.

"Did Claudia enjoy it?"

Driscoll rolled his eyes heavenward. "The food's good, but the company..." He extended a flat hand and waggled it, then crouched down so that he could be at eye level with the seated women. "It was my mistake, you see. All the tables were full up when I got here. She was at that table alone, and I asked if I could sit with her."

"And of course, she couldn't refuse a direct request," said Emily with an understanding twinkle in her eye.

"Not and be polite! Big mistake on my part, though. Woman's got ice water in her veins. She's not exactly, you know, conducive to good digestion."

Emily smiled and mentally corrected his English.

"Now if you'll excuse me, ladies, I'm going to be toddling off—see if I can't walk off some of that fried fish."

He rose and slapped his stomach again, then left them just as the waiter waved in their direction from the newly cleared table.

"Come on, Aunt Marci, the table's ready," said Rebecca.

"I'm hungry," Marcella croaked irritably as she struggled to her feet. The bench didn't have armrests to hold for support, and her niece helped her up. True to form, Marcella snatched her arm away the moment she'd been righted.

Once they were seated they pored over the menus of an extensive selection of traditional British fare, along with some American additions. In the end all four of them ordered fish and chips, a decision which served to further the festive mood. Marcella regained her equilibrium the moment the food arrived, and appeared to delight in the scurrying of the staff and the roar of the crowd.

The fish was deep fried in a thick batter to a perfect golden brown, and the chips were crisp on the outside, hot and soft in the middle. Marcella smacked her lips around the food, enjoying it with obvious gusto. And though the other three ladies might not have been quite as noisy about it, their enjoyment was none the less.

After a dessert of raspberries and cream and a large pot of tea that was shared among them, they left the pub feeling considerably heavier than they'd been when they'd arrived, and considerably more satisfied as well.

Emily could appreciate Bertram Driscoll's desire for a walk after such a heavy meal, and suggested to the others that they take a turn around Main Street before returning to the boat. The idea was met with approval.

All of the shops appeared to still be open, their windows casting a warm glow onto the darkening street, which was now lit with electric lamps designed to look like gaslights. The foursome strolled in pairs up the right side of the street, with Emily and Lynn in the lead. When they reached the cookery shop, Lynn ran in and purchased some of the lemon curd she'd spotted earlier, then they continued their progress.

It wasn't long after that that Marcella stopped suddenly, and with wide, bewildered eyes, said, "We came this way already."

Rebecca stifled a sigh. "You're right, we did. But we're just taking a walk now, remember?"

They started once more, but hadn't gone more than twenty feet before Marcella stopped again. "I'm tired!" she announced truculently.

Lynn and Emily had stopped and turned around, and Rebecca hesitated before saying anything. "It's all right, you two go on, I'll take my aunt back to the boat."

"You don't need to come with me," said Marcella.

"Oh, no, really, I want to."

Emily sighed, attempting to sound weary. "I really should go back as well. I'm quite tired myself. It's been a very long day."

They didn't talk much as they retraced their steps down Main Street, then River, and over the broad lawn to the pier. It had grown considerably darker during their brief walk, and the area leading to the dock was unlighted, though hanging from the nearest post of the pier was an old-fashioned lantern. The boat itself was lit by a row of small white bulbs hung around its perimeter.

Just as the women reached the pier they heard someone approaching, the heavy tread causing the boards to creak, but with the lantern right before them they could see little more than an approaching shadow beyond it.

It was a man who passed by the light. He had a pinched, craggy face and hair that was a mixture of white and bluish gray. He didn't speak to them as he hurried by, and it seemed to Emily that he had tried to avert his face as he passed the lantern. But it wasn't his face that she recognized, it was the red jacket.

"I wonder who that was?" said Rebecca. "He must've been coming from the *Genessee*. It's the only boat docked here."

"Well, the Farradays run the tour all summer," Lynn offered. "They must know people all along their route. He was probably here to see them."

"Or one of the passengers," Emily muttered.

Lynn went with Emily to her cabin, where the old woman sighed heavily and sat down on the bed.

"Did we overdo it today?" Lynn asked.

Emily chuckled. "You sound much like the nurses when I had my heart surgery."

Lynn laughed. "I wasn't using the royal 'we.'"

"Well, in that case, I don't think we exactly overdid it, but I will admit I'm very tired."

Lynn studied her face for a few moments. "Emily, is something bothering you?"

"Not really," she replied slowly. "It's probably just old age, that's all...."

"What do you mean? Don't you feel well?" Lynn sat beside her.

"What? Oh, I don't mean that at all! I'm perfectly all right. No, I was thinking...doesn't it strike you that there's something not quite right about this cruise?"

Lynn's deep brown eyes opened wide. "You mean other than some of the passengers not really liking some of the others? No, I haven't noticed anything at all."

"You needn't look so concerned," Emily said with a kindly smile, "I'm not losing my faculties. It probably is only my suspicious mind."

"Or you've been spending too much time with your favorite detective," Lynn countered. "But I doubt it. If I look concerned it's because when you think there's something odd, there usually is. What have you seen that I haven't?"

"Little things," Emily replied vaguely. "Very little things."

She explained, starting with the exchange she had overheard—or had dreamed—earlier that day on the white deck: the anxious voices she couldn't place talking about a thing that wasn't there, and how that exchange had stopped at the sound of approaching footsteps.

"You probably did dream it," Lynn said lightly.

"I probably did. But somehow I felt that it was real."

Lynn thought for a minute, then shrugged. "You said you couldn't identify either voice."

"That's right. I could barely hear the second one."

"So it could've been two of the crew, who would've naturally been upset if they'd lost something that either belonged to their employers or one of the passengers."

"That's true," Emily said with a thoughtful tilt of her head. "And speaking of the crew, then there's David Douglas, the overly personable head steward."

Lynn's face clouded at the mention of his name. "Oh, him. He's been bothering Rebecca."

"I shouldn't think that was anything serious. I was thinking more of his evasiveness when I asked him about his former employment."

"Why should he be evasive? It was an innocent question." She smiled. "Wasn't it?"

"Of course," Emily said innocently.

"Emily…"

The old woman's eyes were lit with amusement. "Well, I did think that young man a bit too sincere to be true. But as you say, for all intents and purposes, it was an innocent question from an old lady who couldn't possibly cause him any real trouble."

"So why be evasive?"

"Exactly."

"You have some idea?"

"The most obvious one that springs to mind is because the question was so unexpected…at least, from my quarter."

Lynn sat back and knit her narrow brow. "What difference would the quarter make?"

"Sometimes all the difference in the world. There are people whose frame of reference relies entirely on context. I once knew a man—a Mr. Gorden—who lived down the street from my husband and me. Mr. Gorden once ran into his own wife unexpectedly in a store in which he'd never seen her before, and it was several minutes before he could remember her name."

"His own wife?"

Emily nodded. "Oh, yes, that sort of thing happens more often than you think. So it's possible that David has a ready reply handy in case one of the Farradays ask him about his past, but it failed him when the source of the question was someone else."

"Yes, but…" Lynn couldn't keep the note of doubt from her tone. "It may have been nothing. He may have just been distracted."

"That's very true."

They were silent for a while, then Lynn said, "The only thing I can think of that's odd was seeing that stranger coming out of the darkness from the direction of the boat."

"Oh, I wasn't surprised by him at all!"

"You weren't?"

"No. I'd seen him before."

"Where?"

"This afternoon. Talking to Stuart Holmes."

"Really?" Lynn considered this a moment, then shrugged. "But that still probably doesn't mean anything."

"Of course not," said Emily. "Many people from Chicago vacation here. It wouldn't be that surprising for Mr. Holmes or any of us to run into someone we know. But...didn't the stranger strike you as rather furtive when he passed us?"

Lynn tried to picture the scene in her head. "You know, come to think of it, he did kind of turn his face away when he went by the light, didn't he? But...a lot of people do that when they run into strangers, especially in the dark."

Emily sighed. "I daresay you're right, my dear. Maybe I'm just tired. Or maybe I am just getting to be a foolish old woman."

Lynn emitted a muffled snort. "If you think you're a foolish old woman, then you really are tired. You are the most practical person I know."

Emily seemed to be turning something over in her mind. "Well, then, if I were to look at it all from a strictly practical standpoint, I'd have to say that these things I've noticed amount to nothing." A little light flickered in her eyes. "Then, of course, there is the fact that last time I was on vacation in Michigan, there was a murder."

A WAVE OF WEARINESS washed over Lynn once she was back in her own cabin. She didn't want to admit it to herself, and she certainly wouldn't have admitted it to Emily, but she really had been worried about her elderly friend going on this trip. It wasn't exactly rational: Emily was no more frail now than she

was the day they'd met. In fact, since Ransom had hired Lynn
to clean for Emily after the old woman's heart surgery, she was
actually stronger now than when they'd met. And Emily was
a perfect judge of her own limitations. Lynn knew that Emily
wouldn't overtire herself or take on tasks that she knew were
physically foolhardy.

"Unless, of course, she couldn't still judge her own limitations," Lynn said to her reflection in the round mirror over the
sink. Looking into her own clear eyes, Lynn suddenly laughed.

"I'm the one who's not being rational. I'm letting Rebecca
rub off on me."

She experienced a slight pang when she thought of Rebecca,
and shook her head brusquely to dismiss it. As she undressed,
she gave some careful consideration to what she'd been feeling.
Lynn was, in her own way, a very practical woman—though
perhaps not quite so much as Emily. But still, it was possible
for her to put aside her fears and worries and take a clinical
look at herself. And when she did this, she realized that it was
in part Emily's birthday that had brought about her anxiety for
the old woman's well-being. With the day-to-day passage of
time it was easy to forget that Emily had passed into her eighties, but a birthday was a milestone: it brought home the fact
that her friend would not be there forever. Lynn had even found
herself feeling cheated because she'd met Emily so late in life.

She slipped into a pair of sensible pajamas in light green
and white stripes, paused in the act of buttoning up the top,
and sighed with disgust at herself. *What in the hell is going on
with me? It's not like me to think that way! It's morbid!*

She dropped down onto the end of the bed and laid her hands
on her knees as she took stock. When she pushed aside the
cloud of worries, she found that behind them was a simple
truth: she was lonely. It had been a few years since her lover,
Maggie, had died, and despite the bond she'd formed with Emily, who had become like a wise old grandmother to her (just
as she had to Ransom), and despite her friendship with Ransom
as well, she didn't have someone with whom she could truly

share her life. Worse yet, it wasn't until that moment that she was even aware of the desire.

With another sigh she leaned over and switched off the compass lamp on the bedside chest, remarking to herself that the Farradays must've gotten these unusual lamps as a job lot. Then she stretched herself out on the narrow bed. Through the open porthole she could hear the gentle sloshing of the water against the hull, and the occasional call of a bird—gulls, she imagined—from somewhere in the distance. They were peaceful sounds that Lynn expected would quickly lull her to sleep.

But it was not to happen. She lay on top of the blanket for a while, and though exhausted, sleep refused to come. She tried turning on one side, then the other. It wasn't like her to lose sleep over anything, but she couldn't get her newfound realization out of her head. Nor could she dismiss Emily's observations. She knew that Emily was still one of the sharpest individuals she'd ever met. That left her with the belief that if Emily thought there was something amiss, then there probably was. And that thought kept Lynn awake.

She lay on her back again and stared up into the vague blackness, mentally clicking off each of the things Emily had told her. Like most people unaccustomed to sleeplessness, she felt as if she'd only been in bed a short time, so it was a shock when she turned on her side again and saw the luminous dial on the travel alarm she'd placed on the chest. It was twenty after one.

Oh God, she thought as she sat up and swung her feet to the floor, *I'm never going to get to sleep.*

She sat there for a few minutes trying to decide whether to lie back and try again, or to give up entirely and try to find some way to occupy herself until sleep might come to her. Choosing the latter course, she got up and drew on the dark green cotton robe she'd left hanging on the hook on the door, and left her cabin.

The hallway was only dimly lit now by a pair of shielded night lamps at either corner of the hallway, and muted running lights along the floor on either side. She quietly made her way to the staircase and up to the top deck.

The deck was mostly in darkness, except for one dim electric lamp mounted at the back of the wheelhouse, which gave off only enough light to make it the locus of attention for a swarm of insects. The ship's aft was facing out into the harbor, so offered nothing to view but the inky blackness of the water. In the opposite direction, Lynn could see a few stray lights coming from the inns and houses, so she headed forward.

As she rounded the side of the wheelhouse, she thought she could make out a figure standing at the very prow of the ship: against the general blackness of the background, a silhouette that was blacker still.

Lynn sighed inwardly. Caught in her sleepless state she had wanted to be alone to collect her thoughts, but there was no turning back now. The figure had stirred when it heard her.

"I hope I didn't startle you," Lynn said as she completed her approach.

"You did a bit, but it's all right," came the reply.

It was Rebecca, which came as something of a relief to Lynn as she came up beside her at the rail.

"You're up late," said Rebecca.

"I couldn't sleep. What's your excuse?"

"The same."

The weariness in her voice didn't go unnoticed. The irritation that Lynn felt toward Rebecca's aunt rushed back into her memory, tempered by the sympathy she felt for the niece.

"Your aunt runs you ragged."

There was a sigh. "Yes, she does."

"I hope you don't think I'm prying, but I—" Lynn broke off. She suddenly realized that she really didn't know why she was interested in the relationship between Rebecca and her aunt.

"What?" Rebecca prompted. "Go ahead. It's all right."

"I was just wondering if you take care of her all the time."

"No."

When Rebecca went no further, Lynn thought the invitation to ask her question had been nothing more than politeness. She decided not to pursue it. "Well, you're doing a very good job of it. You obviously love her very much."

Rebecca made a sputtering sound, then buried her face in her hands.

"Oh! I'm sorry! I didn't mean to—" The normally capable Lynn found herself at a loss. After a lengthy hesitation, she put an arm over Rebecca's trembling shoulders.

"I'm sorry!" Rebecca's voice was muffled by her hands. "I shouldn't break down like this."

"At the risk of sounding clichéd, sometimes it's good to cry."

Rebecca raised her head and released a shuddering sigh. "God, I wish they'd mentioned this damn cruise in the damn church bulletin! Once Auntie saw the mention, you couldn't get her off the topic!"

Lynn didn't know what to say. She certainly didn't think she needed to remind Rebecca that the church couldn't be expected to refrain from putting notices of events in their bulletin for fear the wrong people might become interested.

Rebecca sighed again. "I know, I'm being stupid."

"No, I think you're being tired," Lynn said gently.

Rebecca was quiet for a very long time, allowing the calming arm to remain on her shoulder. Finally, she said, "My mother died when I was very young, and my father worked all day, so he was never home. Aunt Marci—my mother's sister—she practically raised us. No, there's no 'practically' about it, she *did* raise us." She started to falter. "But…for a long time now, my brother and sister have been saying that we need to put her—that we need to find a place where she could be given proper care. But I know how much Auntie would hate that, and I've stood against them all the time."

"Until now."

There was a long pause, then Rebecca nodded reluctantly. "She insisted on coming to this trip…I had to come with her...." She stopped again and though Lynn could barely see her face, she sensed the surprised knowledge. "I felt I had to come with her, so I suppose I've known...or suspected...how bad things were. I don't see her all that much, you see. Not as much as I should. But it wasn't until spending this past couple of days with her, getting ready for the cruise and...that I've realized how bad she's gotten. I suppose I should say it wasn't until now that I was willing to admit it. I suppose I've known for a long time."

"It's a hard thing to accept," said Lynn.

"Yes, but I have to. It's Alzheimer's disease, you know. She can't help it. She does things that are crazy. You wouldn't believe it. I mean, like, when I was helping her unpack, I found this package in her suitcase—this box wrapped in dirty brown paper that's been sitting around for God knows how long. I was the one who packed her suitcase, so she must've put that thing there sometime when I wasn't looking. I'm sure she doesn't even know why."

"What was in it?"

Rebecca shrugged. "No idea. The minute I asked her about it she snatched it out of my hand like it was a guilty secret. But it's just like her to have packed something worthless."

Up until that moment, the stillness of the night had only been broken by the sounds of crickets singing, and the gentle waves. Rebecca and Lynn had kept their voices relatively low, as if the darkness were a cathedral in which loud voices would be sacrilege.

But the natural sounds were interrupted by the creak of one of the deck's boards. Though not very loud, it was unexpected enough to startle the two young women. Rebecca gave a muffled cry.

"Is someone there?" Lynn asked in a clear voice.

There was no answer, but Lynn thought she heard another creak, this time farther away.

"Must've been someone who didn't want to disturb us," she said as the two of them turned back to the railing.

They were silent for a couple of minutes. Then Rebecca said quietly, "It's so peaceful here, it's hard to imagine anything being wrong."

"What do you mean?"

"I mean, Aunt Marci."

"Oh." Lynn was relieved. For a minute she thought Rebecca was about to tell her that, like Emily, she had been noticing things that didn't seem quite right.

There was a long pause, then Rebecca said quietly, "I wish she were dead."

"What? You don't mean that!"

"Yes, I do." Her sorrow was palpable. "I can't bear the thought of putting her in a home, and...and she once told me that she'd rather die than go into one."

"Everybody says that," Lynn said. "They don't really mean it. And even if they do, a lot of times there just isn't any choice."

Rebecca rested her head on Lynn's shoulder and sighed deeply. They stayed like that for several moments, drawing a sense of peace from the surrounding quietude and the companionship.

Lynn was surprised—pleasantly—by the readiness with which Rebecca seemed to accept her warm shoulder, and found herself wondering what that readiness meant. After a while she smiled inwardly at herself; earlier she'd believed Emily might be reading too much into the little things she'd observed, and now Lynn herself was spinning theories around a simple gesture that was obviously nothing more than Rebecca's need for comfort.

All of these thoughts were abruptly halted when a distant cry rang out in the silence. Rebecca raised her head and the two of them strained in the darkness to make out the source of the sound.

"What is that?" Rebecca asked breathily.

"It sounds like a bird being strangled," said Lynn. "No...wait, it doesn't sound like an animal at all...."

Rebecca gasped. "It's Aunt Marci! Oh, my God! It's Aunt Marci!"

She took off at a run, but promptly collided with the corner of the wheelhouse in the darkness. When she regained herself, she rounded the corner and kept going.

"Rebecca! Be careful!" Lynn called as she followed her.

They scrambled down the rough metal steps from the white deck to the red, and the screaming continued as they descended to the blue deck. When they reached the bottom, they turned to enter the hallway to the passenger cabins, but found the entrance blocked by the impressive bulk of Mrs. O'Malley, the cook. She was clad in a gun-metal gray dressing gown that closely resembled her uniform, and a white night bonnet that made her look like a Victorian housekeeper. Hoke stood behind her clad only in a pair of briefs, and straining to see over her shoulder. David Douglas, who was wearing a pair of sleek, dark blue silk pajamas, was leaning against the doorjamb and contriving to look both uninterested and amused.

"Excuse me! Excuse me!" said Rebecca.

The crew parted as she shouldered her way past them. She very nearly came to a stop inside the hallway. All of the passengers were standing in their cabin doorways watching the show. Marcella was in the middle of her own doorway, her hands braced on each side of it as if she were fighting some unseen force trying to catapult her into the hallway. Her eyes were wide and she continued to let out short, intermittent animal-like screams.

"Miss Hemsley, *please,*" Samantha Farraday was saying with rising exasperation. "If you could just tell us what's wrong…"

The captain looked on from a discreet distance. It was clear that it had been decided between them that a woman's touch was needed here.

It was then that Rebecca came to her. "Aunt Marci!" She spoke calmly but very firmly. "Stop that right now!"

Marcella was held frozen in stunned silence for several seconds. Then she loosed her grip on the doorjamb and flung her arms around her niece.

"Rebecca!" she sobbed, "Rebecca! He was here!"

"Who was?"

"A man! There was a man in my room!" Her chin was resting on the young woman's shoulder, and when she raised her eyes she suddenly recoiled. She let go of Rebecca and took a couple of steps backward, then raised a pointing finger, and said in a tremulous voice, "It was you!"

All eyes turned toward David Douglas.

"What the hell are you talking about?" he demanded, all traces of nonchalance disappearing.

"You know what I mean! You were in my room! I saw you!"

"Like hell you did!"

"David!" the captain said.

"But she's crazy!"

"David…" The captain turned to Marcella. "Miss Hemsley, I don't think it was him you saw…."

For the first time, Rebecca turned her eyes from her aunt to the captain. There was something subtle but unmistakable in his tone: it implied a belief that Marcella hadn't seen anything.

"When you cried out, we all came to see what was wrong. David was behind my wife and me."

"It was him, I tell you!" She said this petulantly, but there was doubt and confusion in her eyes.

The captain allowed a significant pause, then said, "Well, why don't we get this sorted out in the morning? Maybe we'll be able to think more clearly after a good night's sleep."

He left her standing openmouthed in her doorway, and Samantha trailed after him without a word. As they passed by Hoke, he suddenly became aware of his state of undress and cupped his hands over the front of his briefs, then scurried back to his cabin. He was followed by Mrs. O'Malley, and finally by David, who paused in the entryway long enough to exhale with sharp derision in Marcella's direction.

Claudia Trenton stood in the doorway to cabin one clutching the folds of her blue robe around her. She shook her head sharply and then went into her cabin. The other passengers faded as discreetly as possible into their rooms one by one. Rebecca didn't have to try to coax her aunt back into her own cabin. Once Marcella realized that she wasn't being taken seriously, she stormed into her cabin and slammed the door.

Lynn had stopped beside Emily when she and Rebecca arrived, and once the captain had unceremoniously ended the scene, she followed Emily into her room.

"God, I feel so sorry for Rebecca!"

"Why?" Emily asked as she sat at the foot of the bed.

"Why? Didn't you see what just happened?"

Emily sighed and smoothed out the lap of her light blue dressing gown. "Yes, I did."

"I was upstairs talking to Rebecca when we heard the screams. She told me that her aunt has Alzheimer's."

"Yes?"

"You know?" Lynn said with surprise.

"Well, it seemed the most obvious explanation for her behavior."

Lynn crossed the room and sat next to her. "Rebecca says that she's been trying not to put her in a nursing home—that's what the rest of the family wants to do, put her away. Rebecca's been against it but she says she doesn't think she can avoid it anymore."

"It's a very weighty decision for a young woman to have to make."

"Yes, but after what just happened…well, you can see she's right. It has to be done."

"I suppose that's true…."

Lynn pulled back slightly. "You don't agree?"

"Oh, no, my dear, I suppose it would be best for Marcella to be somewhere where she could have constant supervision if she's a danger to herself. But not because of what just happened."

"What do you mean?"

"Only that people with Alzheimer's disease may do many things, but I don't know that they *see* things. Perhaps they do, I don't know that much about it. But I think it's more that they might misconstrue something they see…I don't know that they create phantoms."

"You mean you really think someone was in her room?"

"I think it's entirely possible."

THREE

THE MOOD ABOARD the *Genessee* the next morning was decidedly tense. Irritation born of interrupted sleep radiated off the passengers like waves of heat. Breakfast was eaten in a stony silence punctuated only by the clinking of utensils against plates, and David Douglas's forced brightness as he poured out juice and coffee. Even Bertram Driscoll's customary bluster failed him. Seated at a table by the portside door with Holmes and Brock, he attempted to start a conversation several times, only to find himself turning red in the face over the lack of response.

At the table in the center of the room sat Marcella and Emily with Lynn and Rebecca, the latter of whom was uncomfortably aware of the animosity being directed toward their table. It wasn't just toward her aunt: in the sidelong glances Rebecca perceived the implied criticism that she shouldn't have brought Marcella on the trip at all, or barring that, she should've made it her duty to keep a closer eye on her. Or a tighter muzzle.

While the passengers ate, the captain got the boat under way, heading out of the harbor and up the coast to the next stop on the tour. Rebecca and Marcella had seen him on their way to the dining room, and he'd greeted them with nothing more than a cheery good morning, which made Rebecca realize that the subject of last night's disturbance had been dismissed. Then again, she thought that was probably a good thing, because her aunt had made no mention of the incident since getting up, and for all Rebecca knew she could've entirely forgotten the episode.

After breakfast the passengers retired to the white deck where the chairs were all instantly adjusted to the reclining position.

Emily and Lynn had taken seats along the starboard railing where they could again enjoy the passing scenery. Marcella sat to Emily's right, and Rebecca was beside Lynn. It was less than ten minutes before Marcella's eyes drifted shut, and she began emitting an energetic wheeze that closely resembled steam escaping from an old-fashioned radiator.

"She's asleep," Rebecca said quietly.

"I gathered that," Lynn replied with a smile.

There was a pause. "I don't know what I'm going to do."

Lynn turned her eyes toward her. "About what?"

"This trip. I really didn't realize how bad she'd gotten. I don't know if…after last night, I don't know if we should get off at the next stop and I should take her home."

Lynn experienced an unexpected pang. "I suppose you could do that, but don't you think she'd…resist the idea? Kick up a fuss?"

"You're probably right," Rebecca said with a heavy sigh.

Lynn glanced at Emily, then turned back to Rebecca. "Look, if it makes you feel any better, Emily had an interesting insight about last night's business."

"What's that?"

"She thought your aunt probably did see someone."

"What?" Rebecca said this more loudly than she meant to. Marcella sputtered noisily, then quickly settled back into her regular wheezing.

"I don't mean she saw something shifty going on. Emily just thinks she might have seen something that she misinterpreted—like, maybe somebody heard a noise in her room and just took a peek in to make sure everything was all right."

"But…but why wouldn't whoever it was have owned up to that?"

"As hysterical as your aunt was? Probably out of fear."

Rebecca looked out toward the shoreline as she considered

this. It wasn't long before she began to relax. "You know, I hadn't thought of that. Maybe you're right."

"Not me," Lynn said with a smile. "Emily. And there's no maybe about it. Emily's almost always right."

IT TOOK A LITTLE LESS than an hour and a half for the *Genessee* to reach their second port of call, Macaw. Much smaller than Sangamore, the meager number of year-round residents rated only one mail box, and that was located in front of Friendly's General Store, which also housed the counter that served as the town's post office.

Friendly's was a long wooden structure with its back to the water, and had docks extending outward from it.

"Macaw is a great nature outpost," Samantha explained to the company as the boat slowly flowed into a slip. "Just to the south you'll find a visitor's nature center with maps of the trails through the wooded areas and along the lake. Just in case you're worried that the trails might be a little rough, the people of Macaw and the neighboring villages have marked them out with plenty of benches, so there's a lot of places to sit and rest. There are also campgrounds in every direction so there's usually a lot of people around, and even though it's a little early in the year, the weather is bound to have brought out some. And there's plenty of public facilities should you need them."

"Public facilities," Driscoll said in a loud whisper a few inches from Emily's right ear. "That'd mean a hole in the ground with a box around it." Today he wore a white shirt over tan and white checked pants.

"I see you've regained your humor," Emily said lightly.

"Ha! That's the one thing they can't take away from me!"

"Although there are a few little shops here for those of you who are so inclined," Samantha continued, "there aren't a lot of places to eat, so we'll be serving lunch on the boat at twelve-thirty, and dinner at six."

"It's just after ten," Lynn said with a glance at her watch.

"That will give us time for a nice little walk before lunch," said Emily.

The gangplank was secured in place and the passengers disembarked, much in the same order as they had the previous day, with the single exception of Lily DuPree, who had decided to stay behind and read on the deck. This decision left Muriel bobbing amongst the remaining passengers like a pinball searching for a slot.

Samantha smiled and shook her head as she watched them go, then went down to the dining room to make sure it had been cleared of the breakfast things. She found the room properly cleaned, but was surprised when she heard the clink of glassware coming from the lounge. She went around the corner, stopped and folded her arms. David Douglas was behind the bar, unnecessarily wiping the insides of the glasses.

"David, there's no need to do that now," said Samantha.

"Huh?" He started, and his head snapped in her direction. "Oh, I just like having everything shipshape."

She gave him an indulgent smile. "Yes, I know, but it's time to get the cabins in shape, and Hoke's not supposed to have to do that alone."

"But I thought—"

She shook her head. "Everyone has gone ashore except Miss DuPree, and I doubt if she'll be wanting a cocktail."

David laughed as he came out from behind the bar. "You're probably right."

"Now, come on, David," Samantha said without rancor. "You know you're supposed to help with everything."

"Aye, aye, Skipper! Didn't mean to shirk my duty!"

She laughed. "It's all right."

"Why didn't little Miss DuPree go ashore with the rest?"

"Afraid to, I think. The point of stopping here is for the passengers to go on some nature walks, but I think she's a little too frail. She's sitting up on deck reading a book."

"Ah," he said as they went through the starboard door. "Which reminds me—Neil and I are going for a walk ourselves, so you might want to check on Miss DuPree in a little while and see if she needs anything.''

''Will do.'' He gave her a cheery salute, then hopped down the stairs to the blue deck.

THE PASSENGERS had to make their way down the dock to the back of the general store, which had large barnlike doors that were closed to keep in the air-conditioning, and bolted from within. There were a pair of windows on either side of the doors. A walkway circled the building in both directions, and the passengers split into two groups and started around it. When the group that had gone to the left reached the side of the building, the Millers stopped in their tracks. A narrow, deserted beach stretched north as far as the eye could see.

''*Look* at it!'' Laura exclaimed delightedly. ''Look at all the deadwood!''

''Make for some great pictures!'' her husband agreed.

There was a two-foot drop from the walk to the sand below. Martin jumped down, then Laura took a more tentative leap while her husband held her waist. As he lowered her to the ground he spun her away from the walk. Laura giggled and the two of them embraced, then they hurried away up the beach.

''Sort of like a wrinkly ballet, isn't it?'' said Driscoll.

Emily couldn't help laughing openly at this.

''If I didn't know better, Miss Charters, I would think I was winning you over!''

''I wasn't aware you were trying to.''

Their group came around the front of the store just as the rest appeared at the opposite corner. They converged in the middle, where they lost another member when Stuart Holmes disappeared into the store.

''He said to go on without him,'' Jackson Brock explained. ''He wants to make some calls.''

The group stood there for a moment getting their bearings. The store was on a two-lane paved road, the opposite side of which was bordered by a thickset forest. A handful of shops were nestled among the trees, and a pair of hikers were peering into the window of one of them—a small wooden building above whose door was a slab of driftwood on which the word Leatherworks had been burned.

"That must be the visitor's center over there," Brock said with the tentativeness of someone who doesn't want to be viewed as trying to assume command.

They all looked to the right. Beside the general store was a small parking lot, and beyond that a wide, solidly worn path leading up to an octagonal, gazebolike structure. They moved toward this in an untidy mass.

"This is really an odd place to bring an elderly tour, isn't it?" Rebecca said, keeping her voice low.

"Why?" Lynn asked.

"It's mainly nature trails. All that walking…"

"I'm surprised at you, Becky." She fell into using the nickname without a thought. "None of these people are infirm. You've seen them shop!"

For the first time in their acquaintance, Lynn was treated to the sound of Rebecca's laugh.

"But seriously," Lynn continued, "I think being out in nature is very healthy, and the Farradays seem to have chosen this stop with a lot of care. They picked a place with benches and facilities and people all around. Everything will be fine."

When they reached the visitor's center, Driscoll propped open one of the screen doors and struck a comic salute as the group passed through. Inside, the building was devoid of furniture save for two rustic benches. The walls were covered with slots containing maps of the trails, schedules of summer activities in the area, and brochures advertising everything from fresh fruit to hay rides to guided nature tours.

Claudia Trent, clad in a mint green suit, a pair of dark green sunglasses, and the inevitable sunhat, marched across the room to the rack, grabbed one of the trail maps, then turned on her heel and strode out of the building without a word to anyone.

Driscoll and Brock watched her leave, then Driscoll gave the remainder of the company a quiet once-over. Emily, Lynn, Rebecca, and Marcella were looking through the brochures. On the other side of the room, Muriel Langstrom's lips were moving as she surveyed a notice about campground safety.

"Well, Jackson," Driscoll said as he gave him a genial slap on the back, "looks like it's you and me."

As he said this he unceremoniously ushered Brock toward the door, but he wasn't quite fast enough.

"Oh! Oh! Mr. Driscoll! Mr. Brock! Are you going on a walk?" Muriel sputtered.

"Why, yes, Miss Langstrom," Driscoll replied, not quite covering his dismay. "That's the general idea of comin' here."

"*Could* I go with you? I'm terribly timid about going into the woods! I'm sure I couldn't do it alone."

"Well, we're going to walk pretty fast, I think—"

"Oh, that's fine!" she cut him off eagerly. "I'm a very good walker. I walk all the time! I know I could keep up. It's second nature to me!"

"Don't you think…" Driscoll gave a nod in the direction of the other four women.

Muriel glanced at them, then stepped closer to him and said in a spirited whisper, "I wouldn't feel safe going out into the woods with only *women*. I would just be too frightened. There's no telling what could happen to us. I'd feel much safer with a man."

Inwardly crestfallen, Driscoll had no polite way to refuse, so he acquiesced. "Sure, ma'am. You can come along with us." He called across to the other women. "Emily? Ladies? Would you like to go with us? Make up a good team!"

"Oh, no," Emily said pleasantly. "Thank you for asking, but you go ahead. We're going to take our time."

His puttylike face fell. "Oh. Well. Okay."

He held the door open again, and Muriel took the lead followed by a suitably bemused Brock. Driscoll shot Emily a resigned grimace before trailing after them, closing the door behind him.

Lynn had been looking at one of the trail maps. She said, "One of the trails starts right across the road from here. Why don't we try that one, and just have a short walk this morning? After lunch we can see if we want to try a longer one."

"Sounds good," said Rebecca.

Emily agreed, and Marcella grunted as if she saw a secret flaw in the plan but was unwilling to point out what it was. However, she was happy to be on the move. She led the way, banging out through the screen door and coming to a stop at the edge of the road.

"There it is!" she exclaimed happily when the others caught up with her.

On the opposite side there was an opening among the trees marked with a green shield-shaped sign that said Trail Three.

Marcella started to charge across the road but Rebecca grabbed her arm and pulled her back.

"Wait! I hear a car."

They looked to their right where the road inclined and crested. Driscoll, Brock, and Muriel were walking up a path alongside it toward its top. An olive green sedan came into view and whipped past the three on the path, then past the four women. It stopped quite suddenly when it was even with the parking lot for the general store, then pulled in.

"Now, that is very curious," said Emily.

"What is?" Lynn asked.

"The driver. It was the same man I saw talking to Mr. Holmes yesterday. The one we saw on the dock last night."

"It's all right now," Marcella said irritably as she pulled away from her niece.

"Yes, Auntie," Rebecca replied.

"There's nothing like a good walk, I always say!" Marcella exclaimed as she went briskly across the road toward the trail.

"Aunt Marci, wait! Slow down!" Rebecca called out as she chased after her.

As Lynn and Emily crossed the road, Lynn was struck with a sensation she'd never felt before: it was not foreboding but rather a sense that something significant was happening. Perhaps it was the sudden awareness of the total quietude around them, or it might have been the fact that everyone within her view was disappearing simultaneously: As Marcella plunged between the trees followed by Rebecca, their three fellow passengers descended out of sight on the other side of the rise in the road. Out of the corner of her eye Lynn was aware that the driver of the sedan was passing through the doorway into the general store. She also noticed that the two young hikers had gone as well. It gave her the disquieting feeling that everyone had just been sucked from this dimension. She thought for a moment of telling Emily about this weird sensation, but decided against it.

She's had her own misgivings, Lynn told herself, *I'm not going to make it worse by going all fanciful on her.*

When they reached the opening of the path, Rebecca came running back to them.

"I'm sorry," she said, slightly out of breath. "Aunt Marci seems to think we're on a forced march. I'll try to slow her down."

"It's all right," said Emily. "If you can't we'll all meet back at the boat for lunch."

Rebecca took off down the path. Lynn called after her, "Don't worry. According to the map there's a campground a little over half a mile ahead. She can't really get lost."

Before Lynn could get this out, Rebecca had disappeared around a bend in the path.

Emily and Lynn continued on at a leisurely pace. The path was about four feet wide, very flat and easy to walk. The trees were thick with leaves and the woods smelled pleasantly of musty bark and damp earth. Emily would occasionally stop by a particular tree or plant, examine it, and emit a "hmm," and like any good tourist could not resist stopping and reading the helpful plaques describing the area's plant life.

After about twenty minutes they came upon a bench and decided to have a rest.

"Do you know much about plants?" Lynn asked.

"I remember a bit about them, very dimly, from my ancient past," Emily said with a smile. Her right hand absently went to the gray bun at the back of her head and shifted it slightly. "When I was a girl at school they used to teach us about plants, the various kinds, the different types of leaves, which were poisonous and so on. Of course, back then people communed with nature on a more regular basis, so that kind of information was rather important. I don't know what they teach nowadays."

Lynn wrinkled her nose. "Probably how to buy CTA fare cards."

They fell silent. A warm breeze stirred some of the upper leaves of the trees, which caused a wet rustling sound. From somewhere farther up the path they could hear what sounded like the laughter of a pair of small children, muffled by the natural soundproofing so that it seemed it was reaching them through waves of cloth.

"I'm surprised we haven't caught up with Becky," said Lynn. "I didn't think they'd get that far ahead of us."

Emily's thin brows elevated slightly at Lynn's use of the familiar. "Given the speed with which Marcella was moving, I'd be surprised if her niece has caught up with her yet." She paused, then said, "You like that young woman, don't you?"

Lynn flushed and looked away. "I don't know. Maybe I do. It's hard to tell how much is liking and how much is sympathy."

Emily produced a vague shrug. "Sometimes one can grow out of the other."

Lynn cleared her throat. "Do you want to go on now?"

"Certainly."

They got up from the bench and continued along the path arm in arm. The sounds of children at play grew nearer as the woods began to thin out. The path then opened into a camping area, where the ground among the trees had been cleared somewhat. A handful of tents of various shapes and sizes were pitched at wide intervals. The noise they'd been hearing came from a little boy and girl who looked to be under the age of ten and were gamboling among the trees in a rowdy game of tag.

On the far left side of the campground was a narrow, heavily rutted dirt road. The hiking path continued in a more or less straight line along the right border of the clearing, then continued into the woods through an archway formed by a pair of drooping trees. Lynn and Emily followed the path. As they neared the far edge of the grounds, there loomed to their right, partially obscured from view by a particularly dense knot of trees, a ramshackle wooden structure that housed communal showers and toilets.

"Typical of Americans," Lynn said with a cluck of her tongue. "Roughing it with all the comforts of home."

Emily started to laugh but was cut short when Rebecca came hurrying toward them through the natural archway. She was even more out of breath than before, and perspiring heavily.

"Have you seen her?" she gasped as she reached them.

"What?" replied the startled Lynn. "You mean your aunt?"

Rebecca nodded. "She got away from me."

"How?"

"We stopped here to use the bathrooms. We both went in, but—I don't know if she was finished first or if she just…when I came out of the stall, she was gone! I figured she'd gone on, and I ran and ran that way…." She pointed toward the arch. "But I couldn't find her. I'd gone a long way…and it didn't seem possible that she could've gotten that far ahead of me, so I thought she must've gone back instead of going on!"

"I'm afraid she didn't do that," said Emily. "She would've passed us, and we haven't seen anyone."

"Don't worry," said Lynn, "there's people all around out here. We'll find her."

"I'm going back to the boat," said Rebecca, "to see if she went back there! It's the one place around here that she'd be familiar with.'' She went away from them not running but walking very fast, and was quickly swallowed up by the woods.

Emily watched her with eyes narrowed with concern. ''You should go with her. I don't think she should be alone.''

''Are you kidding?'' said Lynn. ''I'm not leaving you alone in the woods!''

''I'm perfectly capable of making it back to the boat on my own.''

''That's beside the point! I wouldn't leave anyone alone in the woods.''

''Very well. But I do think we should go back.''

They followed Rebecca as quickly as they could. The timbre of Emily's voice when she'd said ''You should go with her'' disturbed Lynn, bringing back to her the unease she'd felt as they'd entered the woods.

''Are you all right?'' Lynn asked when they finally emerged from the woods.

''Quite all right,'' Emily replied, though she did seem a trifle winded.

They crossed the road, and as they reached the other side the captain and Samantha came over the crest of the hill, strolling hand in hand. Emily and Lynn stopped and waited for them.

''Ladies,'' said the captain, a row of straight furrows cutting across his forehead, ''is something wrong?''

''It's Miss Hemsley,'' said Lynn. ''She seems to have gotten lost.''

Samantha said, ''Oh, my.'' She'd tried to sound sympathetic but couldn't manage to erase the note of inevitability from her voice.

''How long has it been since she was seen?'' the captain asked.

''Within the last half hour, I think,'' said Lynn.

''Don't be concerned. She can't have gotten very far away, and there's enough people around here that she'll be safe. She's probably just lost and wandering around. We'll find her.''

"Shouldn't we—"

Lynn's question was interrupted when Rebecca appeared from behind the general store and sped in their direction.

"She's not on the boat," she said. "I checked her cabin and all the decks. I kept calling her name. She wasn't there."

"Had anyone seen her?" Emily asked.

She shook her head. "The only one there was Mrs. O'Malley, and she hasn't seen anyone—she's been busy in the galley making lunch. And Miss DuPree was on the deck, but she was asleep."

"David and Hoke weren't on board?" the captain asked, the furrows growing deeper.

"I couldn't find them. What should we do?"

"Fan out and look for her," said Lynn.

"No," the captain said with calm authority. "I don't think that's a good idea. We don't want anyone else to get lost. Why don't you ladies go back to the ship—"

"No!" Rebecca exclaimed.

The captain was shaking his head. "Samantha and I know the trails. We'll look for her and ask the campers and other hikers—someone's bound to have seen her."

"No! I'm coming with you! I have to! She may not—" Rebecca broke off and choked back a sob. "She might not recognize you, and it would scare her…."

The captain glanced at his wife, who shrugged with resignation.

"All right," he said. "Why don't we head the way you came first?"

"Shouldn't we notify the local sheriff?" Emily asked.

He gave her a deprecating smile. "I don't think there's any need for that. We'll find her."

Emily and Lynn watched as the other three crossed the road and started down the trail. With his wide, loping stride, the captain managed to appear unhurried even though he was moving fairly rapidly. Samantha, almost as tall as her husband, easily kept pace with him, while Rebecca had to walk briskly to keep up.

"The captain is a very strong presence," Emily remarked. "He should be able to keep Rebecca from panicking."

"I guess," Lynn said doubtfully.

Emily considered her for a moment. "We're almost back to the boat now. You really can go with them if you like."

Lynn shook her head. "Becky's aunt would probably be more afraid if a mob came after her in the woods."

Emily slipped her hand back through Lynn's arm and they started toward the general store. They hadn't gone more than a few feet before they heard Bertram Driscoll calling.

"Miss Charters!"

They stopped and turned around. Driscoll was coming toward them down the roadside path he'd taken with Jackson Brock and Muriel Langstrom.

"How're you doing?" he asked as he reached them. "You heading for the boat?"

"Yes," said Emily. "Where are your companions?"

To Emily's and Lynn's surprise, Driscoll turned deep red and looked to the ground, apparently trying to hide his smile.

"Uh...you mean Brock and old Muriel? Well...I don't know."

"What do you mean, you don't know?" Lynn asked. She really didn't like the look on his face, or his forced coyness.

He made a show of shuffling his feet. "Well, me and Jackson, I'm afraid we've been naughty boys. But, I mean, after all, we didn't ask her to come along with us."

"What did you do?" Emily asked.

The redness deepened. "We ditched her."

"What!" Lynn exclaimed sharply.

"We let her take the lead, and she was yakking and yakking, and when we came to a fork in the path, she went one way and we went the other!" His grin had broadened. He was obviously very pleased with himself. "She didn't even notice, at least not that I know. Of course, when we'd gotten far enough away from her, ol' Jackson started feeling sorry for her and went back to get her. But I was too fed up with the whole thing. I decided to come back on my own.''

"That was not just naughty," Emily said after a rather pointed pause, "it was a very dangerous thing to do, leaving someone alone in the woods like that."

"Oh, come on, Miss Charters! The trails are clearly marked. Nobody could get lost out there."

"Somebody has," said Lynn.

This brought Driscoll up short. "Huh?"

"Marcella Hemsley has disappeared. The captain and his wife and Rebecca are searching the woods for her right now."

"Well, yeah, but Miss Hemsley—bless her heart—she's not exactly all there. Muriel's got her wits about her."

"That may be," said Emily, "but anyone can become confused when they're frightened or upset, which is most likely exactly the result your prank has caused Muriel. Really, Mr. Driscoll, I can't imagine what you were thinking!"

This was the closest Emily came to scolding anyone, and it had its effect: Driscoll's smile was replaced by an abject frown. "When you're right, you're right. I'll go back, too. We didn't get that far. I'm sure Jackson caught up with her and everything's all right. But I'll go back."

Emily and Lynn stared at him without speaking. Looking even more abashed, he added, "And apologize."

"I think that would be best," said Emily.

Driscoll turned away and headed back in the direction from which he'd come.

"You have a very good influence on me," Lynn said as she and Emily continued to the boat.

"How so?"

"If you hadn't been here, I'm afraid I would've been a lot less ladylike with that man."

"It really was too cruel of him. Both he and Mr. Brock."

As they crossed the lot to Friendly's General Store, Lynn said, "The car's gone."

"Hmm."

They followed the walkway around to the back of the store, then went down the dock to the boat. The sun shimmered blindingly off the water, and Lynn put a palm across her brow to shield her eyes as they went up the boarding plank.

Lily DuPree was still asleep in her chair on the opposite side of the deck, facing the water, a paperback romance lying open on her lap.

"It's after eleven-thirty," Lynn said after glancing at her watch. "What would you like to do until lunch?"

"Actually, I think I'll go to my cabin and rest for a while."

"Did you tire yourself out too much?" Lynn said, her smooth white forehead furrowing.

Emily smiled rather mischievously. "No, my dear, I tired myself out just enough."

Lynn laughed, then accompanied Emily down to the blue deck. When they reached the bottom of the second staircase, they rounded the corner into the hallway and were surprised to find the door to number 8 ajar.

"Becky must've forgotten to close it," Lynn said.

Emily glanced at her, then went over to the door and pushed it open. Marcella Hemsley lay sprawled on the bed, her face bloated and purplish, and her arms and legs splayed. Her macramé belt was twisted tightly around her neck, and the compass lamp was lying beside her head, a smear of blood on its base. She looked like a huge rag doll that had been carelessly tossed on the bed.

Emily proceeded into the room and laid two fingers on Marcella's wrist.

"Oh, my God, is she—?" Lynn asked.

Emily released the wrist. "Yes. She's dead."

Lynn sputtered. "But—that's impossible! Becky said she just looked in here!"

"I know."

FOUR

"THE WAY I SEE IT, this young lady is the only logical suspect."

The man speaking was Joseph Barnes, sheriff for Allegro County, the small county that encompassed Macaw and its surrounding villages. He was in his early thirties and had reddish blond hair, a full, neatly trimmed mustache, and sallow skin. His face was thin, his eyes light brown. His summer uniform consisted of khaki pants, a matching short-sleeve shirt, and a black tie, the knot of which was never tightened to his throat. The office was a small square with a window to the right of the desk. The window looked out on a clearing less than thirty feet wide. Barnes sat behind the desk, resting his elbows on its top, his finger interlaced.

"I talked to all the passengers and the crew. It doesn't look like anybody really knew Marcella Hemsley other than to nod to, except for her niece."

"That doesn't mean one of them couldn't find a reason to kill her." Seated across the desk from Barnes was Detective Jeremy Ransom. He had driven half the night to reach the town, and was feeling the worse for wear: his joints ached from six hours behind the wheel, and his crystal blue eyes felt dry and stinging from staring so long at the ribbon of highway. And of course, there was the lack of sleep.

"Well, since any number of things could've happened to the old lady," Barnes said amiably, "I suppose some psycho killer could've just happened to choose that time and place to sneak on board to do somebody. But this isn't Chicago."

Ransom smiled. "Even there I've found that psycho killers are relatively few and far between."

Barnes laughed outright. Though his lips were thin and pale, his smile lit up his face. "I suppose you're right. Most murders have a definite reason." He sobered. "But, see, that's just my point. The only one I know of who could've had a reason to kill her is the niece, Rebecca."

"And that reason is...?"

Barnes shrugged. "I don't know. But she was the only one that knew her. And there's the fact that she lied when she said she looked in her aunt's cabin and she wasn't there."

"Are you sure about that?"

He shrugged again. It appeared to be an automatic gesture for him, indicating a certain embarrassment at being right. "The other ladies, your friends Miss Charters and Miss Francis, they said they were in there right after meeting Rebecca, and they found the body."

"Did Miss Charters offer any observations about the matter?"

The sheriff produced an apologetic smile, the type that implied one had to make allowances for the elderly. "Oh, yeah, she had a lot of things she noticed. Bunch of little things that don't add up to anything. You know how old people get. They don't have much to do with their time, so they watch everything going on around them and build up something in their heads."

"Hmm," said Ransom. "I don't know that much about other elderly people, but I've known Emily long enough to know that one ignores her observations at one's own peril."

There was a beat. "Have you talked to her yet?"

Ransom shook his head. "Just briefly. On the phone. Not long enough for her to go into details."

Barnes pursed his lips, then drew them to one side. "You might change your thinking when you've had a talk with her...but I guess the fact that you rushed up here proves what you say."

Ransom considered him for a moment. Though Barnes was free of what the detective would term urban polish, he had an intelligent face and a notable lack of rural wariness. "You know, Sheriff Barnes, it strikes me that you're being uncommonly gracious with someone who's butting into your territory."

Barnes laughed and sat back in his chair, resting his hands in his lap. "Detective, we don't get a lot of murders up here. Mainly I catch kids doing drugs in the woods, and now and then I get a big catch, like when we get hold of somebody running drugs to the Upper Peninsula or thereabouts. When we do get a murder, it usually just means we find a body that somebody's dumped in the woods, or someone's been killed there and left. I don't usually have a boatload of suspects."

"A boatload?" Ransom replied, raising his right eyebrow.

"Figure of speech. Like I said, the niece is the only one we have any evidence against."

"The fact that she lied."

The sheriff nodded. "And there's only two sets of fingerprints on the lamp—hers and her aunt's."

"Hmm. But you don't mind if I…nose around?"

"Uh-uh."

Ransom smiled and shook his head. "There, you're being gracious again, which I take to mean that you have your doubts about Rebecca."

"She swears her aunt wasn't in that cabin when she looked. If she's lying it's a really stupid lie, given what happened."

"Then why do you think she would do it?"

"There's only one reason I can think of. She killed her aunt in the cabin, and didn't want the body found for a while, so she sets up this hue and cry, says she can't find her aunt, intending to send everyone off looking for her out in the woods. Then when they come back and find the body they all think somebody got in the boat while they were all gone and killed the old lady. So Rebecca insists on going with the captain and his wife to search so that she'll have a perfect alibi. It was just her hard luck that your friends decided to go back to the boat when they did, and that the door was open.''

''Isn't it possible that somebody else killed the aunt after the niece left the boat?''

''Who?'' Barnes replied with a shrug. ''There were only two people on the boat at the time—the cook, who'd never seen the Hemsley woman before, and this lady, Lily DuPree, who you could practically snap in half just by looking at her.''

Ransom sighed. ''So, your explanation of the event sounds logical...impausible, but logical...given the way things look. So what's the problem? Why do you have your doubts about Rebecca Bremmer?''

Barnes sighed very deeply. ''It's such a stupid crime! Why do all that? Why go back to the boat and do her there? She and her aunt went off in the woods alone. She could've done her there, then gone to the others and said she'd lost her aunt, and when they find her she's dead! Then it could've looked like some stranger came on her in the woods and killed her. Much easier than all the other rigmarole.''

''Except that since she'd have been alone with her aunt in the woods, she would've been the chief suspect.''

''Yeah, but she is anyway, and this way it's even stronger. That's why it doesn't set right.''

Ransom uncrossed his legs then got to his feet. ''So, as to my nosing around...?''

''Nose away!'' Barnes replied, rising. ''Miss Charters and Miss Francis are out front.''

''Yes, I saw them on my way in. What about Rebecca Bremmer?''

''I'm going to be holding on to her for the time being—she doesn't want to stay on the boat in any case—and give you a little while to see if you can find out anything. But not too long. I'm going to have to turn her over soon.''

''I see.'' Ransom started for the door.

''Detective?''

He stopped and looked back.

"I've told the passengers on the *Genessee* that they can't leave the area until I say so. But you know as well as I do that I can't hold them here very long, if at all. The minute one of them starts squawking about leaving…" He let his voice trail off suggestively. "'Course, I understand this was some sort of church party, and if someone *does* make a stink, I'm going to remind them how they should want to help us find the person that murdered their 'sister.'"

The right corner of Ransom's mouth crooked upward. "Thank you, Sheriff." He opened the door and went out.

The outer office was large and low ceilinged, with walls painted pale yellow and dingy white acoustical tile overhead. A long counter in front of the wall to the left of Barnes's office was manned by one of the deputies, while another sat in a chair to the side reading the paper. Ransom stepped up to the desk and spoke to the mousy-haired young man sitting behind it.

"Is there somewhere around here to eat?"

The young man turned up a pair of eager brown eyes. "Yes, sir. Well, there's a lunch counter at Friendly's—that's the general store—then there's Golda's. That's a restaurant about a mile up the road. Those're the two closest places."

"Thank you."

Emily and Lynn were seated on a rough wooden bench that spanned the north wall of the room. Ransom crossed to them and sat beside Emily.

"What did the sheriff say?" Lynn asked anxiously.

"It's as you thought, Emily. The only case he has is against Rebecca. He's not really going to go beyond that."

"Then he's an idiot!" Lynn exclaimed, sitting back abruptly.

Ransom eyed her curiously. "I would probably do the same thing he's doing under normal circumstances. But the sheriff is at a disadvantage. He doesn't know Emily." He turned to the lady in question. "What was your impression of the sheriff?"

Emily pursed her lips pursed. "I thought him quite capable."

"Emily!" Lynn exclaimed.

"He's young, so he's a bit narrow in his thinking, but that will change with age and experience. What was your impression?"

"Pretty much the same as yours. I think he's very intelligent...and he's not quite as narrow as you might think. He's open-minded enough to let me look into this."

"That's great!" Lynn's face brightened.

Ransom curled his lips into a self-deprecating smile. "Well, we'll see how great it is. Why don't we get out of here? I'll take you someplace where we can have something to eat, and you can fill me in on the lay of the land." He had risen and gave his hand to Emily.

"I'm staying here," said Lynn.

"Why?"

"For God's sake, Ransom, Rebecca's in jail in a strange town. I'm not going to desert her!"

Emily now at his side, the detective looked at the seated young woman with a return of his curious gaze. "In order to get her out, I'm going to need all the information I can get. So come with us now, and when we've had something to eat, I'll bring you back here, if you like."

She stared at him for a moment, then huffed impatiently and got to her feet. "You're right, I guess."

He held the door open for them and they passed out into the harsh sunlight. The sheriff's station was separated from the road by a large parking lot. Though it was not quite eleven o'clock yet, the temperature was already in the high eighties, and the lack of rain in recent days caused dust to rise beneath their shoes as they crunched the gravel underfoot.

Ransom led the two women to the "previously owned" dark blue Camry he'd bought a couple of years earlier, and unlocked the doors. With great care Emily climbed into the front seat, while Lynn stood by with a hand on the door. Once Emily was secure, Lynn tossed herself on the backseat, closing the door behind her.

Gravel spat from beneath the tires as Ransom hung a right

and headed north. The right side of the road was bordered with thick forest, while the left was lined with trees through which could be seen snatches of the lake, as if through leafy tendrils, shining placidly in the sun.

The three of them remained silent, apparently through a tacit understanding that they would not discuss the case until they were situated at the restaurant. Emily sat with her hands neatly folded in her lap, eyeing the passing scenery with the interest she always seemed to manage no matter what the circumstances. Lynn rested an elbow on the windowsill, her head lolling against her hand. Her fingers had wound their way into her tawny hair, a grim frown marring her normally bright visage as she stared out the window. The trees passed in a muddy-green-and-brown blur.

"There it is," Ransom said.

A clearing on the right side of the road revealed a glass box encircled by another gravel parking lot, most of which was empty. The glass was tinted blue, and the roof extended several feet beyond the front wall and sloped upward, forming a blank billboard across which Golda's was spelled out in pink neon.

The interior of the restaurant was L-shaped. The long end of the L was taken up by a counter in front of which stood a row of stools with pink padded seats, like powder puffs perched on pedestals. Behind the counter there were rows of old-fashioned Coca-Cola glasses and dessert dishes, and beyond them a wall that looked to be brightly polished stainless steel. In the center of this was a rectangular hole through which orders could be picked up by the waitresses. The entire place was scrubbed so clean it fairly sparkled in the inescapable sunlight.

"Welcome to Golda's," said a raspy voice as Ransom, Emily, and Lynn came through the door.

The voice belonged to a rather wide woman who barely made the five-foot mark. She had black hair interwoven with white threads, cheeks that were doughy both in color and consistency, and black, bloodshot eyes that were magnified through the thick lenses of her glasses. She waddled up to them, cradling a stack of menus in her arms. "There's three of you?"

"Yes," said Ransom.

"You want a booth or table, I guess." Despite the fact that the place was nearly empty, she sounded as if it would be a great inconvenience if he assented.

"Yes. A booth, if possible."

It was a moment before she moved. She blinked once, her enlarged lashes brushing the back of her lenses like frayed windshield wipers. She then pivoted and led them around the corner into the dining room. Ransom couldn't tell if the walls were actually painted blue or it was merely the result of the sunlight filtering through the tinted windows. The booths had vinyl seats the same shade of pink as the stools, repeated again in the Formica table tops. Only three of the two dozen tables were occupied.

"You might as well have this one," the hostess said, coming to a stop at a choice booth at the center of the side window. She peeled three menus off the top of the pile and unceremoniously dropped them on the table, then waddled away.

"You go in first," Emily said to Lynn with a smile, "that way I won't have so far to slide."

Lynn complied, shifting herself over to the window somewhat gracelessly, then Emily sat beside her. Ransom took his place across from them.

A rail-thin, pockmarked waitress in a pink uniform with a blue apron approached the booth with the tip of her pencil already poised on her small green pad.

"This all one check?" she asked.

"Yes," said Ransom. He ordered eggs and bacon, and Emily ordered a club sandwich. Lynn declined any food at first, until Emily insisted that she eat in order to keep up her strength. Lynn consented to have the same as Emily, and the waitress slumped away.

"So," said Ransom, folding his hands on the table, "why don't you start at the beginning and tell me what happened?"

Emily started to say something but Lynn cut in. "First of all, Rebecca didn't do it!"

Her two companions looked at her.

"That's what I'm here to look into," said Ransom.

"It's no good unless you have it right from the beginning," said Lynn, surprised at her own intensity. "You have to start out knowing that Rebecca didn't do it!"

"You seem awfully sure of that."

"I am sure! She couldn't kill anyone, let alone her aunt."

"You're fond of her?"

Lynn's cheeks turned red. "I like her."

"I see."

Her eyes flashed. "No, you don't see! I don't know her well, but I do know that she adored her aunt. She wouldn't have killed her." She glanced at Emily and her redness deepened when she saw something close to pity in those aged eyes.

"So, Emily," said Ransom, "all you told me on the phone was that this woman had been murdered, and you thought the police were interested in the wrong person. Possibly. Do you have a—" His eyes shifted for a split second in Lynn's direction. She was looking down at the table. "—particular reason for thinking that?"

Emily adjusted herself in her seat. "I suppose I do, but nothing that you would call conclusive. I imagine it's possible that Miss Bremmer killed her aunt—" Lynn raised her eyes and started to say something, but Emily headed her off. "I know, my dear, it would be a terribly hard thing to accept, but I'm talking in terms of conjecture." She turned back to Ransom. "As I said, I suppose it's possible. Marcella Hemsley had become—through no fault of her own—a difficult and rather disagreeable woman, and Miss Bremmer was facing the prospect of putting her in a nursing home, a thing she was loath to do. I don't think it's outside the realm of possibility for someone in that position to..." She allowed her voice to trail off, finishing with a suggestive shrug.

"You mean mercy killing," said Ransom.

"But she loved her aunt!" Lynn objected.

"Exactly. She loved her very much. We all witnessed how patiently and devotedly she cared for her aunt."

After a beat, Lynn looked away from her, and Emily turned back to Ransom.

"You see, a few things have happened in the two days we've been gone that, in lieu of any sort of explanation, look a bit odd. Now, if Rebecca did indeed kill her aunt, then I suppose none of these things really matter. But if she didn't kill her, then there are things that need to be looked into. And you see, Jeremy, Sheriff Barnes didn't quite see the importance."

"And what are these little things you're talking about?" Ransom asked.

She shook her head slowly and gave him a self-deprecating smile. "I'm afraid you're going to think I'm very foolish...."

"I doubt that."

"Well—"

They were interrupted by the arrival of the food. The waitress held a plate in each hand and had the third precariously balanced on her left forearm.

"I remember you're the odd man out," she said as she placed the dish full of eggs and bacon in front of Ransom. She then put the other two plates in front of the women.

"I'll be back with coffee," the waitress said over her shoulder as she walked away.

"This looks very nice," said Emily, eyeing the three-decked concoction that had been cut into triangles, each of which was speared with a toothpick topped with crinkles of colored cellophane.

"You were saying?" Ransom prompted.

"Oh, yes. The first thing might've been a dream—at least in part, because I'm almost sure I was at least partially awake." She related what she remembered of the anxious conversation on the white deck, then told him of the meeting she'd witnessed between Stuart Holmes and the stranger, and the stranger's reappearance that night on the dock.

Ransom had been listening to her thoughtfully. "I wouldn't think it was that unusual to run into someone you know in Sangamore. And, having done that, would it be so odd for his friend to visit him later on the boat?"

"But the way that guy acted at the dock," Lynn cut in. "He turned his face away when he passed under the light. Emily called it furtive, and that's certainly the way it looked to me—like he was afraid of being recognized."

A new thought occurred to Emily. "Recognized...or described. He did look familiar to me, some" She lost herself in thought for a moment, then shook her head. "But, Jeremy, that in itself wouldn't seem strange except for one other thing. The stranger showed up here just as we all set off on our hikes. And he went into the general store where Stuart Holmes was waiting."

"Hmm," he said, raising his right eyebrow a fraction of an inch. "Is there more?"

"Well, of course, the big event—other than the murder—is that the night before last, our first night out, Marcella woke everyone on the boat screaming that someone had been in her room."

"You don't think she was a reliable witness."

Emily shook her head. "Wholly unreliable, I should think. But I wouldn't dismiss the possibility that there really was someone in her room—even though it may just have been one of the stewards looking in to check on her."

"She accused David Douglas," Lynn said, her brittle tone surprising the detective.

"Did she?"

Lynn smiled for the first time since the murder had occurred. "I wish you'd stop doing that."

"What?" he asked innocently.

"Responding to me as if I'm the world's most questionable witness."

"I'll be glad to oblige...if you'll tell me what you have against David Douglas."

The smile disappeared and her jaw hardened. "Nothing. He's just a pest."

"How so?"

"He…just is. He's one of those overly friendly people who don't have a sincere bone in their bodies."

He turned to their elderly companion. "Emily?"

"He's quite an ingratiating young man," she said with a hint of a twinkle in her eye.

"You are perhaps the only woman I know who could make that sound damning."

Lynn said, "But Becky's aunt did say it was David she saw." She paused, then added grudgingly, "But it couldn't have been him. The captain himself—and yes, before you ask, he is a reliable witness—said that David followed him and his wife into the corridor where the passenger cabins are."

"Yes, he did say that," said Emily, "and I'm sure the captain was being completely honest. But that doesn't mean that it wasn't David Douglas who was in Marcella's room."

"If someone was," said Ransom.

Emily nodded. "Granted."

"How is that possible?" Lynn asked.

"Well, we were all woken from a sound sleep. It took us all a bit of time to respond to Marcella's cries, and I'd imagine even longer for the captain, whose cabin is at the other end of the boat. The boat isn't all that long—surely if it was David that Marcella saw, the moment she woke and started screaming he would've taken off for his own cabin."

"How long are we talking about here?" Ransom asked.

Emily offered a genteel shrug. "Before anyone got to the corridor? I don't know…thirty seconds? Sixty seconds? Maybe longer. It wouldn't take nearly that long for someone like David to have run to the back of the boat."

"Wouldn't he have been heard running?" Lynn asked.

Emily shook her head. "I don't think so. Not in the confusion."

"All right," said Ransom, "so we have the incident in the

night, the stranger visiting Stuart Holmes, and the conversation you think you overheard but might have dreamed. Is there anything else?''

Emily raised her head and looked off in the distance as if something were niggling at the back of her mind. ''There was one other odd thing...if I could remember what—'' Her face suddenly brightened and she looked Ransom in the eye. ''Oh, yes. It seems very unimportant—and it probably is—but it struck me as peculiar at the time. When we were in Sangamore, Lynn and I met Marcella and Rebecca for dinner at a pub.''

''A pub?'' Ransom echoed with a grin.

''Yes. It was very crowded, and far in the back of the room there was Claudia Trenton, who has made a point of keeping herself aloof from her fellow travelers—which in itself does make me wonder why she would choose to come on a trip like this, since a certain degree of camaraderie is to be expected....''

''Emily...''

''Oh, I'm sorry. Claudia was having dinner with Bertram Driscoll.'' Having imparted this bit of information, Emily took a bite of her sandwich.

''Is that significant?''

She finished chewing and swallowed. ''That's just the thing. I don't know if it is or isn't. Miss Trenton and Mr. Driscoll are polar opposites, and the last people one would expect to see dining together under any circumstances. It was just another thing that struck me as not quite right.''

''But he explained that,'' said Lynn, who had been eying Emily curiously as she'd related this.

''Yes, he made a point of explaining it, when it wasn't really necessary.'' Emily's brow knit slightly. ''I would've thought Claudia would've been the one who would want to explain....'' Her face cleared. ''But, no matter. The other thing is, Mr. Driscoll was the one who woke me up when I was overhearing the conversation on the deck.'' She paused and looked at Ransom significantly.

"I see," he said, nodding. "So since Claudia was the only one on deck, it's reasonable to suppose she was the female voice you heard, and Driscoll was the one she was talking to."

"It's possible. It would be unlike him to be so quiet, but it would make another instance of the two of them together, in a situation that could be thought questionable."

Ransom was looking down at his half-finished eggs and slowly drumming his fingers on the pink tabletop. "And you told all this to Sheriff Barnes?"

"Yes, and he didn't think anything of it!" Lynn snapped.

"Well, in all honesty, Lynn, if I didn't know Emily, I don't think I'd make much of it, either."

Emily sighed. "I'm afraid it does all seem rather inconsequential. And as I said, if Rebecca is guilty, it all amounts to nothing. It may do that either way. But if she's innocent, then these things bear looking into, don't you think?"

FIVE

RANSOM WASN'T AT ALL sure that it did warrant looking into. Emily was usually unfailing in her ability to sense when something wasn't quite right, but she herself readily admitted that on this occasion her observations seemed trivial. Ransom could sympathize with Sheriff Barnes…and yet, even the sheriff had sensed that something was wrong with the setup.

A half-overheard conversation, an encounter with a stranger, the wrong people dining together: things that might have the ominous quality of the beginnings of a nightmare where minor occurrences are infused with an inexplicable foreboding before something terrible happens.

But that was exactly what happened, wasn't it? Ransom thought. *Minor forebodings, and now a woman is dead.* With an inward sigh he admitted to himself that Emily was most likely right.

They dropped Lynn off at the sheriff's station, then headed south for the dock which was a little over a mile away.

"This isn't exactly going to be an easy task, is it?" Emily observed.

"Well," Ransom replied, "I can question Holmes about his friend, of course. As for the rest of it, I don't know what point there would be in asking Trenton and Driscoll about their dinner, since they'd just give me the same explanation he gave you. And if there was something fishy about it, asking them would put them on their guard. Are you sure it was Claudia Trenton you heard on the deck?"

"Not for a moment," Emily admitted candidly. "I do wish

I could be more definite. Claudia was the only one there when I drifted off, and she was still there when I woke. The conversation was stopped by the sound of approaching footsteps coming up the steps…the starboard stairs, I believe. The next thing I knew, Bertram Driscoll was standing over me, waking me up. When I turned around to see who had been talking, Claudia was in her deck chair, presumably asleep. Mr. Driscoll said he hadn't seen anybody else. It could very well be that Claudia was talking to someone else, and Mr. Driscoll came up the stairs and the other person fled down the port stairs, not wanting to be seen with her. When the footsteps sounded, the woman said 'wait,' and there was nothing more after that.''

"Hmm. Has it occurred to you that perhaps Driscoll was the one she'd been talking to, and he came over to make sure you were asleep?''

"Yes, it has. But if it's true, that would mean Bertram Driscoll is very clever.''

"Why do you say that?''

She smiled. "Because he *told* me that was what he was doing.''

When they reached Friendly's, Ransom turned right into the parking lot and came to a stop at the ridge of trees that bordered the lake. He switched off the engine and sighed deeply. "Emily, I'm really sorry this had to happen on your vacation.''

"I shouldn't be,'' she replied with Victorian spirit. "It's been a very interesting trip so far.''

He laughed. "I suppose if no one had been murdered, you'd feel slighted.''

She made a gently deprecating noise. "What do you propose to do first?''

"I don't suppose I could convince you to leave the boat and stay at the motel.''

She shook her head. "I couldn't leave Lynn alone on the boat.''

"I meant both of you.''

"I can assure you Lynn will not leave the boat," Emily said solemnly. "She is determined to clear Rebecca."

Ransom turned to face her with one brow upraised. "What's going on there? Did Lynn know Rebecca before now?"

"No, I'm sure she didn't."

"Then how on earth did they form this bond so quickly? It's only been a couple of days."

Emily smiled at him with grandmotherly affection. "Have you ever heard of a shipboard romance?"

"Has it gone that far?"

"I suppose right now you would call it a strong affinity. But think of Lynn's character. Rebecca is someone who needs support—she was caring for a difficult relation, and under a great amount of strain. Lynn likes to help people who are in need. That's simply her nature. Remember, when her lover, Maggie, was terminally ill, Lynn quit her job and went to work as a very efficient cleaning woman so that she could command her own time." Emily paused and her eyes wandered out through the windshield. "I suppose it's my good fortune that she decided not to go back to the corporate world once Maggie was gone."

"So you think the relationship between them is nothing more than Lynn wanting to help someone in need."

Emily quickly came back to the present and looked at him pointedly. "No, I think that may have been the basis of it. But for Lynn it goes deeper than that."

Ransom ran a hand over his close-cropped blond hair, then rested his arm on the back of the seat. "Emily, have you been playing matchmaker?"

She looked mildly affronted at the suggestion, though her smile belied the offense. "Certainly not! Of course, I've been gracious about having Marcella and Rebecca accompany us...."

Ransom laughed. "Oh, I'll bet you have! Now, to get down to the matter at hand, you can give me the lay of the land."

"How do you mean?"

"We know that Marcella was killed sometime after you all started on your outing. Can you tell me where everyone was?"

Emily sighed with frustration, folded her hands again, and rested them in her lap. "That's just the problem, and I'm afraid it's not going to make your task any easier."

"Hmm?"

"Virtually everyone was on their own just before we discovered the body. Lily DuPree had decided to stay onboard rather than hike—which is not at all surprising because she's rather frail and I don't think she would've been able to manage the trails very well."

"She stayed on the boat?" Ransom said with interest.

"Yes, but from what I understand she claims to have fallen asleep and didn't hear or see a thing—which is also not surprising. The boat is small enough that you do feel the motion of the water. It's an amazingly effective soporific. Add to that the fact that our sleep was interrupted the night before, and there you are."

"I see. Go on."

Emily raised her chin and took a deep breath. "The Millers were the first to leave the group...." She went through the roster of passengers, relating when each of them had split off from the main group. "The only other people we saw at all was the stranger that drove up in the green car, and a pair of hikers looking in those shops over there."

"Hikers?"

"Yes. Apparently that's what they were. They were there when we first came along, and gone when we came out of the visitor's center."

"Hmm. So the Millers were off on their own," Ransom said, ticking them off one by one, "Claudia Trenton, Lily DuPree, and Stuart Holmes were each on their own. Muriel Langstrom, Jackson Brock, and Bertram Driscoll were together for a while but separated. Were the last three alone long enough to go back to the boat and kill Marcella?"

Emily sighed again. "It's a very good question, but I don't

have an answer. I don't know about Muriel or Mr. Brock. I would imagine Mr. Driscoll was on his own long enough— though of course, we did meet him on his way to the boat.''

''Do you have any idea exactly where any of them were?''

She shook her head. ''Sheriff Barnes did talk to everyone briefly, but everyone said they were off hiking when it happened. He didn't go much further than that.''

''I see,'' Ransom said as he pulled his cell phone from the inner pocket of his jacket. He flipped it open and punched in a series of numbers.

''Who are you calling?'' Emily asked.

''The rest of the cavalry.''

After three rings his call was answered by a voice that Ransom always thought of as having the consistency of watery pudding.

''Detective White.''

''Hello, Gerald.''

There was a smile in his partner's voice when he replied, ''Hi, there, Jer.''

''Everything all right there?''

''Newman's doing a burn over you taking time off out of the blue, but he'll get over it.''

Ransom curled his lips. Sergeant Newman was their immediate superior, and after years of dealing with the aftermath of murder and mayhem he was more likely to be upset over an impromptu vacation than over an eruption of violent crime.

''He's probably only miffed because I won't be there to disturb him.''

''How are things in the northern woods? Peaceful?'' Gerald asked.

''The woods themselves, yes. However, it seems that one of Emily's fellow passengers wandered off into them and somehow managed to turn up dead back on the boat about an hour later.''

''Back on the boat? Jeez! How is Emily? Is she all right?''

''Oh, yes,'' Ransom said broadly. ''She's fine. She's more

than fine. She's refusing to leave the boat. Perhaps you can talk some sense into her.''

Gerald burst out laughing. ''I wouldn't even try!''

''You're very wise. It would be a waste of breath. But I want you to talk to her about something else.''

''What?''

''She's here with me now. I'm going to have her give you a list of the passengers and crew of the *Genessee*. I want you to run them and see if you turn up anything.''

''Sure thing.''

Ransom handed the phone to Emily. She gingerly held it to her right ear and said, ''Hello?''

Ransom smiled inwardly. She always sounded tentative when talking on the phone, as if somewhat awed by the idea of voices traveling over wires. But she sounded even more so when on a cell phone, the removal of the wires seeming to add to the bafflement.

''Miss Emily?'' Gerald said. ''How are you?''

''I'm perfectly all right. I trust you're not going to try to talk me into moving off the boat.''

He laughed again. ''Wouldn't dream of it.''

After making polite inquiries about his wife, Sherry, and their two daughters, Emily proceeded to provide him with the list. When she was finished, she said her goodbyes and handed the phone back to Ransom.

''You get all that?'' he asked.

''Taking notes is what I do best,'' Gerald replied flatly. Ransom could picture the smile on his partner's pale round face. ''I'll get back to you as soon as possible, but it might not be until tomorrow.''

''As soon as you can,'' said Ransom.

''Oh, by the way, Jer,'' Gerald said quickly, ''how is the local law taking you being there?''

''Surprisingly well. I don't know if that will last, though. We'll see.'' Ransom signed off and slipped the phone back into his pocket, then turned to Emily. ''Shall we?''

He climbed out of the car, went around to open the door for her, and helped her out. He then closed the door and gave Emily his arm.

"The dock is just around there," she said, crooking a thin finger in the direction of the back of the general store.

Ransom guided Emily onto the walkway and they went around back to the dock. The *Genessee* was still moored alone in one of the slips, its boarding plank in place. As they approached, through the windows of the wheelhouse they could see Captain Farraday leaning back in his chair reading a newspaper. His wife was at the railing on the port bow, staring fixedly out at the water. Her long dark hair and the skirt of her white cotton dress fluttered in the warm breeze.

Ransom walked Emily slowly up the ramp and onto the deck. Lily DuPree was lying in the same chair she'd occupied the day before, and were it not for the change of clothes it would've looked as though she'd never moved. She now wore a light blue dress with tiny, dark blue flowers that uncomfortably resembled a hospital gown. Muriel Langstrom was on a chair on the other side of the deck, uncharacteristically alone. Her eyes were hidden behind wide glasses with smoky gray lenses, her mouth hanging open and drooping to one side. She emitted loud snorts at irregular intervals. Nobody else was on the deck.

"I'm going to need to talk to the captain," said Ransom.

She didn't quite hear him, her attention elsewhere.

"Emily?"

"What? Oh! Yes, you should talk to Captain Farraday. Lily is alone. I think I'll go over and have a little chat with her."

Ransom went around the starboard side of the wheelhouse, gave a gentle rap on the door, and opened it when he heard the sturdy voice from inside bid him to come in.

"Captain?"

Farraday laid down the newspaper and rose from his chair, extending a hand. "You must be Detective Ransom. The sheriff radioed you'd be coming over."

Ransom shook his hand. The captain's grip was firm and strong, much in keeping with his general appearance. The erect posture, steel gray hair with its white-flecked temples, and the unwavering gaze all supported the impression of dignified authority.

"Pull up a seat," the captain said with a gesture toward the plain wooden chair sitting in the corner. Farraday resumed his seat behind the wheel as Ransom complied. But before the detective sat down, Mrs. Farraday came in through the port bow door.

"Ah. This is my wife, Samantha," Farraday said. "Sam, this is Detective Ransom. From Chicago."

"My husband told me you were coming. Pleased to meet you." She folded her arms and rested her back against the door.

Ransom inclined his head slightly, then sat down. "Captain, as I'm sure Sheriff Barnes has told you, I'm going to look into this murder."

"Yes. And I welcome that if it will get us under way any sooner."

"This delay is awful," said Samantha. "It's bad enough a murder had to happen at all, but then to be stuck here. I don't want to sound unfeeling, because after all, a human being is dead—but I can't think what this is going to do to our business. And everything we have is tied up in it."

After a calculated pause, Ransom said, "Given today's climate I should think it would help business."

There was a barely noticeable jolt through Samantha's body, as if a reaction were stopped abruptly almost before it started. Her face froze in incredulity. Apparently she couldn't decide if she should be affronted by this suggestion, welcome it, or be horrified.

"It would help us," the captain said calmly, "if we could continue the tour as soon as possible. I don't have a lot of confidence in Sheriff Barnes's abilities."

"Why is that?"

"He already has Rebecca Bremmer. I don't see any reason for him to keep us here. He should let us get on our way."

"Even if there's a murderer on board?"

"What?" Samantha said sharply, her dark eyes widening.

The captain hadn't reacted openly, but Ransom could've sworn his spine had grown even more stiff.

"You mean there's some doubt about who murdered Miss Hemsley?" he asked.

Ransom shrugged nonchalantly. "That's why I'm here. The sheriff must've told you that."

"No, he didn't go into details…it's just…I thought our being held here was more a formality than anything else."

"The sheriff is not completely satisfied that Rebecca Bremmer is the murderer. And after talking to him, neither am I. Now, I realize that you've only been with these people a couple of days, but can you tell me if you've noticed anything out of the ordinary going on between any of the people on board?"

Farraday was silent for a moment, then laughed lightly. "Detective, Miss Hemsley was strangled, and she wasn't exactly a petite woman, either. This is a seniors' cruise. The passengers are, for the most part, pretty old to be doing something like that. I would say only two of the passengers are young enough and strong enough to have strangled someone, and one of them is her niece. The other one is that friend of Miss Charters."

"But there are other people on board," Ransom said after a beat.

"What?"

"Besides the passengers…"

"What are you saying?" Samantha demanded as she came up behind her husband and laid her hands on his shoulders.

Farraday reached up and placed his hand on his wife's, never taking his eyes off Ransom. "Wait, Sam. Detective Ransom is just doing his job. Thoroughly. Yes, you're right, there are also three crew members."

"And yourself."

The captain smiled. "And myself, and my wife."

"Now, getting back to my original question. Did you notice anything out of the ordinary going on between any of the people on board and Marcella Hemsley?"

"Sam would probably be the best one to answer that—I've spent most of my time in here." He looked over his shoulder at his wife, who hesitated before answering.

"Well...I don't know any of them, so it's hard to say what would be out of the ordinary. They seemed to form little groups, but I assume that's because they were friends...or at least knew each other before."

"What were the groups?"

"Um...as far as Miss Hemsley goes, she spent most of her time with Miss Charters and her companion, and of course, her niece. The three men—Mr. Brock, Mr. Driscoll, and Mr. Holmes—stayed together for the most part...."

So she doesn't know that Holmes had a tendency to break off from the rest, thought Ransom.

"Which I guess stands to reason. Uh...the Millers keep to themselves, mostly." Here she stopped and smiled. "They're that kind of couple. And Miss Trenton, she keeps to herself, too, when she can."

"What about Muriel Langstrom?" Ransom asked.

Samantha rolled her eyes. "Oh, God! The chatterbox! She's latched on to Miss DuPree, who I don't think has the spine to resist her."

"And how did they all relate to Marcella Hemsley?"

She sighed. "I didn't see them pay much attention to her at all. She was...she wasn't the easiest woman to deal with. I think there was something wrong with her—with her head, I mean."

"What makes you think that?"

"She was...I guess you'd call it cranky. I didn't have much time to notice her, myself—there's a lot to do on a trip like this, you know—but she reminded me of how my grandmother was late in her life, always irritable. We found out later she was hard of hearing, and was acting that way because she couldn't really keep track of what was going on around her.''

''But you said you thought there was something wrong with Miss Hemsley's head. I took that to mean a mental problem.''

''Well, yes,'' Samantha assented reluctantly. ''Mainly because of that incident the other night. Honestly! Screaming like that in the middle of the night, she almost scared the life out of me and everyone else on the boat! And for nothing!''

''For nothing?'' Ransom looked at the captain. ''So you didn't look into it?''

Farraday looked blank for a moment, then shook his head. ''No, there wasn't really anything to look into.''

''Didn't she accuse your head steward—David Douglas, I think his name is—of having been the one in her room?''

''Yes, but David came out of his room after we did. There was no reason to think he actually did anything. Hell, there was no reason to believe she saw anything in the first place.''

''Except that she said she did.''

The captain leaned forward a fraction of an inch. ''Detective, David followed us into the corridor. When Miss Hemsley accused him, he denied it.''

''Naturally.''

''The point is, what would be the good of asking him if he really had been in there? I don't believe that there was ever anyone there. She was either dreaming or imagining things. If I'd questioned him, which I think would've been totally unnecessary, he would've denied it again and then felt he wasn't trusted. I wasn't going to do that for nothing.''

''So…Douglas has worked for you before? You're sure of his honesty?''

Farraday sat back. ''No, as a matter of fact, he signed on just before this trip. We scheduled this at the last minute, and needed to get somebody fast.''

''What's his background?''

''He has had a lot of jobs, various kinds. He's been a waiter, a bartender, he's even worked in a nursing home. So we thought he'd be good.''

''Hmm,'' Ransom said with a half smile. ''Sounds like he was everything you were looking for.''

''Yes…''

''That was very convenient. However, someone who's had a lot of jobs doesn't sound all that promising as an employee.''

Farraday smiled, which deepened the crow's feet around his incisive eyes. ''It's a temporary job. A summer job.''

''Did you check his background?''

''You can't seriously think he had anything to do with this!'' Samantha interjected. ''Why would he kill Marcella Hemsley?''

Ransom produced an unreadable smile. ''As your husband said, I'm just being thorough.''

''In answer to your question,'' the captain said, ''no, we didn't check his references. We didn't have a lot of answers to our ad, so there wasn't a lot of people to choose from. But I met with him. Interviewed him. He seemed all right. A bit of a glad-hand, maybe, but that can be an asset in this type of job.''

''I see. And the rest of the crew?''

''Hoke—Joaquin Vasquez—he's the other steward. He was with us last summer.''

''He's a very nice and sweet-tempered young man,'' said Samantha. ''Very eager to please.''

''The only other crew member is Mrs. O'Malley, our cook,'' said the captain. ''She's been with us since the beginning, and I'd vouch for her all the way.''

''Um-hmm. Well, what can you tell me about the relationship between Miss Bremmer and her aunt?''

''She ran the poor girl into the ground,'' Samantha said with feeling. ''Rebecca walked on eggshells around her, trying to keep her happy despite…the way she was…and running interference for her with everyone else.''

There was a pause, then Ransom said, "You seem to have observed a lot more than you thought you did."

Samantha's face flushed a deep crimson. "You only had to look at the poor girl to see how exhausted she was. I wouldn't blame her if—" She broke off, and though it didn't seem possible her face grew even more red.

"If she'd killed her?" Ransom said.

"Everybody has a breaking point. Even with people they love."

"That was obvious as well?"

"That she loved her aunt? Yes."

The detective unexpectedly rose from his seat. "Well, I think I have all the background I need for now." He swung the chair back into its position in the corner. "Thank you for your help. I'll be talking to the passengers and crew—"

"Mr. Ransom," Farraday said, rising from his chair, "Detective…please keep in mind that the passengers have already been very upset by this business. I'd appreciate it if you'd be…circumspect in the way you talk to them. I don't want them to be more upset than they already are."

"So far the people I've talked to agree that Rebecca Bremmer adored her aunt, despite her aunt's problems. It's probably already entered at least some of their minds to doubt whether or not she is guilty. And if that's true, I would think they'd feel much safer if they were *sure* they were not traveling with a murderer."

"I guess that's so," said the captain, "but still—"

Ransom stopped him with a wide smile. "I'll be a gentle as a lamb." He started for the starboard door, but before opening it stopped and turned around. "Oh, one other thing. The two of you, I understand, went for a walk of your own while the passengers were on their hikes."

The captain's visage hardened to granite. "Yes?"

"Did you leave the boat just after the passengers?"

"Why do you ask?"

Ransom contrived to look perplexed by his reaction. "Because if you stayed onboard for a while, you might've seen someone come back, and even if not it would help narrow down the window of opportunity the murderer had to kill Miss Hemsley.''

Much to Ransom's surprise, the captain reddened slightly. ''Oh. Well, actually, I'm not sure I remember....'' He looked to his wife.

Samantha ran a hand through her long dark hair. ''It was a around ten-thirty when we left, I think. I checked my watch because we had to be back to do the lunch.''

''And nobody came back to the boat while we were here,'' said the captain. ''At least, if they did we didn't see them.''

''Good enough,'' Ransom said genially as he opened the door.

While Ransom had been questioning the captain and his wife, Emily was having a much more relaxed conversation on the deck. After Ransom left her, she wandered over to Lily DuPree in a tentative manner meant to disguise any trace of design. She sighed heavily as she sat on a chair beside the frail old woman.

Before Emily could begin the conversation, Lily roused herself. ''Who was that handsome young man you came on board with?'' Her tone betrayed a prurient interest.

''He is a police detective from Chicago with whom I'm acquainted.'' She had chosen to downplay their relationship for fear of arousing even more of her elderly friend's interest. ''He was kind enough to give me a ride back to the boat from the sheriff's station.''

''It's terrible, isn't it? Just terrible!'' Lily said, obviously eager for another opportunity to discuss the tragedy. ''To think that something like this could happen on our little trip.'' The avid light in her normally dull gray eyes belied the idea that she felt any grief over the event.

''Yes, it is. Of course, Marcella was quite old, and not in perfect health, but that seems to me all the more reason to be allowed to enjoy every day you're given, rather than having your life snuffed out prematurely.''

"Well… Well, I don't know about that,'' Lily replied, some of the light dimming as her tentative manner returned. "I don't like to think it, but…well, I've seen a lot of people go the way Marcella was going, and I'm sure she would've ended up in a nursing home…and I think…well, I've often thought that I'd rather die than end up in one of those places.''

Emily looked at her with an appraising eye. *Yes,* she thought, *so many people say that, but when it actually comes time would you give up even an hour of your life?*

"It's terrible to say it, I suppose,'' Lily continued, "but her niece probably did her a favor.''

Emily leaned in closed to her and whispered confidentially. "From what I heard at the station, they're not completely sure it was Rebecca who did it.''

"Really?''

Emily could almost hear the other woman's heart flutter with excitement. She nodded. "No, they're not completely sure.''

Lily tried to lean in closer herself, but the slight hunch to her back made it something of a struggle. She was finally able to do it by tightly gripping the arm of her chair. "The sheriff questioned me, you know. Because I stayed here in the boat. He wanted to know if I'd seen or heard anything.''

"Really?'' Emily said with zestful interest. "And did you?''

Lily's brow twisted with disappointment. "No…no, I was so tired, you see—that dreadful to-do the night before! It was hours before I was able to get back to sleep, so I was very tired when I was lying up here. I'm afraid I fell asleep. Just lightly, mind you. I do think I heard footsteps coming and going, but…'' The effort to keep herself pulled forward became too much, and she lowered herself back against the chair.

"It seems so odd that nobody stayed on the boat,'' Emily said. "The crew, I mean. You would think someone besides Mrs. O'Malley would stay to mind the store, so to speak.''

"Yes, I agree." The corners of her mouth turned down in a slight frown that didn't go unnoticed by Emily.

"Did you see them leave, by chance?"

"Yes, I was still awake then….I imagine the captain and his wife have to get off the boat now and then and stretch their legs. They're very attentive, don't you think?"

"Yes?" Emily replied, hoping to prompt her to continue.

Lily pursed her lips in a disapproving manner. "But I shouldn't have been surprised when that steward left…when the cat's away, as they say."

"You mean David?"

"Who? Oh, no, no, the little one—the dark one."

"Ah. Joaquin."

"Yes. Then the other one left as well. David." She paused and smiled. "His mother must be very proud of him."

"Why do you say that?" Emily asked, completely mystified.

"He has such nice posture, doesn't he?"

Emily cleared her throat. "I hadn't noticed."

"Anyway, I just didn't think that was quite right. It seemed like somebody should be on the boat, just as you say. I mean, after all, our things are here! Just anyone could come on and do anything!"

"Yes, they could," Emily said thoughtfully. "Lily, you were sitting just where you are now, facing the water with your back to the deck. Did you actually see these people leave?"

"Oh, yes! You know how it is—I heard footsteps and glanced over my shoulder."

"But you didn't see anyone later—Rebecca or Marcella?"

She shook her head slightly. "No. After that…Joaquin left, that was when I really started to doze. Isn't it funny? I stayed behind and ended up being right where the action was, even if I was asleep."

"Yes, it is."

Muriel Langstrom chose that moment to emit a louder snort than usual. Lily started to look back over her shoulder but winced slightly and checked herself. She then leaned closer to

Emily. "You know, I do feel sorry for Muriel. I think it really was too bad of Mr. Driscoll and Mr. Brock to do what they did. And as difficult as her life has been."

"Has it?" Emily said, prompting her to continue.

"She's the type of person who drives people away. Her daughter will have nothing to do with her—she told me she's never even seen her own grandson. Isn't that sad?"

"Yes...," Emily said vacantly. "A grandson...he would probably be in his twenties now, wouldn't he...."

"I suppose so."

"Yes...that would explain it...."

"Explain what?" Lily asked blankly.

"Something I saw on Navy Pier when we sailed. I hadn't thought about it until you mentioned this. There was a young man who showed a great deal of interest in our little group, or somebody in it. I was just thinking that if a boy that age had never seen his grandmother and was curious about her, that is probably the way he would do it...though how he would've known she was well..."

"How mysterious!" Lily exclaimed breathily.

"Oh, it's probably not at all," Emily replied airily. "It's just another odd thing." She adjusted herself in her chair. "Now, tell me, Lily, in your tenure as church secretary, you must know most of the people on this boat."

"The passengers, yes."

"I got the impression that there was some problem between the Millers and their grandchildren. When they were taking pictures as we sailed, Martin said something about their grandchildren, and Laura became very upset."

Lily was shaking her head. "I don't know about that. The Millers joined the church after I retired. I think I've heard that they're estranged from their children, but isn't that always the way with children nowadays?"

"I don't know about that. My late husband and I were never blessed with children. What about the other passengers?"

"Well, Stuart Holmes is divorced," Lily replied, more than

willing to provide the information. "I don't think he and his wife had any children. That, if you ask me, was one of the problems. That man was all work, and his wife couldn't stand for it. Mr. Driscoll's wife passed away a few years ago. Nearly ten now, if I remember correctly. They never had children. And poor Mr. Brock never married. I don't think he ever met the right woman."

"I see," said Emily. Then she asked, "Marcella told me that Claudia's grandson had had some problems."

"Drugs," Lily said darkly. "Although you'd never think it to look at her."

"I beg your pardon?" Emily said, drawing back slightly with surprise.

"I mean that that sort of thing would happen in her family."

"Oh, yes, well. One never knows what one will find in anyone's family."

"That's very, very true," Lily agreed eagerly.

Ransom emerged from around the far corner of the wheelhouse. He paused for a moment to survey the scene, then approached Emily and Lily.

"Hello again," he said to Emily, then turned to the other woman. "Hello, Miss...?"

"DuPree," Lily said, her eyes brightening. She made an attempt to straighten herself in her seat, but ended up in the same position. "Are you really the police?"

He smiled. "Yes. The boat looks deserted. Any idea where everyone is?"

With difficulty, Lily craned her neck around the side of her chair, a process that appeared to be quite painful given the way the muscles in her face tightened.

"Well, that's Muriel Langstrom," she said. Then she lowered her voice conspiratorially. "She seems to be...not herself today, although that's to be expected, under the circumstances. She's stayed to herself all morning."

"And the others?" Ransom asked.

"No, I'm afraid I haven't been paying attention. I heard

some of them going off in dribs and drabs earlier, but I didn't look to see who it was. Anyone who's not gone will either be in the lounge, which is the next deck down, or in their cabins,'' said Lily.

"And everyone should be back soon. It's nearly lunchtime,'' Emily concluded.

"Thank you, ladies,'' Ransom said cordially. He started to walk away, then paused. "By the way, which cabin belonged to Miss Hemsley?''

"Number eight,'' Emily answered.

"Thank you.''

He crossed the deck to where Muriel Langstrom lay on a chair that had been reclined to a forty-five-degree angle. She was so still that Ransom thought for a moment that she might be dead—an impression that was instantly dispelled when he cleared his throat and she started violently.

"What? Who are you?'' Her right hand had gone to her throat as if to ward off an imminent attack by Marcella's strangler.

"I'm so sorry to startle you, Miss Langstrom. I'm Detective Jeremy Ransom. I'm looking into Miss Hemsley's murder.''

"Oh.'' Her tone was lifeless and her body immediately relaxed once she had the explanation. Her eyes were barely visible behind the dark glasses, but Ransom could see enough to know that she was staring straight ahead rather than looking at him.

"Did you know Miss Hemsley well?''

"No. Only to speak to.''

"And you didn't get to know her any better on this trip?''

"No.''

He moved around to the foot of her chair, by the railing, blocking her view. "I'm trying to get an idea of where everyone was when Miss Hemsley was killed. Can you tell me where you were?''

"In the woods.''

"I see. Were you with anyone?''

Three evenly spaced, shallow lines appeared across her forehead. "What?"

"I asked if you were with anyone."

She swallowed. "Yes. I—for a while. We got separated somehow."

"Would you happen to know what time it was when that happened?"

"I wasn't wearing a watch." She said this without emotion, so Ransom was surprised to see a tear slowly emerge from beneath the right lens of her sunglasses. It disappeared into the corner of her mouth, leaving a wet trail behind.

"How long were you alone?"

"I don't know. It seemed like hours. I was…I was…sort of frightened."

"I'm not surprised."

"But it was probably only about twenty minutes or so." She sniffed and ran a meaty wrist beneath her nose. Then she straightened herself up a bit and made an attempt to sound lighter. "I don't know how it happened! One minute we were together—Jackson Brock, Bertie Driscoll, and myself—and then suddenly I was alone. I was talking—" She broke off and there was a noticeable hesitation before she continued. "I was talking and we just somehow got separated."

"And you were alone for about twenty minutes, you think? That's quite some time. Why didn't you just retrace your steps and come out of the woods?"

She sniffed again, and it was apparent that it was difficult to explain this without breaking down completely. "I got all turned around. I started…I thought I'd started back in the right direction, but somehow I got the idea in my head that I was going farther into the forest, so I turned back again, and pretty soon I didn't know which way was out."

"Aren't the trails marked?"

She nodded. "But they're the same on both sides. I went this way and that, and after a while I just sat down on a tree stump. I know it sounds silly, but…I was frightened. And then Jackson caught up with me.''

"And he explained to you what had happened.''

Her assent was barely audible.

"So it was only about twenty minutes when Mr. Brock reappeared and you never saw Mr. Driscoll again?''

"That's right.''

"Thank you,'' Ransom said kindly. He felt much less pleasantly disposed toward Brock and especially Driscoll. ''You've been a great help, Miss Langstrom.''

"Have I?'' She lifted her head slightly, some life returning to her voice.

"Most definitely.''

He left her and went to the starboard staircase. As he started down the steps he glanced across the deck and noticed that Emily had gone. At the bottom of the stairs, he found himself outside of the dining room. Although he didn't see anyone through the windows, the long table along the portside wall was in the process of being laid out for lunch: it had been covered with a white cloth, and a stack of bread on a silver plate was at the far end. He pushed open the door and stopped just inside at the sound of voices coming from around the corner in the lounge.

"That's all right, Mr. Driscoll, that's what I'm here for!'' said a voice that Ransom found excessively cheerful. ''Just yesterday I was telling Mrs. Farraday that they always need me to man the bar, just in case!''

"Don't usually start so early in the day,'' a second voice said, presumably belonging to Driscoll. There was a huskiness and age to it.

Ransom came around the corner and found a young man, blond, well shaped, and wearing a broad grin that looked like a permanent fixture working behind the bar. He twisted the cap off a bottle of beer and plunked a glass onto the bar.

"Don't need a glass, David,'' said Driscoll, who sat on a stool with his back to the detective. ''I drink it straight.'' He laughed heartily at his own joke, and Douglas joined in dutifully. It was then that he noticed Ransom over Driscoll's shoulder. His smile waned and his eyebrows went up.

"Who are you?"

Driscoll swiveled around on his stool.

"I'm Detective Ransom," he said, coming into the lounge. Any residual amusement Douglas had been displaying completely vanished. "Huh?"

"I'm here looking into Miss Hemsley's murder."

"I thought the sheriff got the murderer," Douglas said as he wiped his hands on a black towel.

"We just want to be sure."

"Detective?" said Driscoll. Ransom noticed that his face was rather flushed. "I didn't know they had detectives in these parts."

"They don't. I'm up from Chicago."

"Um, would you like a drink?" Douglas asked.

"No, thank you."

Douglas hung the towel across the tap on the bar's small sink. "If you'll excuse me, I have to get back to getting lunch on the table."

"I do want to speak to everyone."

"Yeah, I know, but..." His eyes shifted for a split second in Driscoll's direction, a move that caused Ransom to raise an eyebrow.

Ransom said, "I can talk to you later."

With a look of relief profound enough to shake even the most doting mother's confidence in his veracity, Douglas disappeared through the door behind the bar.

Driscoll spoke to Ransom's reflection in the mirror behind the bar. "That young fellow's about as genuine as a plug nickel!"

"Is he?"

Driscoll screwed up his mouth. "I could tell you stories! Here, pull up a stool." He gestured to the maroon padded seat next to him. The directive was figurative since the stools were anchored to the floor, but Ransom accepted the invitation and slid onto the seat.

"Bertram Driscoll," the older man said, offering him a hefty paw to shake.

"What stories could you tell me?" Ransom asked.

Driscoll grimaced. "You're probably too young to remember the sort of thing—carnivals, hucksters—you know the type of thing I'm talking about?"

The fortyish Ransom entertained an inward glow at the idea of being thought too young to remember something. "Yes."

"That's what that Douglas reminds me of. Those guys that could smile in your face, butter not even meltin', while they take your money. He's the type of man who, if he shook my hand I'd check to see if my watch was still there after."

"Really?" Ransom knit his brow slightly. "Has he actually done something to make you think he's dishonest?"

"Oh, no, no," Driscoll backpedaled quickly. Then he leaned over toward the detective. "But he always looks like he's going to."

Ransom studied him as Driscoll laughed at his own joke and took a swig of beer. It was a self-conscious action, calculated to punctuate the punch line, like a failed repertory actor.

"So, Mr. Driscoll, I'd like to ask you a few questions about what happened yesterday."

"Awful business, that," Driscoll replied soberly. "'Course, I don't really know anything about it."

"Maybe not directly," Ransom said smoothly, "but I'm checking on everyone's movements, just in case they might have seen something...without realizing it, perhaps?"

Driscoll turned from the reflection to the original. "You think I might've seen or heard something? Sorry, can't help you. I was off in the woods."

A smile played about the detective's lips. If Driscoll had been more astute, he would've noticed a hint of malevolence in it. "So I understand. Now, you went off with the rest of the party originally, is that correct?"

"Yeah."

"And you split off from the larger group with Jackson Brock and Muriel Langstrom."

"That's right."

"I understand that after hiking for a while, you…became separated from them?"

"Uh-huh."

"How did that come about?"

Driscoll hesitated before answering. "Well, I…you know, we…thought we'd play a little joke on Muriel. She was walking up ahead of us, and when we came to a fork in the path, she went one way, and we went the other."

"You and Brock decided this together?"

His ruddy complexion turned darker. "Well…no, I guess. I just sort of pulled Jackson over to the right and clapped a hand over his mouth, and after Muriel was out of sight, I explained I thought it would be a fun trick to pull."

"And he went along with it?"

"Yeah, yeah. That old milquetoast would just about go along with anything rather than put up a fuss."

There was a beat, then Ransom said, "It didn't occur to you that what you were doing might be dangerous?"

"No! 'Course not! No way anybody could get lost out there! The trails are clearly marked." Driscoll said this broadly, but his face grew even redder and he shifted on his stool. "Listen, I'll tell you. Muriel is a good woman, but God, can she talk! Yakety-yakety-yakety! It's like to drive you crazy! I mean, it was just a joke, our going off! I wanted to see how long it would take her to realize we weren't there any more."

"I see. How long would you say you and Brock were apart from Ms. Langstrom?"

"Not more than ten or fifteen minutes."

"I understand Mr. Brock went to find her."

"He's a class-A mama's boy! Got all worried about Muriel. Said we shouldn't have done it."

"You didn't go with him."

Driscoll swatted the air with his right hand. ''By that time I was tired of the two of them. I thought I'd just stay on my own. What's this got to do with Marcella, anyway?''

''I just need to check where everyone was at the time of the murder.''

Some of the redness began to drain from Driscoll's face. ''See? Like I said, I was off in the woods.'' He lifted the bottle to his lips and took another drink.

''How long were you on your own?''

''No idea.''

''Did you check your watch at all?''

''My—?'' He stopped, his expression creased with puzzlement. Then it lightened as he laughed. ''Oh. No, I don't wear a watch. What I said before about checking to see that my watch was still there, that was just a figure of speech, as they say.''

''Um-hmm. Could you estimate how long you were on your own?''

''I'm…really bad at things like that.''

''Ten minutes? Fifteen? Twenty?''

''Oh, I'd say at least twenty, I guess.''

''Could it have been half an hour?''

''I suppose.''

Ransom pursed his lips reflectively. ''Hmm.''

''What?'' Driscoll asked apprehensively.

''Well, Mr. Brock did find Ms. Langstrom, so they can alibi each other—''

He went completely white. ''Alibi!''

Ransom ignored the interruption and continued pointedly. ''But what you're telling me is that you had possibly a half hour or more in between the time Brock last saw you and when you met Ms. Charters and Ms. Francis—which would be just after the murder—during which you can't account for yourself.''

Driscoll stammered, ''But…but I was heading back to the boat when I ran into Emily.''

Ransom shrugged again. "Nothing could be easier than to go up the beach from the boat, then come back down the path by the road and appear to be just returning."

The old man looked positively horrified. "You can't believe I'd do something like that!"

"It's a theory. Of course, I still have a lot of people to question before I come to any conclusions."

Ransom slid off his stool and looked at Driscoll meaningfully. "It's really a shame you didn't stay with your friends."

Pleased with himself, he left Driscoll gaping after him and went out through the starboard door of the dining room. Then he went down the stairs to the blue deck.

At the bottom he turned into the small vestibule between the passengers' and crews' cabins. He pulled aside the heavy curtain that closed off the section to his left and found the crew's quarters: two doors on each side, and one at the end of the brief hallway. He closed the curtain, turned around and went into the passenger's corridor.

Ransom opened the door to cabin 8 and was surprised to find Emily seated on the chair next to the nightstand, her hands patiently folded in the lap of her light blue dress, rather like a schoolmarm waiting for a tardy pupil. Ransom went into the room and closed the door.

"You took longer to get down here than I expected. Did something happen?"

"I ran into Mr. Driscoll in the lounge."

"Ah, well, I wanted to show you how we found the body. She was here." Emily gestured along the bed. "Her head was against this corner, and the lamp was on the pillow by her head—a lamp shaped like a compass, with a very heavy base. There's one like it in my room. I assume it was tossed there, since she certainly must've been struck down before she was strangled."

"Hmm."

There was a pause, then Emily asked, "What did Mr. Driscoll have to say for himself?"

"The same thing he told the sheriff. I left a rather large flea in his ear."

"Indeed?"

"Yes. I pointed out the fact that his little prank left him without an alibi."

She broke into an amused grin. "I see."

He sighed. "The trouble is, as much as I'd like to find him guilty of something other than being a clod, I don't think Mr. Driscoll works very well as a suspect."

"How so?"

"The coincidence factor. If he planned to kill Marcella Hemsley, I could imagine him coming up with a reason to ditch his friends and making it seem like a spur-of-the-moment thing…even picking a fight with one of them and storming off would've done it. But this elaborate plan of ditching them?…Could he have counted on Jackson Brock to leave him to go looking for Miss Hemsley?"

"Well, of course I don't know Mr. Brock very well, but actually that's exactly what I would've expected him to do. He's the type of man who can be swept along in the moment, but who I think can be relied upon to feel remorse and try to set things right."

Ransom shrugged. "You would know best."

"There is one thing I'm sure of," said Emily. "Mr. Driscoll did not expect Muriel to be accompanying them. She rather forced herself on them. In fact, he asked the rest of us if we would come along."

"That seems to let Driscoll out."

"Does it?" Emily said rather vaguely. "Hmm…I wonder…"

"What?"

"If it had been Mr. Driscoll's *plan,* I think it would've been fairly easy for him to lose Jackson Brock in the woods. Under most circumstances, it would've been far more difficult for him to disappear with a third person there to notice. But having Muriel's presence thrust upon him, don't you think it would be safer for him to have the rest of us? It would be far easier for him to lag behind and disappear from a group who were all chatting together.''

"Perhaps," Ransom said doubtfully. "It would be taking an awful risk.''

"Yes, but Jeremy, I don't think anyone planned to kill Marcella—"

"Ruling out her niece."

"Yes, ruling out Rebecca."

"How do you figure that?"

"Because nobody expected Marcella to be on the boat. She was supposed to be off on a hike.''

"Oh, of course." He sighed again. "That being the case, the most logical scenario is that she came back to the boat and surprised someone in her cabin. And since you all had left the boat, except for Miss DuPree, who I could hardly imagine throttling anyone, the most likely people to suspect would be the crew, except that they were all gone as well, except for the cook." He paused and a grin spread across his face.

"Why are you smiling like that?" Emily asked, noting the impish curl to his lips.

"I had a very brief word with David Douglas. He seems a very natural person to suspect.''

"Ah, yes," she said with a nod. "Mr. Douglas strikes me as rather the lovable rogue; perhaps harmless, perhaps not, but I would say almost completely disingenuous. Although I think—" She stopped abruptly and her face lit with surprise, her right hand going absently to her cheek. "Oh, dear! I hadn't thought about that!"

"What?" Ransom said with some frustration when she didn't continue. It was a rare taste of the treatment he usually gave to Gerald.

"Something that I noticed without realizing that I'd noticed it. At our first meal on board—it was lunch, the day we left. It was the first time Marcella made something of a scene…''

"I'll never know unless you tell me, Emily," Ransom said after a pause.

"Oh! I'm sorry. It's just—like so many things I've noticed, it might be nothing…and yet…" She suddenly shifted in her seat as if getting down to business. "Well, you see, David was moving among the tables serving drinks. After he'd left ours, I asked Rebecca what she thought of him—"

"You did?" Ransom said, raising his right eyebrow.

Emily went a bit pink. "Yes. Anyway, Marcella interrupted and said, 'He's a tart,' I believe it was, and Rebecca attempted to shush her. But Marcella added something to the effect of 'I know the type and I've seen them before.' I just happened to notice Mr. Douglas glancing at her from over his shoulder in a way that certainly didn't inspire confidence."

She stopped and sat looking at him.

"Yes?"

"Oh! I forgot that you didn't know Marcella. She had a habit of talking in a rather countrified manner. What she actually said was, 'I've seen 'em before."

After a pause, Ransom said, "I'm sorry, Emily, I'm still lost."

"You see, I understood what Marcella was saying. I know his type, I've seen *them* before. But she abbreviated the word, and Mr. Douglas was overhearing it. It's possible he thought she said, 'I've seen *him* before,' and that's what prompted the look."

"Yes," Ransom said doubtfully. "Or the look could've meant that he thought she was being a nuisance."

Emily sighed. "Unfortunately, that is a very real possibility."

"So what we're left with is the crew, only one of whom was on-board when Miss Hemsley returned, or Rebecca, who was at that point the only one we know of who went back to the boat…."

"Oh, I wouldn't say that," Emily said after pursing her lips for a moment. "Any of the passengers, with the possible exception of Muriel and Mr. Brock—unless they're in it together…I suppose the same would be true of the Millers—could've come back to the boat after the captain and crew left, and have been caught by Marcella.''

"Unseen?''

"It's possible.''

Ransom pursed his lips. "What does your little sentinel, Lily DuPree, have to say about the comings and goings aboard ship? I take it you managed to have your chat.''

"Actually, she confirmed that she was dozing, so didn't know anything for certain. She saw the captain and his wife leave, and Joaquin and David, but after that she doesn't know anything definite. She has some vague memory of hearing footsteps later, but that could easily be something she's imagined since the murder. Lily is the type who rather enjoys a scandal.''

Ransom sighed heavily, slowly shaking his head.

"What's the matter?'' Emily asked.

"Whether or not someone was here when Marcella Hemsley returned, the idea of her walking in on someone doesn't explain why Rebecca didn't find her when she—''

He broke off suddenly at the sound of a light rap against the wall beside the bed. Both he and Emily froze in place, but the sound didn't repeat. Ransom sprang off the bed.

"Stay here,'' he said to Emily.

He went out into the hallway. It was empty, but the door to cabin 6 was ajar. He went to it slowly and quietly, careful not to make any noise. He listened at the door for a moment and could hear movement within. Then with his hand on the door handle, he slowly pushed it open. A diminutive young man with black hair and a white uniform was bent over the bed, smoothing out the navy blue blanket.

"Excuse me,'' said the detective.

The young man jumped sharply and wheeled around in a way so reminiscent of British farce that Ransom almost laughed.

"You must be the steward, Joaquin Vasquez?''

"Yes," Hoke answered, nodding his head like a dashboard doll.

"I'm Detective Ransom. I'd like to speak with you."

"You would? The sheriff already talked to me. I don't know anything."

"Let me be the judge of that." Ransom came in to the room and gestured toward the bed. "Please, sit down."

"There?" Hoke sounded as awestruck as if he'd just been asked to accede to a throne.

"Yes. It will be all right."

There was a lengthy hesitation before Hoke complied, and even when he did he lowered himself onto the bed with a great deal of reticence. He sat on the edge with his back painfully straight and his hands on his knees. The fear was unmistakable behind his bright brown eyes.

"After the passengers left the boat yesterday," Ransom asked, "what did you do?"

"What did I do? Why do you ask me that? I didn't do anything. I've never been in any trouble!"

Ransom couldn't help smiling. "I'm just trying to get a line on where everyone was at the time of the murder."

"But—"

He raised a palm to stem the tide of protest. "And you can help me do that. Since you were on the boat after the passengers left, you may have seen or heard something important."

"I didn't hear anything."

"All right. What did you do after the passengers left?"

"Just what I do now. I clean the cabins and make up the beds."

"Were you aware that Captain and Mrs. Farraday had left the boat?"

He nodded. "David tell me—told me."

"And while you were still working, you didn't hear anyone come back to the boat?"

"No. I told the sheriff. No."

"You didn't hear Miss Hemsley return?"

"No."

"And since you were working down here, you would've heard her if she came back while you were still here?"

There was a hint of a smile on Hoke's face. "I think so. Unless she was sneaking."

"Hmm?"

"She was kind of noisy, usually."

Ransom returned the smile. "I see. I understand that you and David left the boat."

"Yes. I was done with my work—for now. I mean, for then."

"Did you go together?"

"No. David said he was going to go ashore. When I was through with the rooms, I looked for him, but he'd already gone. So I went."

"What did you do when you were ashore?"

"Me? I didn't do anything," Hoke said anxiously, as if he thought he were being accused of something.

"No, what I'm trying to find out is if you saw anyone while you were off the boat. Remember, I told you I'm trying to figure out where everyone *else* was at the time of the murder." He had stressed the word in order to allay the steward's obvious fears, and hopefully enlist his aid.

"Oh." Hoke blinked and appeared somewhat mollified. "I went to the store " He cocked his thumb in the general direction of the dock.

"Friendly's?"

"Yes. I had a soda. I didn't see anyone there. And there are a few shops on that road out there. I went into them and looked around. There isn't really much to do here."

"And you still didn't see anyone?"

He shook his head. "It wasn't until I came back to the boat that I hear something is wrong."

"How long were you off the boat?"

Hoke frowned and squinted as if trying to read an imaginary clock. "I don't know. Maybe an hour. Less, probably."

Ransom nodded. "Thank you very much."

"That's is all?" Hoke said with surprise as he jumped to his feet. He was unable to hide his delight that the ordeal was over.

"That's all," Ransom said with a shrug. "Oh, except one thing. You seem like a very observant young man...."

"I do?"

"I was wondering, what has it been like working with David Douglas?"

"What do you mean?"

"He seems nice enough. I was wondering what you thought of him."

"David?" A tiny bit of fear returned. Clearly he didn't relish the position in which the detective was putting him. "I don't know."

"Surely you must have some opinion."

"David is very nice."

"Um-hm. But I notice you're down here 'doing the rooms' alone."

"He...he has other duties."

"Like bartending."

"Yes!" Hoke had brightened again, as if greatly relieved to have thought of one.

"Did he help you with the cabins yesterday?"

"Um...yes. Some."

Ransom smiled with understanding. "Like today."

"Yes."

Ransom turned to leave, then turned back again. "Do you know what time it was when you left the boat?"

Hoke scrunched up his nose and squinted. "Not exactly. No. It was after ten-thirty. Not very long after, I don't think."

"But before eleven."

He nodded. "Oh, yes."

Much to Hoke's relief, this time the detective did leave.

Ransom went back into Marcella's cabin where Emily was waiting.

"Who was it?" she asked.

"Joaquin Vasquez."

"Ah. A very nice young man."

Ransom smiled. "And with that considered assessment may we strike him off the list of suspects?"

"Well, I should be very surprised—and distressed—if Joaquin had anything to do with it. But that's just the trouble. If Marcella was murdered because she walked in on someone, then I *suppose* we have to consider him." She frowned. "But I would hate to think it."

"I wouldn't worry about it. Both he and Douglas were off the boat before eleven. And it wasn't until around then that Rebecca lost her aunt, wasn't it?"

They were silent for a few moments, each lost in their own thoughts.

"So, what do we do now?" Emily asked.

Ransom glanced at his watch. "It's nearly twelve. The rest of the passengers will be coming back for lunch. I think I'll join them."

SIX

THE CELLS AT the sheriff's station were located in a large, blank room behind a door to the left of the desk in the outer office. Only one of the cells was occupied.

Rebecca Bremmer sat on the narrow bed against the rear wall of the ten-foot square, surrounded on three sides by bars. After Ransom dropped Lynn off at the station, Sheriff Barnes had bent the rules enough to allow her to sit in the open cell beside her. They spent the remainder of the morning talking in between long lulls.

"I don't know what I'm going to do," Rebecca said, breaking one of the silences by a return to a theme she was finding hard to let go of. "I suppose I should call a lawyer, but...I don't know one."

"You don't have to do that yet," Lynn said reassuringly. "Ransom will sort this all out and find out who really did it. He's very good. I wouldn't admit it to him, but he is."

Rebecca didn't appear to have heard her. "That Stuart Holmes is a lawyer. I suppose I could ask him to help me...."

"You can't do that. He's one of the passengers."

Rebecca looked up. "So?"

"So that makes him a suspect."

"But why would he—oh, it's no use!" She had animated for a moment, but now the energy drained from her again.

"You shouldn't think like that. Ransom really will get to the bottom of this. He's a regular Mountie—he always gets his man, or woman." Lynn was aware that she'd said this too brightly. She knew that if she'd been in Rebecca's situation, it would've sounded like an offer of false hope.

Rebecca's cheeks were stained with drying trails of tears. Her dark hair had gone limp, and her face was deathly pale. "I miss her already," she said softly.

"I know."

"It's funny, the past few days I've been with her…the way she was acting…I can't really picture them in my mind. All I can see now are the good times. The woman I knew when I was younger, who baked muffins and bread and made some of her own clothes, and who was stern but never harsh. She never had a bad word to say about anybody."

"I know," Lynn said quietly. "When my lover died—she'd been sick for a long time and had physically withered away. She never really lost her faculties, but it was hard to see someone I loved physically deteriorate like that. After she died, it was funny…I could only picture her the way she'd been when she was sick if I tried really hard. What came easy was seeing her healthy and happy. I guess that's probably some kind of blessing that we're given at times like that."

"Your lover…so you're…?"

Lynn hadn't been thinking of the implication when she'd said this—that she would be revealing something about herself that could potentially destroy the budding friendship with this woman. Despite the circumstances, her heartbeat quickened when she realized that it mattered to her how Rebecca responded.

"Uh-huh," Lynn said, her eyes leveled at Rebecca.

"Same here," she replied vacantly.

Lynn cleared her throat and tried to slow her heart. "Anyway, remembering those good times should be a blessing."

Rebecca looked down at the hands she'd folded in her lap, her slender white fingers looking pale against the rust-colored dress. A fresh onslaught of tears ran down the tracks on her cheeks. "I guess they should, but…I feel so guilty."

"Why?"

"Because I wanted her to die," she replied without looking up.

Lynn shot a glance at the door leading to the outer office and wondered whether or not their conversation could be heard. "You shouldn't say that."

"You know it's true. I told you just the other night."

"You told me something that was very human. Everybody feels that way when someone close to them is suffering."

Rebecca looked at her with wide, watery eyes. "Did you feel that way?"

The normally direct Lynn averted her eyes. She didn't think it would help the situation if she were to break down. "Yes, sometimes."

"I'm sorry."

Lynn looked up. "It was a long time ago now. Look, it's natural to feel the way you did."

They fell silent for quite some time.

"Lynn, could you do me a favor?" Rebecca said at last.

"Anything."

"Sheriff Barnes said that they'd gone through my things and Aunt Marci's at the boat. Could you pack them up for me and bring them here?"

"Well, sure," Lynn replied, though the idea made her heartsick. She took Rebecca's request as a sign of acquiescence to her fate—or at least, that Rebecca could see that the matter wasn't going to get cleared up quickly. This caused a dent in Lynn's reserve. She felt as if something were slipping away.

But she knew her own feelings made little sense. Surely the tour wouldn't go on now. And if it did, and Rebecca were of necessity left behind, Lynn didn't have to go with it. Having made a tentative start, she wondered if offering to stay behind would look as if she were rushing a relationship that had barely begun at the worst possible moment. At the same time, she mentally kicked herself for even thinking of these things while the object of her newborn affection was in this predicament.

Right then, more than anything, she wanted to get away for a little while and get a grip on herself.

"I'll take care of it," she said.

RANSOM SAW Emily back to her cabin, where she wanted to freshen up before lunch, then headed for the red deck. He'd only gotten as far as the staircase when he ran into Stuart Holmes, who came to a halt three steps from the bottom at the sight of the unfamiliar face.

"Who the devil are you?"

"Detective Ransom. I'm here looking into Miss Hemsley's murder. And you are…?"

"Stuart Holmes." He descended to the bottom and extended a hand with a distinct lack of grace. "I thought the case was all settled."

"Not quite," Ransom said lightly as he shook the hand. "I'd like to ask you a few questions." Holmes looked as if he were about to protest, and Ransom added quickly, "As I'm doing with everyone."

"All right," Holmes said after a beat.

"Your cabin?"

"No, over here, if you don't mind." He was already moving over to the brief expanse of railing to the left of the stairs. "The cabins on this boat are awfully small. I feel claustrophobic enough in it myself. I don't think I could take it with another person."

"I understand." He'd had only a moment to assess the retired lawyer, but Ransom thought the old man cut quite a dignified, if slightly starchy, figure. Holmes was dressed, as always, in a lightweight suit and tie. The crisp whiteness of his shirt made his skin look a bit yellow and his powderlike hair seem dingy.

"I first should say," Holmes began, planting his palms on the railing and looking out over the side as if making a speech, "that I, of course, had nothing to do with the murder. I hardly knew the woman. And from our brief acquaintance—if you could call it that—I wouldn't have wanted to know her."

"She was that difficult?"

"From what I could see."

"Well, what I'm most interested in getting from the passengers is an account of their movements after leaving the boat yesterday, through the time the body was discovered."

"Yes, of course. I was in the general store."

Ransom's right eyebrow elevated. "The whole time?"

"Yes. I suppose it doesn't do me any credit, but I was already tired of the mob and wanted to be away from them. Didn't particularly want to go walking in the woods, either, so I stayed there and had a cup of coffee."

He sounds like he's rehearsed this, thought Ransom. "I'm a bit confused. You see, Joaquin—Hoke, the steward—went into the store and he didn't see any of the passengers."

Holmes didn't turn a hair. "Boy can't see his own nose."

Ransom waited, silently staring at the side of Holmes's face. The former lawyer lasted for a while under the scrutiny, but finally faltered. "Well, I might've gone out and looked at those little shops across the way for a while. Yes, I did do that, come to think of it."

"You don't sound very sure."

The old man turned toward the detective. "Hoisted on my own petard!"

"I beg your pardon?"

"I used to be a lawyer. Used to hear from my peers how when they asked people where they were at the time of the crime, they'd say they were so shocked they couldn't remember. After all these years I'm damned if I don't find myself in the same state. Heard one of our members had been murdered, and everything else went out of my head." A smile slid across his face. "And like they say, I didn't know I was going to need an alibi."

"You were a criminal lawyer?"

Holmes looked completely surprised by the question. "No.

I did…other kinds…most other kinds of law. But I know some criminal lawyers. Fellows I went to school with.''

"So you were on your own when the murder occurred.''

"Probably was. But as I said, except for on this trip, I didn't know the woman at all.''

"Um-hmm.'' Ransom cleared his throat. "I'm also checking up on any strangers who might've been in the vicinity.''

The detective thought he noticed a split second during which the former lawyer froze in place. "Yes?''

"Some members of the tour saw a man drive up and go into Friendly's while you were there.''

"They did?'' Holmes said lightly. His eyes had gone blank, and his tone was vague. Ransom thought this was a technique that had probably served him well in his practice. "I don't remember seeing anybody.''

"You don't? That's interesting….''

"Why?''

"Because the people who saw him arrive told me that it was a man they'd seen before…talking to you on the street in Sangamore.''

There was a longer pause, this time during which Ransom could hear the gears turning in the old man's head. "You know, I do remember somebody coming in. He sat by me at the lunch counter.''

"And was it the same man?''

"As a matter of fact, it was. But he's nothing to me—just somebody I got into a conversation with in Sangamore.''

Ransom was finding Holmes's responses more and more puzzling. There was no doubt in his mind that the former lawyer was lying, and pretty badly, at that. But what possible reason he could have for doing so under the circumstances eluded the detective.

"Mr. Holmes, if you'll forgive me for saying it, you're not very good at this.''

"What?'' Holmes exclaimed, his lower jaw dropping with an odd click. "What do you mean?''

"As a lawyer, you should know the importance of telling the absolute truth in a murder investigation, regardless of whether or not you practiced criminal law."

"Are you calling me a liar?"

"You were not just seen talking to this man, he paid a visit to the boat late in the evening that you were in Sangamore. Then he showed up here. Unless he's a stranger who has suddenly become obsessed with you, you must know him."

Holmes couldn't look him in the eye. Instead he looked back over the water and sighed. "You're right. I'm not a very good liar. But if I give you my word as a gentleman that this has nothing to do with the murder, can we let it go at that?"

Your word as a gentleman who has been lying to the police? Ransom thought. "I'm afraid not."

"So be it," Holmes said curtly. "If you must know, that man is a client of mine."

"I understood you were retired."

"A former client. I just…ran into him in Sangamore, and offered to give him some advice. Professional advice, I mean. That's all I can say about that." He gave a single nod, indicating that was an end to the matter. "Now, if you'll excuse me, I'm going to go wash my hands for lunch."

Ransom watched with a certain degree of admiration as the back of the rail-thin beige suit disappeared around the corner. He disliked being lied to, and disliked even more being stonewalled regardless of whether or not he was convinced of the validity of his own investigation. But he couldn't help admiring the fading dignity with which Holmes had managed to accomplish it.

Ransom went up the stairs and glanced into the dining room. Douglas was just laying a platter of decoratively arranged meats and cheeses on the buffet table. After he set it down a short, stout woman who Ransom took to be the ship's cook made a slight adjustment to it, then followed David back in the direction of the kitchen. Lily DuPree was already seated at one of the tables waiting for service to begin, and Bertram Driscoll was leaning against a portside window, drink in hand, staring out at the scenery.

Ransom continued to the top deck, which he found empty. Rather than remain idle he went down the boarding plank and followed the path around to the front of the general store. The door opened with a loud *sproing* occasioned by the large, long metal spring used to pull it shut. Nothing had been done to disguise the warehouse origins of the store: the walls were knotty, age-worn bare wood, the rafters exposed, and the lighting provided by low-hanging fluorescents of the type that Ransom associated with turn-of-the-century newsrooms. Long rows of shelves contained everything from potholders to beef jerky, to Bon Ami, to disposable cameras: a sign that though the store might be old-fashioned, the proprietors knew enough to carry whatever would sell. An antique, top-loading Coca-Cola cooler was just to the left of the door, though Ransom was rather disheartened to find it filled with canned sodas of every variety.

Along the north wall there was a low counter with stools. A hand-printed menu was tacked to a corkboard on the wall behind it. The menu consisted of three different kinds of sandwiches, none requiring cooking, and a choice of coffee or soda. The store was empty except for a woman seated at the counter looking down at an open newspaper, her blasé expression indicating that the news of the world was providing a very unexciting diversion. She was a solidly built woman with a round face. Her hair was dark gray and she wore it pinned in a loose bun on top of her head so that it resembled a wilting chef's hat. Over her gray dress she had tied a stained, bibbed apron. She hadn't looked up when Ransom came in, apparently accustomed to tourists who would look around and leave without making a purchase. She didn't raise her eyes from her reading until he was at her side.

"Yup? Can I help you with something?"

"Mrs. Friendly?"

"Uh-huh?"

"My name is Detective Ransom. I take it you've heard about the murder that happened yesterday on the *Genessee?*"

"Joe Barnes was in here, already talked to me about it."

"Sheriff Barnes has kindly allowed me to do a little investigating of my own," he said lightly.

"You don't say?" The dint that appeared between her eyebrows was the only indication she gave that this news had made any impression on her.

Ransom noticed the windows at the back of the store. They faced out toward the dock but were covered by faded floral curtains.

"He asked you if you saw anything? Anyone going to or from the boat?"

She nodded, the pile of hair moving out of sync with her head. "Uh-huh."

"And did you?"

"Nope. Nary a soul."

"Too busy?" He asked with a smile.

She grinned. "I'm never too busy here. Just not interested. And I always have the curtains back there closed in the morning. Sun's just too damned hot."

"No, I meant too busy because I understood you had some customers yesterday morning...from the boat?"

"Hoke was here," she said.

"You know him?"

She nodded again, causing the same disconnected motion of her hair. "I know who he is. *Genessee*'s been here now and again this past couple of summers. I know the Farradays, too."

Ransom's right eyebrow went up. "Did they come in yesterday?"

"Nope. But I know them just the same."

He smiled. "Of course. Now, the people I was referring to were two men who came in sometime before the murder and had coffee."

"Oh, yeah," Mrs. Friendly replied, her face lightening.

"Guy with white hair and one a little younger, not so gray. Nervous guy."

"How long did they stay, do you remember?"

"Well, the younger one come in first, and asked for a cup of coffee. The second one, he come a little bit later, and he had one, too."

"But how long did they stay?"

She pursed her lips. "Only so long as to finish the coffee. Not long. They didn't linger over it or anything."

"Did you happen to hear anything they talked about?"

"No 'happening' about it. You can see how quiet it is here. You can't help but hear what people are talking about, even if they try to keep their voices low."

"Anything you think might be important?"

"Naw. They didn't say much of anything except chitchat about the weather and such like, and the drive up here and all."

"I see."

"What're you looking for, anyway?"

Ransom heaved a sigh. "I wish I knew. Anything that might shed some light on what happened."

She flapped a flabby hand. "Joe got that all sewed up."

"He's done a very good job," Ransom replied. Despite his abhorrence of soft-soap, he wasn't above using it when called for. "But it's always best to be sure where murder is concerned."

"Hmm." Mrs. Friendly gave a slight nod, which caused the mass of hair to lurch forward, where it stayed until she shoved it back with her right palm.

"So, the two men were here for only a short time, and didn't say anything of importance. Did they leave together?"

"Oh, yeah," she replied broadly. "They were in a hurry to get back to the one's motel to have a talk."

"Oh, so one of them was staying here?"

"Not the white-haired one, I don't think. It was the younger one that said they could go back to his motel room, I think."

"Which motel would that be, do you know?"

She shrugged her massive shoulders. "Imagine the Lake-view. It's the closest. Isn't another motel for at least ten miles. 'Course, that don't matter with a car. You want to know where it is?"

He shook his head. "That's where I'm staying. One other thing. Did you happen to see a pair of hikers yesterday morning?"

"In here?" she said. "No. It's a little early in the season for them."

Ransom returned to the boat feeling anything but satisfied. Despite Sheriff Barnes's doubts, Emily's concerns, and Lynn's hopes, the detective didn't think he'd made much progress in disproving Rebecca Bremmer's guilt, or learning anything of importance, for that matter.

Once back on the boat Ransom went down to the red deck and looked in the window. Lunch was now being served, once again buffet style. Lily DuPree was at the table where Ransom had seen her earlier, and Emily had joined her. Muriel Langstrom was at a table across the room from them in the company of a man to whom Ransom had not yet been introduced. Also strangers to him were the man and woman seated at the table next to Lily's. Stuart Holmes and Bertram Driscoll were at the buffet table helping themselves to the various dishes, and Hoke and David were serving.

Emily glanced toward the window, and when she saw Ransom she gave him a meaningful nod, then pushed back her chair and got up. She came out and joined him.

"Oh! Jeremy, good, you're back," she said in the slightly abstracted way she sometimes lapsed into when something was on her mind.

"Who's the man with Muriel?" he asked.

"What? Oh! That's Jackson Brock...."

"And the couple—that would be the Millers?"

"Yes...but before you talk to them, I thought you should know that Claudia Trenton hasn't been seen this morning."

"What do you mean she hasn't been seen? Do you think something's happened to her?"

"No, not at all," Emily replied with surprise. "She's not dead."

"You sound disappointed."

"Now, Jeremy," she said in a mildly reproachful tone. "When Claudia didn't appear for lunch I asked Joaquin if he knew where she was. He said she hasn't been out of her cabin. She didn't even allow him in to make up the room. Now, that seems rather significant to me. Does it to you?"

"Not necessarily. Someone's been murdered. She could just be very upset."

Emily's eyebrows peaked. "Claudia Trenton? You think that because you haven't met her yet. As far as I know, she barely knew Marcella Hemsley. And I know she found her rather irritating." A hint of a smile appeared. "At any rate, she isn't having lunch. Perhaps this would be a good time to talk to her."

Ransom emitted a sigh of resignation. "All right."

He started down the stairs, but stopped and turned around when he realized she was following him. "Shouldn't you be having your lunch?"

"I thought I'd come with you. If she *is* so upset about the murder that she hasn't left her cabin, having a stranger appear at her door might upset her even more."

He grinned. "And here I thought you were just curious. Come along."

He preceded her down the stairs and gave her his hand as she stepped off of them.

"Which cabin is she in?" he asked as they went down the corridor.

"Number one."

It was located at the far end on the left, and when they reached it Ransom raised his hand to knock, but Emily stopped him.

"Let me." She gingerly tapped on the door with her finger-tips. When there was no answer, she did it again.

"If she's asleep she's not going to hear that," Ransom said, growing impatient.

It was then that they heard the voice from within the cabin. It was distinct but devoid of energy. "Yes?"

"Claudia? It's Emily Charters. Can I have a word with you?"

There was a long pause before the lifeless voice replied. "Come in."

Ransom stood to the side as Emily opened the door. Claudia was lying on the bed in the same light green suit she'd worn the day before, its wrinkles showing it had been slept in—if sleep had ever come to her. One hand lay limply at her side, the other was draped just below her breasts. She was staring at the ceiling.

"Claudia? Are you all right? I haven't seen you today. I was worried."

"I'm not hungry."

Emily's brow knit questioningly at the incongruous reply. "No, I imagine not. Are you feeling unwell?"

"No." There was a brief pause. "Yes, I suppose I am."

"Is there anything I can do for you? Do you need to see a doctor?"

"No, no," Claudia said wearily. "I just want to be left alone."

Emily had remained by the door during this exchange. Now she came into the room and quietly crossed to the bed. Once she was closer to Claudia, she could see that her eyes were bloodshot and her face very wan.

"Are you sure you're all right?" Emily asked.

"Yes. Please…all I need is to be left alone."

"Yes," Emily said kindly, "I understand that. However, we do need to speak with you."

For the first time the other woman turned her head and looked at Emily. "We?"

"Yes. The police are still looking into poor Marcella's death. They're asking all of us additional questions."

"The police?"

Emily didn't miss the tremor in her voice. "Yes. A very nice young man from Chicago is helping Sheriff Barnes. He's waiting outside to talk to you." When Claudia shot a nervous glance toward the doorway, Emily quickly added, "He's already talked to most of the rest of us. There's nothing to be anxious about. I'll stay here with you."

There was a brief but unmistakable spark of gratitude in Claudia's eyes. But then her face hardened as if unexpectedly caught by an Alberta clipper. She sat up, though not quickly, and planted her feet on the floor.

"I suppose you can stay if you like," she said as if conferring a boon upon one of the peasants.

"Thank you," Emily replied, smiling inwardly. Then she looked toward the door. "Detective Ransom?"

As he came into the room Emily could sense the increased tension emanating from Claudia.

"Miss Trenton?" said Ransom. "Are you all right? We were worried about you."

"I'm fine," she said in the manner she used to let people know they were being held at arm's length. But after a beat, she continued uncertainly. "I'm…it's just that I've had a very bad headache this morning. I'm subject to migraines."

"I'm sorry to hear that. Did you take something for it?"

"Of course. But the best thing for me to do would be to lie down and be left alone."

The right corner of Ransom's mouth twisted upward. "I'll try not to bother you any more than I need to."

"It's this awful business that's caused my headache to begin with," Claudia said forcefully, apparently having decided that mounting an offense was her best course.

"I wasn't aware that you were that close to Marcella Hemsley."

"I wasn't. I was referring to the fact that she was murdered not thirty feet from where I'm sitting. If we hadn't been made to stay by that sheriff, I would've left the boat and this tour immediately.''

"You must realize,'' said Emily, "that we would be asked to stay until the investigation is complete.''

"I don't even understand why there is still an investigation going on!'' Claudia replied haughtily. "They have the Bremmer girl in custody. They know she murdered her aunt.''

"Hmm,'' said Ransom. "Then you have nothing to worry about, do you?''

There was a startled pause. "What?''

"If the murderer is in jail, you shouldn't have anything to worry about, should you?''

She stared at him blankly for a moment. "I didn't say I was worried. It's the idea that a murder took place here. It's not a very pleasant thought.''

"Yes, I see. Now, Miss Trenton, could you tell me where you were at the time of the murder?''

"I don't know when the murder happened.''

Ransom's eyes narrowed. If she chose to be difficult, he would have no compunction about responding in kind. "I believe you do.''

Claudia caught herself just short of a gasp. "What?''

"Surely Sheriff Barnes asked you about the time period around eleven-thirty.''

"Oh…yes.'' She had visibly deflated with relief. "I was out walking, just like everyone else.''

"Alone?''

"Yes?'' She voiced this as a question, challenging him to make something of it.

"Don't you think that was a bit dangerous?''

She produced a brittle smile. "No. It seems it was much more dangerous to be on the boat.''

He smiled. "Very good. I'm just a little surprised. It seems odd to me that you would not want any company on a walk in a strange place. You've never been here before, have you?''

"No, of course not!"

"Claudia," said Emily, whose keen blue eyes were leveled at the other woman, "you went with us to the visitor's center, took a brochure, then left in a manner that I could only term…abrupt. One might've called it purposeful."

Claudia had involuntarily faded back slightly, as if in a slow-motion recoil. Her jowls seemed to grow heavier. "No," she said after a long pause. "If anything, I was trying to avoid those dreadful men." She turned from Emily to Ransom. "They've been following me around, trying to accompany me everywhere."

"Mr. Driscoll, Mr. Brock, and Mr. Holmes?" he asked.

"Yes. Very tiresome people. They seem to think they need to keep me company, I suppose because I'm on my own."

"Yes, we saw Mr. Driscoll having dinner with you in Sangamore," said Emily with no particular emphasis.

"That was not of my choosing. I don't want company. That's not why I came on this trip."

"If we could back up for just a moment," Ransom said, noting that Claudia had seemed relieved to have moved on to the safer area of airing grievances, "you say you went for a walk, alone—"

"I don't just say it, that's what I did."

"I understand that. Where exactly did you go?"

"What?" Her eyes had gone blank again.

"Which trail did you take?"

"I— What possible difference could that make?"

He shrugged. "We're trying to trace everyone's movements, including the dead woman."

"What does that have to do with me?"

"If you saw one of your fellow passengers, and could estimate when that was, it would help."

"Oh. Well, I didn't see any of them. Not at all."

"And which trail were you on?" Ransom pressed with elaborate patience.

"Oh. It was…" She shot an uncertain glance in Emily's

direction, then the corners of her mouth drooped as if something very disheartening had just occurred to her. "It was trail three, I believe. Yes. It's just..." There was a short silence while she did a mental calculation. "It's just north of the shops."

"And did you see anyone?"

Claudia emitted a sharp, frustrated sigh. "I already told you—" He raised a palm to silence her. "Not passengers. I mean did you see anyone at all?"

"What?"

Emily eyed her curiously. "You must have seen that young couple hiking. We all did."

Her brow furrowed. "I...I may have done. Oh, I don't remember! So much has happened since then! Why are you asking all these questions? That sheriff didn't ask so much. He was happy enough to arrest that tiresome woman's niece! Why do you have to pester me like this? I've told you I'm sick! This whole trip has been just...ghastly!"

"Claudia," said Emily, "why *did* you come on this cruise?"

Her eyes widened. "What do you mean? I have every right to go where I please! Normally."

"Yes, but this seems like such a peculiar choice for someone who wants to be left alone—to be thrown so closely together with other people."

"I thought..." Claudia was at a loss for a moment, then gained confidence as she formed the idea into words. "I suppose I thought the boat would be bigger. I thought it wouldn't be difficult to keep to myself...I thought—wrongfully, of course—that the other passengers would leave me alone!" She grimaced and put a hand to her forehead. "Now, if you will please, please allow me to lie down."

ONCE OUT in the corridor, Ransom said quietly, "Emily, did you tell me you had a map of the trails?"

"Yes, from the visitor's center."

"Do you still have it?"

She nodded, then led him to the other end of the hall and into her cabin. He closed the door as she retrieved the map from the nightstand. When he crossed to her, she handed it to him and sat on the bed. He sat beside her, opened the map, and stared down at it.

It was crudely drawn with little in the way of detail, though it marked the road, the trails, and the campgrounds. The clearest landmark was the prominently featured general store. As Claudia had said, trail three began just north of Friendly's on the opposite side of the road.

"What are you looking for?" Emily asked.

He sighed. "I don't really know. But you said that Claudia looked as if she had some purpose when she left you, and she claimed she was trying to get away from your pesky fellow passengers."

Emily clucked her tongue lightly. "She wasn't very kind about it, but Jeremy, I have to admit they did rather pester her. I'm sure they behaved like gentlemen around her—"

"Even Mr. Driscoll?" he cut in.

Emily smiled. "As much as that is possible. But the point is, more than once they joined her when, if she is to be believed, she didn't want them around. So, she could very well be telling the truth."

"Except for one thing."

"Hmm?"

"When I pressed her about which trail she took, she looked as if she wanted to lie, but was afraid you might've seen which way she went."

"I see," Emily said with a thoughtful nod.

Ransom drew his attention back to the map and studied it. The three trails closest to the docks were numbered out of order, with three just to the north of Friendly's, then six, then trail number one, the one Driscoll and company had taken, beginning just past the rise in the road. A large area marked Campground was in the center of the eastern portion of the map. Trail number six ran along the right side of the campground and continued on, while trail three was a short distance from the ground's north rim.

"Where was Marcella last seen before Rebecca lost her?" Ransom asked.

"The rest rooms were here." Emily tapped her index finger on the upper right-hand corner of the campground.

"Hmm. So presumably she came out of the rest room, and since she didn't go back the way she came and didn't go forward…" He traced a diagonal line toward the northeast. "She must've cut across the campground and gone down here." His finger followed the track drawn from the grounds to the road, which came out not far from the entrance to trail number three.

"That makes sense," said Emily said. "The entrances to either end of the trail are somewhat covered compared to the campground, which is partially cleared. If she came out of the rest room and was confused, she probably took the line of least resistance…the clearest route."

"Which if I'm not mistaken, would've taken her back to the boat fairly quickly." He looked at the map awhile longer, then emitted a sound through his nose.

"What is it?" Emily asked.

"There's nothing marked on these trails."

"What do you mean?"

"No sights, no rest areas, no landmarks…"

She smiled at him benignantly. "Jeremy, you really do need to get out of the city more often. The map is simply meant to show the basic overview, if you will, of the paths—so that you can make sure you're going the right way…something that's hardly necessary since the trails themselves have plentiful markers. There aren't landmarks along the way, but there are some plaques describing the flora and fauna. And it isn't really necessary to mark rest areas since, as the Farradays told us beforehand, the locals have installed benches along the paths, so there are many places to sit down and have a rest."

"Yes, but look at this." He pointed to a small circle outlined at a kink in the line that formed trail three. "Lookout Point" was printed next to a circle at the edge of the trail in tiny lettering that had bled when being reproduced so that it was difficult to make out.

"Is that significant?" Emily asked, her narrow brows arching.

"It might be. You know I would accept your impressions over the facts any day. Your impression was that Miss Trenton left the group in a purposeful manner after going with you to the visitor's center."

"Yes, it was."

"Of course, this is just conjecture, but it would look as if she went to the center to get the necessary map, and then went directly to trail three—the only one with a landmark—which might suggest she had a rendezvous of some sort."

"It is conjecture," Emily said with a considering tilt of her head, "but it is logical."

Ransom was still looking at the map, his lips pursed. "But we're left with the problem of what on earth that would have to do with Marcella's murder, even if it were true. And if she was meeting someone, could she have gotten back to the boat in time to do the murder?"

"Oh, but there's something else. If she was meeting someone it must've been an outsider—someone other than a passenger."

"What makes you so sure?"

"There wouldn't be any reason for such a roundabout, furtive meeting with one of us. The walls here may be thin, but if you keep your voice down you can easily have a conversation without being overheard."

They were silent for quite some time, then Ransom rose and offered his hand to Emily. "Well, you're long overdue for lunch, and it's time I spoke with the remaining passengers."

Back in the dining room Ransom and Emily found that many of the passengers were still in attendance. Lily DuPree was still picking at her food with quiet, birdlike movements, and the Millers were chattering away at each other between spoonfuls of chocolate pudding. Jackson Brock was sitting alone at his table sipping coffee.

"When I'm finished with lunch, I'll go back to my cabin," Emily said quietly. She then rejoined Lily and continued her interrupted meal, and Ransom went over to Brock.

"It looks as though Miss Langstrom has deserted you," the detective said without a hint of irony.

The startled Brock grasped the inference immediately and his cheeks colored. "Yes. She went to her cabin."

"May I join you for a moment?" Ransom asked as he took a seat. "I imagine you've already heard that I'm Detective Ransom, and I'm looking into Miss Hemsley's murder."

"Yes," Brock replied blankly. "Yes, I thought something was wrong."

"I beg your pardon?"

"When we weren't allowed to leave the area, I mean."

"That was a normal precaution under the circumstances, but there is some doubt as to Miss Bremmer's guilt."

"I'm glad to hear it. She seems like a very nice young lady. And she took very good care of her aunt. It's nice to see that sort of thing in this day and age. You don't often."

"Um-hmm. Now, Mr. Brock, I've already heard about the little escapade in which you took part yesterday—"

Brock's face flushed, and he looked down at the remnants of his lunch. Despite his obvious discomfiture, which Ransom had calculated to produce, the older man protested. "It was not my escapade. I didn't have anything to do with it. I wouldn't have…wouldn't have…done anything like that!"

"How did your participation come about?"

"We came to a Y in the trail, you see. The trail split in two. It was very woody, there. You could clearly see the trail signs on the left, and Muriel was in the lead, so she went that way. But Bertram pulled me to the side. He clapped a hand over my mouth and said 'Be quiet! Don't let her hear you!' He was already guiding me up the other leg of the path, the one to the right, before I knew what was happening. I tried to get him to turn back, and he just kept on going. He thought it was very funny, what he was doing.''

''What you both were doing,'' Ransom corrected.

Brock's cheeks reddened again. ''But I didn't really know what was happening! And when…when I finally got Bertie to stop, and I told him I was going back, he was just…not nice at all about it. He called me several things that I won't repeat, most of them having to do with my manhood, and said I could just go my own way…but I don't think there's anything particularly manly about deserting a woman in the woods, do you?''

''No.''

During the short silence that followed, Ransom did a quick assessment of Mr. Brock: the wide-set eyes, his blank expression, and his weedy physique made his explanation plausible. He was like a feather that could be caught in an updraft and carried along a great distance before its own weight would bring it to the ground.

''So, I went back to the…to the fork in the path. We'd gone much farther than I thought. And I tried to find Muriel.''

''How long did it take?''

''What?'' Brock said, blinking.

''I mean, how long were you on your own?''

He sat back in his chair and touched the fingers of his right hand to his chin. ''Oh, I don't know….''

''An estimate?''

''I'm really terrible at that sort of thing. I really don't know…. Did the others have any idea?''

''Yes, but I'm asking you.''

''Well, whatever they said, they were probably right.''

Ransom smiled. ''Please, Mr. Brock, just a guess.''

''A guess…'' he said slowly, his gaze trailing off into another dimension. As he thought he tapped his fingertips just beneath his lower lip. ''A guess…I don't know…ten minutes? Maybe twenty? It seemed a very long time.''

''But you did find Miss Langstrom again.''

He nodded. "Yes. She was in quite a state. She was crying, very much so. It was a terrible thing to do. I felt ashamed of myself, and very angry with Bertie."

There was a long pause, then Ransom said, "Mr. Brock, while all these…hijinks…were going on, did you see anyone else? Any of your fellow passengers?"

"No. It took a while to get Muriel calmed down, and then I walked her back to the boat. We didn't see any of the other passengers until we got there." There was a pause, then he suddenly remembered something. "Oh, we did see that steward fellow, though."

"The steward? Which one?"

"David Douglas, the blond one."

"Where was this?"

"On our way back. He came up from behind us when we were coming down the road. He joined us."

"From behind you," Ransom said with some surprise.

"Yes. And then we got back here and heard about the murder." He shuddered.

Out of the corner of his eye Ransom saw the Millers rise and start to depart. He thanked Brock, then quickly moved to intercept the retreating couple.

"Mr. and Mrs. Miller?" he said, catching them just by the starboard door.

"Yes?" the husband said brightly. "Oh, is it our turn?"

Ransom smiled. "I'm afraid it is. Why don't we go into the lounge and have a word before you leave."

"Sure thing." Miller put his arm around his wife, whose forced smile showed that she was more apprehensive about this meeting than her husband. Ransom preceded them into the lounge, and they sat at a table by the port windows.

"Nice view here," said Ransom offhandedly, glancing toward the beach.

"It's getting old," said Miller, "but aren't we all!"

Ransom winced internally. The encroaching gray in his own

close-cropped hair was enough of a reminder. "Your names are Martin and Laura, correct?"

They nodded.

"Did you know Marcella Hemsley at all?"

They both shook their heads, but it was Martin who spoke. "Only by sight. We've seen her at church."

"I see. So you didn't have any personal knowledge of her."

They both shook their heads again. "Haven't spent any time with her at all. Don't think we've ever said hello to her before this trip."

"Ah. Now, as for the trip, what were your impressions of her?"

The Millers exchanged glances, then their mouths simultaneously melted into nearly identical, regretful frowns.

"Sad, very sad," said Martin.

"Very, very sad," his wife added.

"Her mind was obviously going. That poor girl, her niece, she did everything she could to make her way easy, but everyone on the boat—the older ones, I mean—could recognize that Marcella was going to have to go into a nursing home."

"Only thing to do," Laura said, shaking her head remorsefully.

"You seem fairly observant," said Ransom cordially.

Martin shook his head. "Didn't really have to be observant."

"We've seen the same sort of thing time and time again," his wife added.

"Hmm," said Ransom. "I was just wondering what you thought of Rebecca Bremmer, and how she took care of her aunt."

"The girl seems very nice," said Martin. "And she was good to her aunt."

"Better, I think, than most could've been," added Laura. "Her aunt wasn't overly nice to her."

"The girl was tired, though. Very tired. Worn out."

"Did she strike you as the kind of person who could've done this? Maybe…out of mercy?" Ransom asked.

The Millers exchanged another glance, which seemed to convey a mutual admonition for caution.

"I wouldn't say that," said Martin. "I wouldn't have thought it. But you never know what someone will do, do you?"

"When pushed beyond the limits of their endurance," his wife added quickly.

"Is that how it struck you?"

Husband and wife stared at him for a moment, then blinked.

"What?" Martin asked.

"That Rebecca Bremmer was being pushed beyond her limit."

"Ho, no," Martin replied with a nervous laugh. "We aren't psychologists or anything like that! And we don't know what the young lady's limits are!"

"Point taken," Ransom said after a beat. "Now, I understand the two of you were the first to split apart from the others."

"Yeah! Bunch of old fogeys!" Martin exclaimed, though not unkindly. "Laura and me, we like to keep really active. No ol' nature walks for us!"

"Where did you go?"

"Right out there," Laura replied, bending a finger toward the beach.

Martin chimed in. "Minute we saw all those dead tree formations, we knew we had to get some pictures." He stopped and gave a rueful glance toward the scene. "Funny, though, now that we're stuck here, all those twines of dead wood seem like a…like a…web or barricade or something. Helluva place for us to have to stay, know what I mean?"

"Honey, don't," said Laura.

"The detective knows what I mean." He turned to Ransom. "Don't you?"

"I think I do. How far up the beach did you go?"

"Oh, a ways away!"

"You didn't get out of sight of the boat, though."

"Well, that's hard to say...."

"We did go some way," Laura offered, "but...I don't know that we got completely out of sight." Her eyes did a quick sidelong glance at her husband, and her cheeks colored slightly.

"You see," said Ransom, "if Rebecca Bremmer didn't murder her aunt, given the time element involved, she had to have been killed by someone who was either already on or near the boat."

The Millers remained silent.

"What exactly were you doing on the beach?"

"Um...just taking pictures, like we said," Martin replied. "You know, of the different...various...tree formations. Dead tree formations."

"They're very beautiful," Laura said quickly. "I suppose many people might not think so, but we...we see the beauty."

"So you were taking photos," said Ransom. "Only of the trees? Did you take any of each other?"

"Well, yes...of coursc. I guess we did," said Martin.

Ransom's brow had creased. "So you must've taken at least some photos in the direction of the boat."

"Uh...maybe. I don't know, though. Besides, we were far away. What difference does it make?"

"Surely you can see that," Ransom replied with a puzzled smile. "It could make all the difference in the world. I'm going to have to ask you for the film."

"The film!" Laura exclaimed. "Our film? No! You can't have it!"

"Why would you want it?" What does this have to do with us?" Martin asked with the wariness of someone who is naturally a bit afraid of the police.

"I should think the answer is obvious. You may have accidentally captured the murderer returning to the boat on film."

"But we were too far away!" Laura protested, her tone becoming shrill. "We couldn't have caught anyone!"

Ransom's expression showed his bafflement at her reaction. "Even if the image is very small, it might help us a great deal." He turned to Martin. "Mr. Miller...you wouldn't be trying to shield someone, would you?"

"No! Of course not! We don't want to lose our pictures, is all. I don't want anybody messing them up. I do all my own developing, you know. I don't trust anyone else, not even photo labs."

"I'm sure you can make an exception in this case. We'll develop them for you, and once we've examined them will give you prints and the negatives. For free." In the back of his mind Ransom hoped that Sheriff Barnes had the capability for doing this.

"I—" Martin stopped when confronted with the eyebrow Ransom had raised in answer to further protest. "All right."

As he rose from the table, Laura put a hand on his arm. "Martin, don't, please!"

"Mrs. Miller," said Ransom. "Think of this: All of the passengers knew you were going up the beach to take pictures. It may be that what I'm suggesting will occur to the murderer. Keeping the pictures yourself could prove dangerous."

She looked at him with large, anxious eyes.

Martin said, "Honey, I don't see any way around it."

He went away from the table, leaving his wife alone with the detective. She attempted a smile. "We're enthusiasts, you see. We like taking pictures."

"I understand," said Ransom, though in truth he was still perplexed over the level of her anxiety. "There's one thing I forgot to ask you. While you were up the beach, did you yourself see anyone?"

She shook her head. "We told you. We were too far away."

"No, I don't mean at the boat. I meant up the beach where you were."

"No. I didn't see anyone."

Having exhausted the subject, they fell silent until her husband returned. It seemed to Ransom that Martin Miller was walking a bit more slowly as he rounded the corner from the dining room and came into the lounge.

"Here," Martin said as he handed a small black canister to the detective. "Please…uh, be careful with them."

"I will." Ransom rose from he seat. "And I'll get the pictures back to you as soon as possible."

"And the negatives."

"Yes," Ransom said after a beat.

Martin gave his hand to his wife and she got out of her chair.

"Thank you," she said to Ransom, averting her eyes.

The couple left the lounge, exiting the dining room through the starboard door. As they went down the stairs to the blue deck, Laura said anxiously, "Did you switch the rolls?"

"Fah!" Martin exclaimed. "Of course not! They can see what the landscape looks like! They would know if I didn't give them the right film." When they reached the bottom of the stairs, Martin took his wife by the shoulders and turned her to face him. "Laura, are you really upset about this?"

There was a short pause, then her lips spread into a broad smile. "No. I'm excited!"

SEVEN

RANSOM WATCHED AS the Millers made their exit, then stuck the film in his pocket. Jackson Brock had left the dining room, and Lily DuPree had finished her lunch and was chatting with Emily as she did the same. Ransom crossed to the back of the bar and went through the door behind it, assuming it led to the kitchen. He found himself in a large but crowded galley lined with cupboards and the usual fittings for preparing and storing food. The plump woman in the gray uniform, her hair held in place with a black net, was busy wrapping the remainder of the lunch meats and cheeses for storage.

"I told you to wait for the rest until I got this lot put away!" she said without looking up.

"Mrs. O'Malley, isn't it?" said Ransom.

The woman jumped and turned, letting out a scream. Her eyes goggled at him.

"My God! You gave me the fright of my life, sneaking up on me like that! Who are you?"

"I'm so sorry, I didn't mean to startle you," he replied smoothly. "I'm Detective Ransom."

She finally allowed herself to exhale. "Oh, yes, I was told you'd be talking to me. You gave me quite a turn."

"I'm sorry."

"I took you for David. You mind if I go on working while we talk? I have to get this lot refrigerated. Ha! The cheese is going limp as it is!" She held up a slice of Swiss for him to see, and it had, indeed, lost some of its body.

"Go right ahead. I understand that you were here on the boat when the murder occurred?"

She slued her eyes at him as she slapped the cheese back onto the plate and began to pile the rest on top of it. "Yes, and don't think that helps me sleep any too good at night, either!"

"I can imagine."

"To think of me being alone with a murderer!" She grabbed up a long rectangular box, measured a length of cling wrap, and stripped it off, replacing the box. "'Course, the one thing that gives me any peace is knowing that it was someone getting murdered in particular, and not some random thing—" She stopped abruptly. "Not that I'm happy the poor old thing is dead. Everybody should be let to live out their lives, with no interference from any outside source." She turned back to her work and began folding the wrap around the cheese. "Still and all, I hate to think of me alone in the boat when it happened."

"Are you sure you were alone?"

She turned to him again, paling as if she thought he was suggesting that the killer had been hiding in one of her cupboards.

Ransom shrugged. "I mean, since you were working in here, you wouldn't have seen anybody."

Her round face relaxed. "Oh, no, I didn't see nobody. I knew the Farradays had left for their walk, and David and Hoke left, too—though strictly speaking, they shouldn't have, but what can you do these days? Young people come and go as they please and don't have any sense of duty to their jobs, and barely ever do an honest day's work." She stopped again and smiled at herself. "Still, David and Hoke are good boys. They seem to work more than others. 'Course, I think that's because Hoke is foreign and David's...old enough to know better. I mean, old enough to know what it means to work. And there's the money."

"The money?"

Her shoulders went up and down briskly. "He's at an age

where he shouldn't be taking a summer job—I guess he needed the work.''

"I see," Ransom replied, pleased that it didn't require an effort to get the cook to talk. "You're sure that Hoke and David left before the murder?''

"I didn't hear them anymore after they said they were going.''

"So they left the boat together?''

Her lips formed a doubtful pout. "I don't think so. David tells me he was on his way a little while before Hoke left. 'Fact, Hoke came in here looking for David, 'cause he'd wanted to go together.''

"Hmm.'' Ransom knew that Emily was not going to like this news. "And you heard nothing after that.''

"Well, I wouldn't, you see. A boat's got a lot of creaks and bumps and what-have-you when it's on the water. But I didn't hear anything out of the ordinary.''

"So as far as you knew, you were alone on board.''

She nodded. "Except for Miss DuPree. Before they left, the Farradays told me she was the only one that stayed behind, so she should've been all.''

"I'm sorry, should've been?'' Ransom asked with a raised eyebrow.

"Well, of course! But Miss Hemsley must've come back, and her niece, too.''

"You didn't hear them?''

"No, like I said.'' She stopped and slapped her forehead. "Wait! You'll be calling me a liar! Miss Bremmer did just poke her head in and ask if I'd seen her aunt, but that was all.''

"And you're sure you didn't hear Miss Hemsley at all.''

She shook her head. "No, but I wouldn't have, would I, closed in here? I wouldn't hear anyone unless they came in the lounge and was making some noise.''

Ransom was about to excuse himself when David Douglas popped open the galley door.

"Mrs. O, are you rea—" He broke off when he saw Ransom, and the color drained from his face. "Oh. Sorry. I didn't mean—" He turned to withdraw but Ransom grabbed the door, holding it open. "It's quite all right, Mrs. O'Malley and I are finished with our talk. However…" He turned to the cook. "You're not ready for Mr. Douglas to bring in more things yet, are you?"

Her cheeks puffed with a knowledgeable smile. "No, it'll be a few minutes yet."

Ransom turned back to Douglas. "So we have time to talk now."

Douglas's square jaw worked for a moment before any sound came out. "I—I still have a lot to do."

"Then we should get to it so that you can get back to work."

"Oh. Yeah. Sure."

"Let's go into the lounge."

As they exited the galley, Ransom glanced over his shoulder and said, "Thank you, Mrs. O'Malley."

"Anytime," she replied with a careless wave of her hand.

He followed Douglas into the lounge. "Why don't we have a seat at the bar?"

"Okay."

They each perched themselves on stools. Out of the corner of his eye, Ransom noticed that Lily and Emily had left the dining room, and Hoke was cleaning up.

Once face-to-face with Douglas, Ransom's impression was much the same as Emily's had been: the youthful appearance was belied by finely etched crow's feet and lines at the corner of his mouth, neither of which were evident at a greater distance.

Douglas attempted his usual ingratiating smile, but fell short. "I suppose people usually feel nervous when they get questioned by the police, huh?"

"Some do," Ransom replied.

He glanced at the floor. "Uh, thanks for waiting to talk to me. I didn't want to talk in front of Mr. Driscoll. I don't have anything to hide, not at all—but I didn't think it was right to talk to me in front of a guest, you know what I mean?''

''I think so,'' the detective replied with an opaque smile. ''Now, Mr. Douglas, let's start with the obvious questions. You stayed on the boat until all the passengers had left, is that correct?''

He nodded eagerly. ''Yeah. All except old— All except Miss DuPree.''

''And you left the boat at what time?''

''I'm not exactly sure. I'd say some time before eleven.''

''Alone?''

''Yeah.''

''Hadn't you planned to go ashore with Joaquin?''

Douglas emitted a derisive snort. ''He said something about wanting to go, too, but I didn't want him trailing after me.''

''Why is that?''

The smile vanished. ''What?''

''Why didn't you want anyone with you?''

''Well…well, I didn't say I didn't want *anyone* with me. But, you know, me and Hoke, we're together all the time.'' A hint of the smile reappeared. ''I suppose I could've asked Mrs. O'Malley if she wanted to go for a walk with me, but she's not exactly my type.''

''Where did you go?''

''I went—'' He stopped suddenly, and his brows made a sharp downward turn. Ransom thought it was not unlike watching a coin that had been dropped in a sorter trying to find the right slot. The glitch, if it could be called that, lasted only a matter of seconds.

''I went up the beach,'' Douglas replied. ''Or rather down it. I went south. The Millers went north.''

Ransom allowed his eyes to widen slightly. ''Oh, then you saw them go.''

''I was on deck when they left, yeah. Does…does that mean something?''

"I don't know what anything means as of yet, Mr. Douglas."

This answer didn't appear to afford the steward much satisfaction.

"Was there any particular reason you were on the deck when the passengers left?"

Douglas returned to his usual manner. "Not really. Just that they were all leaving at the same time, and they're not very young, and they had to manage the gangplank and the dock and all. I thought it was best to keep an eye on them, just in case somebody fell or something."

"I see. Did you see anyone when you went on your walk up the beach?" He already knew the answer to this, but wanted to hear what Douglas had to say.

"Not a soul!"

"And when did you come back?"

"Um..." He now sucked in his lower lip, then pushed it out again. "I don't know exactly what time it was, but it was after Miss Hemsley was found. I mean, I think most of the passengers were back by then." He gave a single laugh. "If they hadn't had a murder to worry about, the Farradays would have chewed me out but good for not being back before the passengers."

Ransom leaned his right elbow on the bar and studied the steward, allowing a long enough interval to ensure his discomfort.

"Is...there a problem?" Douglas asked at length.

The detective smiled. "Forgive me, Mr. Douglas, you just seem very urban to me."

"I don't know what you mean."

"You just don't seem the type who would be interested in a long nature walk."

Douglas smiled. "There's not a hell of a lot else to do around you know...a beach isn't like traipsing through the woods. Not like the old folks were doing."

"The problem is," said Ransom in an alarmingly casual tone

of voice, "that since you left the boat without Joaquin and went off on your own, you don't have anyone to corroborate your whereabouts at the time of the murder."

Douglas was silent for a moment. "You make it sound like I wanted to ditch Hoke so I could be on my own for some…purpose. Well, you're right, but not the purpose you think it is."

"Indeed?"

Douglas leaned in toward him. "Ever since this trip started I've had my eye on this one cutie we got on board."

"Yes?"

"I mean, God knows there's not a lot to pick from. Most of the female talent on this boat got one foot in the grave! It was lucky for me that there was at least a couple of nice-looking women on board." He stopped and rubbed his palms against his thighs.

Ransom stared at him for several seconds. "I'm sorry, I'm not following you."

"Oh!" Douglas exclaimed, his eyes going wide. "What I meant to say is, I went out for a walk because I was hoping to run into that cutie. But, you know, I didn't get started till too late, and I didn't know which way any of them went when they got past the store, so it was hopeless. Of course, now that we know she's a murderer, I suppose I'm better off."

"Ah. So the object of your affection was Miss Bremmer."

"Uh-huh."

"And did she return your interest?"

"Not yet. But it's only been a couple of days. And her aunt was taking up all of her time."

"Hmm," Ransom said thoughtfully. He drummed his fingers on the bar for a moment. "How did you feel about Miss Hemsley?"

"Didn't know her."

Ransom produced a sly smile. "You didn't know her niece, either, but you'd formed an opinion."

"Yeah, but Rebecca's nice to look at. I didn't pay her aunt any attention."

"Really? I understood that Miss Hemsley paid *you* some attention."

"What? What? You mean the other night? When she said I'd been in her room? What would I be doing in her room in the middle of the night? And the captain and his wife vouched for me. They knew I didn't do it. That Hemsley woman was nuts!" He raised an index finger and tapped his temple

"Had you ever seen Miss Hemsley before?"

Douglas screwed up his face. "No. When would I have seen her?"

"I was just curious. It was suggested to me that you might have known her before this voyage."

"What? Who said that? I've never seen any of these people before!"

"I believe it was at the first lunch on board," Ransom said lightly. "I was told that Miss Hemsley made some sort of unpleasantness about you, and that she said something like 'I've seen him before'?"

There was a stunned silence, then Douglas made the effort to readopt his causal attitude. "If she said that, that was just something she made up in her own head. She really was losing it, the poor old thing. Anyone can tell you that."

"They have."

"So you know."

"Yes. You seem very forgiving, given that you had the misfortune of being the object of some of Miss Hemsley's 'fancies.'"

Douglas smiled. "You have to be, with old people."

"Hmm. The captain tells me you have prior experience of working with the elderly."

There was that glitch again: fleeting, but clear and unmistakable. "Yeah, I did. I worked in a nursing home."

"For very long?"

"Yeah. Yeah. For a while. I don't remember exactly how long. You know how time is."

"Yes, I do," Ransom said airily. "And I imagine the name of the place and dates are on your resume, anyway."

"Yeah, they are," Douglas replied. All of the humor had gone out of his face.

"Good!" said the detective as he slid off his stool. "One other thing—I noticed that the beach is lined with trees. While you were walking, did you happen to notice whether or not there was any way to get from the beach to the road?"

"You mean, what? Like paths? Yeah, I saw a couple of paths. I took one of them."

"You did?"

"Well, yeah! I told you I was hoping to run into the cutie. There's a path way down that way." He waved a hand in the general direction of the south. "I was bored with the beach. I took the path out to that road. Didn't work, though—didn't see her. Only people I saw was old Miss Langstrom and Mr. Brock on their way back here."

RANSOM LEFT DOUGLAS sitting on the stool and went out through the starboard door. He hesitated at the foot of the stairs, debating about whether or not to go down to Emily's cabin and report what he'd learned so far—something he would normally do with her over dinner in the kitchen of her small, comfortable bungalow during the course of one of his investigations. The desire to do it now was even stronger, deprived as he was of the company of his usual sounding board, his partner, Gerald White.

However, it had also been quite some time since he'd had a cigar, something of which Emily did not approve, and in the end it was the latter desire that won out. He went up to the white deck. The only passenger there was Lily DuPree, who had resumed her seat on the port side where she lay emitting a short, rhythmic hiss through slightly parted lips, evidence that she had fallen asleep. Samantha Farraday was in the process of straightening the deck chairs. Ransom said, "Where is everybody?"

"It's nap time. Most of them are in their cabins," she replied.

"Their cabins? I would've thought they'd do that up here."

"Normally they would have. You're to blame for that."

"I am?"

She laughed. "As if you didn't know! I think our passengers decided to take their little siestas in their cabins instead of on deck so they wouldn't risk running into you!"

"Really?" Ransom said innocently. "I don't seem to scare Miss DuPree."

Samantha shot a none-too-kindly glance in the direction of the sleeping old woman. Then she leaned into Ransom, lowering her voice. "I think Miss DuPree finds the whole thing very exciting."

Ransom shrugged helplessly. "Some people react that way."

"She can afford to. Her business isn't in jeopardy."

"Do you mean to say you're in financial trouble?"

"I don't—" She faltered, then began again. "I shouldn't have said that. We do all right. But a scandal like this…I know you think it'll bring us customers. Maybe it would eventually. But if passengers stayed away for very long, it would be the end of us."

"I don't think people would necessarily blame you because someone gets murdered on board your boat. Especially if it turns out that it really was Rebecca Bremmer who killed her aunt."

"Maybe not," Samantha said after a long pause. "Look, Mr. Ransom, I really don't mean to sound unfeeling. I know it's a terrible thing, murder."

"It's perfectly natural that you would be concerned about your livelihood."

She searched his face, then smiled. "Thank you. Now I'd better go down and check that the dining room has been cleared."

Before she could walk away, he raised the cigar he'd been holding between two fingers. "By the way, do you mind?"

"Not at all. You're free to smoke on this deck. Just please don't do it on the lower decks."

"Thank you," he said with a tilt of his head.

Ransom stuck the tip between his teeth, pulled the lighter from his right-hand pocket, and lit the end of his cigar. He replaced the lighter, leaned on the ship's rail, and took a long, satisfying drag. He then blew a heavy stream of smoke into the air, silently contemplating what Samantha Farraday had just told him. He had smoked in peace for several minutes when he saw Sheriff Barnes come around the rear corner of Friendly's General Store, accompanied by Lynn Francis. They came down the dock and up the boarding plank.

"Have you found out anything?" Lynn said unceremoniously when they reached him.

"Nothing concrete."

"Anything at all?"

He didn't fail to note the degree of anxiety in her voice.

"I'm afraid not. Not yet."

Lynn's lips tightened. "Rebecca asked me to pack up her things, and her aunt's. Sheriff Barnes was good enough to give me a lift."

"Oh," said Ransom. "I believe Emily's in her cabin. I'm sure she'd like an update on how Rebecca is doing."

Lynn hesitated a moment before leaving them. From the doubtful expression on her face, it was clear she thought he knew something more than he was telling, and equally clear that she didn't want to leave without hearing it. But she'd known him long enough to realize that pressing him would do no good.

"I'll go see her, then."

She crossed to the stairwell and disappeared down it.

"Where is everybody?" the sheriff asked.

"Hiding. Apparently they're afraid of me."

Barnes humphed. "I didn't have that problem. They probably think I'm Barney Fife."

"From what they've told me, they all seem to think you're very capable—and they all think you have the right person in jail. Or they want to believe you do."

Barnes ran one of his large hands through his reddish hair, then bent forward and rested his forearms on the railing. "So, now that your friend is gone, you want to tell me if you learned anything?"

The right corner of Ransom's mouth inched upward. "I was telling Lynn the truth. I haven't learned anything new."

"'Concrete' was what you said. How about something that's not concrete?"

The detective heaved a frustrated sigh. "Everything that everyone has told me so far seems plausible enough. All of them—I should say, most of them—were a bit nervous when questioned, which as you know isn't unusual. I'd have to say that on the surface of it, you are perfectly right in assuming Rebecca Bremmer's guilt."

"I'm not sure I like it when you put it like that."

Ransom laughed lightly. "Sheriff, you have her in jail."

"Yeah…," Barnes replied, dipping his head to one side.

Ransom eyed the side of the sheriff's face for a moment: it was a kind face, strong and firm but not excessively angular. "My guess would be that you honestly believe she's guilty, but feel sorry for her."

Barnes smiled rather sheepishly. "Your guess would be right."

"Don't sound so embarrassed. Pity isn't necessarily a bad thing."

"I wouldn't let it keep me from doing my job."

"Obviously."

"But Detective…uh…pardon me, but despite what you're saying, you don't sound like you think Bremmer's guilty."

"It's not that," Ransom replied with another sigh. "It's that…after questioning all the people, I think Emily's right."

"About what?"

"Something just doesn't smell right on this boat."

"Maybe it's that thing you're smoking," said Barnes with a grin.

Ransom laughed. "I'm sorry, is it bothering you?"

"No, I was just joking."

Ransom took a puff from the cigar and blew the smoke away from Barnes. "I know it's vague, but something here just doesn't feel right. I don't know if it has anything to do with the murder. That might be a completely separate issue."

"So what doesn't feel right?"

"I wish I could say. You did question them all, didn't you?"

Barnes nodded. "Uh-huh."

"And your impression was?"

He puffed out his cheeks, held the air there for a moment, then pushed it out between his lightly closed lips. "Have to say, they all seemed pretty shocked. All except the Farradays, and the crew. And your friends, of course. I got to hand it to that old lady of yours. She can really keep her head."

"Yes, she can. In far more difficult situations than this," Ransom responded rather proudly. "What strikes me is that the things these people say they did yesterday seem fairly odd. Driscoll with his little prank on Langstrom, Trenton going off on her own in a strange place, Holmes and his mysterious client…"

"Wait a minute—what?" Barnes said, knitting his brows.

"Stuart Holmes, the former lawyer, was seen talking to the same man in Sangamore, the boat's first stop, and here. He denied it at first, but when pressed he told me that the man was a client. He wouldn't go farther than that. Didn't Emily tell you about the mysterious stranger?"

"Yes, yes she did."

"And what did Holmes tell you?"

"Just that he didn't know the guy. It was someone he ran into both places. That's not hard to believe. People from Sangamore come through here all the time on their way to the U.P.''

"But you didn't press him on it?"

Barnes shook his head. "No, I didn't. I'm afraid I didn't take Miss Charter's views very seriously. Seems I should have.''

"Many people have made that mistake, Sheriff," Ransom said, calling to mind his first encounter with Emily, when he'd taken her for a doddering old woman. "Even myself." He paused to take another drag from the cigar. "So assuming that Holmes is telling the truth and the stranger is simply an old client and not someone with whom he has hatched a diabolical plot to kill a harmless, senile old woman that neither of them knew, that leaves us with next to nothing."

"You see my problem, then?" said Barnes.

"I saw it from the start."

Barnes straightened up. "I've got another bit of bad news for you. Coroner's report is in, and he found a lump on the old girl's head, of course. He says it means it's likely she was clocked on the head before being strangled, which is what I figured."

Ransom nodded. "That doesn't come as a surprise."

"Yeah, I know."

"Was it a strong blow?"

"Strong enough."

Ransom smiled. "And why is that bad news?"

Barnes shrugged his broad shoulders. "It means for sure that the girl could've done it."

"It also means anyone else could have," Ransom said. "Some of the passengers might not have been physically up to strangling a struggling woman of Miss Hemsley's size while she was conscious, but I'll wager most of them could manage it if she wasn't."

Barnes pursed his lips thoughtfully. "I hadn't thought of that."

"That's because, despite your feelings, you're thinking in terms of evidence against Rebecca Bremmer."

Barnes smiled. "Well, you're thinking about evidence against anyone else."

"No," Ransom replied without emotion, "I'm just focusing, for the moment, on the evidence against others."

"But you haven't found anything."

"Not really." He reached into his pocket and pulled the film out, which he handed to the sheriff. "Only this."

"What's this?"

"The Millers are amateur shutterbugs. They were up the beach taking photographs around the time the murder took place. It's an outside possibility, but they might have caught something on film, though they claim they were too far away. Can you have these developed?"

"Sure." Barnes squeezed the canister in his fist for a moment, then stuck it in his pocket.

"Good. I know I don't have to say this, but be careful with it, please. The Millers were very anxious about them. I told them you'd make copies for them."

Barnes emitted a single laugh. "Okay, sure."

"Other than that, all I've found is the same thing you did: it seems unlikely that any of these people committed the murder. Most of them have fairly good alibis, and even the ones who don't, I haven't found any reason they would want to kill Hemsley. All of them claim that they had very little acquaintance with the victim, and knew nothing of her other than the fact that she was getting senile and was running her niece ragged. All of them claim to like the niece, but they all think she did it."

Barnes sighed. "Well, if that's the case, I'm afraid I'm going to have to let them go on their way. If you don't have anything more."

"Hmm," Ransom said in a tone of understanding. He had, perhaps, a little more information than that, but despite the generally amicable relationship he'd formed with the sheriff, he didn't want to share the possibilities that occurred to him. "When will you let them go?"

"Not till morning."

"SHE'S VERY NICE…she's just very nice, that's all," Lynn said. She held a blouse up by the shoulders and shook it. It was light plum with tiny white buttons.

"That's the way she struck me as well," said Emily, who was seated on the bed next to the case. They were in Rebecca's cabin. "And something more as well."

Lynn folded the blouse and laid it in the suitcase. She looked down and her elderly friend. "What's that?"

"The way she looked after her aunt spoke volumes about her character. Whatever Marcella might have been when Rebecca was a younger woman, she had through no fault of her own become quite disagreeable. The way Rebecca looked after her was admirable. She must be a very strong young woman."

"Yes, she is," Lynn said in a tone so odd it caused Emily's eyebrows to rise. Lynn slowly went over to the closet and retrieved another blouse, this one white, and began to fold it as she recrossed the room.

"What is it, my dear?" Emily asked. "What's troubling you?"

"Emily…Rebecca is the first person I've cared about since Maggie died—I mean other than you and Mr. Detective. I don't think she could harm anyone."

"Lynn, what is the matter?"

The young woman draped the blouse over the upraised back of the suitcase, then sat down beside Emily. Hesitating, she laid her hands on her knees and looked down at them.

"The other night—the night her aunt made the fuss—Rebecca was talking to me about her. Unburdening herself, I guess you'd call it. She told me…she told me that she wished her aunt was dead. She knew she would've been miserable in a nursing home, and wished she would just die."

"Very natural to feel that way."

"She asked me if I felt that way when Maggie was dying. I told her I did, but I lied. I didn't. I didn't want Maggie to die, no matter how badly off she'd become. Do you think that...wanting to hang on like that makes me selfish?"

Emily laid her right hand on Lynn's left. "No, my dear." She allowed a silence, then added, "But there's something more, isn't there?"

"No...no, I don't know what you mean."

"Lynn, just because Rebecca expressed those feelings, that doesn't mean that she killed her aunt."

An involuntary impulse caused Lynn to gently pull her hand away. "No. I don't think that."

"Oh. Well, of course not," Emily said lightly. "It's only that that, too, would be a natural thing to fear about someone one with whom might be developing feelings...because in such early days, and in such dire circumstances, you might realize that you didn't really know that person."

The two women were startled by the sound of a throat being cleared.

"Oh, God!" Lynn exclaimed, looking over to the doorway and finding Ransom standing there. Her eyes narrowed. "How long have you been standing there?"

"I just arrived. I haven't been listening in on your conversation, if that's what you're afraid of."

She flushed and lowered her eyes. "Sorry."

"Lynn, you must stop thinking of Jeremy as the enemy," Emily said. "He's here to help find out the truth."

"Assuming that the truth is what you want," said Ransom.

"Of course it is!" Lynn said defensively. "So why wouldn't you tell me what was going on up on the deck?"

"Because Sheriff Barnes was there, and I didn't feel it appropriate to share views with him that might needlessly cast suspicion around."

"Then you have learned something?" Emily said with interest.

He pulled the small wooden chair out from the corner, turned it to face them, and sat down. "Emily, outside of Rebecca, it doesn't seem that anyone else could've done it—"

"There has to be!" Lynn exclaimed.

Emily patted her hand. "Please."

Ransom continued. "Apparently nobody could have, with the possible exception of Mrs. O'Malley, though why she should kill a perfect stranger is a mystery. Or Lily DuPree, except that even I still doubt she could've wielded anything with enough force to knock out the victim, let alone be able to strangle her."

Emily was looking at him intently, a half smile on her face. "There's something more, isn't there?"

"Yes…and I know you're not going to like it."

"What?"

"You're friend Joaquin."

"What?" Emily exclaimed with surprise.

"He was the last to leave the boat. You all left first, the captain and his wife, then Douglas, and last was Joaquin."

Emily knit her slender brows. "Really. I seem to remember…." She searched her memory, then shifted slightly. "Lily DuPree said that she saw Joaquin leave *before* David…of course she was very vague."

Ransom shook his head. "She was half-asleep. Both Mrs. O'Malley and Joaquin himself verified that Douglas left first. But that leaves Joaquin here on the boat for a time, and we have only his word for when he left. It's possible that Miss Hemsley came back to the boat and found him doing something he shouldn't have been doing."

Emily sighed. "I'd hate to think it. Of course, I've seen enough of life to know that anything's possible. But…Joaquin?"

"It's those Bambi eyes of his, Emily. That's what's getting to you."

She smiled. "'Bambi eyes' rather denotes innocence, doesn't it?"

He laughed. "So, say Joaquin managed to leave the boat

without killing Miss Hemsley. What does that leave us with? That somebody came back to the boat and did her in? The problem with that is first of all, everyone is alibied for at least part of the time, if not all of it. The notable exceptions are Claudia Trenton, who went off on her own, Bertram Driscoll, who was alone part of the time, and Douglas, who claims to have been walking on the beach.''

''I see,'' said Emily, sitting back.

''And I think we can rule out Driscoll.''

''How so?''

''You remember we wondered if it would've been possible for him to come back to the boat via the beach, kill Hemsley for whatever reason, then double back and 'run into' you?''

''Yes?''

''Well, Douglas headed south on the beach, sometime between ten-thirty and eleven.''

Emily nodded thoughtfully. ''Ah, yes!''

''I don't get it,'' Lynn said testily.

''You see, my dear, if Mr. Driscoll had come down the beach, he would've run into Mr. Douglas.''

''Oh, yeah,'' Lynn said. Then her visage darkened again. ''That's assuming Douglas is telling the truth!''

''Of everything he's said,'' Ransom replied, ''there's one thing I'm sure of. He was telling the truth about going down the beach.''

''How can you be sure about that?''

He shrugged. ''Why lie about having been alone for so long? It would only cast suspicion on him. And someone could've seen him. He knew that.''

''Who would've seen him?''

''Lily DuPree might have, for one. And possibly the Millers.''

''Did he know they'd gone up the other end of the beach?'' Emily asked.

Ransom nodded. ''He saw you off. And then there's the

possibility that Joaquin could've seen him as well, since he left after Douglas.''

"Oh, dear," Emily said, her eyes widening.

"What is it?" Lynn asked.

"I've just realized that anyone who planned on coming back to the boat was running a great risk of being seen—the passengers all thought that the Farradays, the rest of the crew, and Lily were on the boat, and the Millers were in view of it.''

"Yes," said Ransom. "And even the crew knew that DuPree and the cook were on board, and the Millers were nearby.''

"It really does look bad for Joaquin in that case, doesn't it?" said Emily.

"Yes. Hemsley could've come back, surprised Joaquin doing something, he killed her, then went to the shops to establish something of an alibi.''

"Why didn't you want to tell the sheriff that?" Lynn asked warmly. "That must be it! That has to be it!"

Ransom and Emily glanced at each other.

"No, Lynn, that couldn't be what happened," Emily said.

"Why not? He just said—"

"Yes, yes, I know," said Ransom. "But Lynn, the thing is, Joaquin *did* go to the shops. At least we know he went to the general store.''

"So what if he did?" Lynn demanded.

"If Rebecca didn't kill her aunt, and her aunt really wasn't there when she looked in, then Miss Hemsley had to have been murdered between the time you spoke with Rebecca after she left the boat, and when you discovered the body. That lets Joaquin out because we actually know that he at least went to the general store—Mrs. Friendly confirmed that. If he'd left the boat after Rebecca, you would've seen him.''

"That would also definitely let Mr. Driscoll out," said Emily, "since it was during that time that we spoke to him.''

The young woman's lips trembled. "Then I don't see how it could've been done." She gave a forlorn sniff, working at keeping herself under control. But it proved too difficult. She rose from her place on the bed and without raising her eyes, said, "I should get Miss Hemsley's things together," and left the room.

Ransom sat down beside Emily and sighed. "What she really meant is she doesn't see how anyone other than Rebecca could've done it."

"The poor dear," said Emily. "I know it's only been a short time, but she really does seem to care for Rebecca."

He turned as curious eye toward her. "A short time? Maggie's been dead for a few years now, hasn't she?"

Emily bestowed a smile on her ersatz grandson. "I meant a short time since she's met Rebecca."

This correction occasioned a rare blush from the detective. "Ah. Of course."

"I suppose people do form bonds quickly nowadays, just the way they do everything else. Especially under such extraordinary circumstances. In my day things would've always been taken more slowly."

Ransom produced an impish grin. "Emily, in 'your day' a respectable elderly lady would not have been playing matchmaker to two women."

She laughed. "Yes. As you would say, touché!"

The detective's smile quickly faded. "The trouble is, I'm afraid Lynn is going to be disappointed. I'm not a magician. And…no matter how she may feel, you realize she doesn't really know what Rebecca's capable of."

Emily nodded. "And she knows that, too."

They fell silent for a time, each lost in thought. Then Emily said, "You know, there is one other possibility, as far-fetched as it sounds."

"What's that?"

Her shoulders elevated slightly. "That the murder was done by someone who has nothing to do with the tour. They watched the boat, waiting for an opportunity to come aboard, perhaps to rob it? And they could've taken the opportunity and been caught by Marcella.''

''And then what? When they left the boat, if they went north up the beach they would've run into the Millers, south would've taken them to Douglas, and if they'd gone around the general store they would've run into you.''

''I know,'' Emily said with a cluck of her tongue, ''it's very vexing. But you know, it is possible. There was that incident quite some time ago when a man strolled into Buckingham Palace, walked the length of it, went up the stairs and wandered into the queen's bedroom.''

''Yes, I remember that.''

''Well, as unlikely as it may be, someone could've watched the boat until after Joaquin had left, seen that Lily was asleep, and took a chance that so near to lunch the cook would be busy in the galley, just as she was. Then he or she could've come onto the boat, been discovered by Marcella when she returned, killed her, and fled. You said that Mr. Douglas left the beach?''

''Yes.''

''Then couldn't it have been a stranger who came on, committed the murder, then went a little way down the beach and disappeared into the woods?''

Ransom heaved a sigh. ''I grant you, it's possible. But I don't like it.''

Emily nodded ruefully. ''It doesn't seem likely.''

''It's not just that. I have enough trouble with the suspects we have without bringing a mysterious stranger into it.'' He got up from the bed. ''And speaking of which, the one last thing I have to do is check up on Stuart Holmes's friend, or client, or whatever he is. I'll be back to take you and Lynn to dinner.''

''Oh, no, I don't think you should do that,'' said Emily, getting to her feet with his help.

''Why not?''

''I think it would be better if we dined with the rest of the passengers—Lynn and I, I mean—because we might be able to get some useful information.''

Ransom smiled. ''All right. I'll be off, then.'' He started for the door, and she followed, intending to go to her own cabin. But Ransom stopped short. ''Oh, one other thing. The sheriff plans to tell the captain that you're all free to go in the morning.''

''Oh, dear,'' Emily said quietly.

LYNN HAD GONE from Rebecca's cabin to Marcella's, where she proceeded to fold the old woman's belongings. It was with some effort that she'd managed to pull herself together after leaving Ransom and Emily. She was at once embarrassed by her loss of control and disgusted with herself for allowing her feelings to grow so strong for someone she really didn't know.

That was the thing that really plagued her mind: that no matter how she felt, no matter what she thought of Rebecca, she didn't really know her. She couldn't. Not after such a short time.

Packing up the things that had been so recently worn by someone who had been alive not forty-eight hours earlier brought back the dreadful period after Maggie had died. The loneliness and unnatural stillness of the garden apartment they'd shared for so many years. Lynn had given up her job as a high-paid corporate personal assistant and taken on the role of what she'd called charwoman to the rich and famous, a high-priced and terribly exclusive cleaning woman for equally exclusive Gold Coast clients. She'd done this so that she could arrange her time flexibly and be able to take care of Maggie at home.

But after Maggie died, that same freedom worked against the healing process. Without having to be somewhere at a specific time, with being able to come and go more or less as she pleased, and not having to really deal with many people, she found herself feeling even more adrift and lost: perhaps more than she would have if career demands had forced her to work her way back into life and the world in general.

She held one of Marcella's faded peasant dresses at arm's length and looked at it. It reminded her of when she'd finally been able to bring herself to pack Maggie's things. She had held Maggie's favorite violet evening dress just the way she was doing this now. It was like looking at a ghost; a lifeless shell that had once contained her beloved friend. It had been a comfort to keep Maggie's things for a while, but when the time came to do something with them, they seemed to mock her with their familiarity. She had pressed that violet dress to her cheek, dappling it with her tears, and found that Maggie's scent still clung to it. It had been almost too much to bear.

And do you want to go through that all over again? she thought to herself now. *Get involved with someone else. Love them, care for them, spend years with them, and then lose them? Again?*

She shook her head briskly. "You're being ridiculous," she said aloud. She carefully folded the peasant dress, placed it in the bottom of the suitcase, then retrieved another from the closet.

Emily's right, she thought. *I don't know Becky at all…not enough to know what she's capable of.*

She stopped as she slipped a light brown dress off a hanger. "But I know she's not guilty of murder," she said firmly, answering her own thought.

EIGHT

BEFORE GOING BACK to the motel, Ransom decided to take a walk on the beach. He went down the dock to the point where it circled the general store, turned to the right, and at the corner of the building jumped down onto the sand, then headed south.

On the deck of the *Genessee,* Hoke bent beside the chair on which Lily DuPree was reclined. "Would you like something, Miss DuPree? Could I get you something cool to drink from the bar?"

"What?" she said in her breathless whisper, startled by his unexpected appearance at her side. "Oh! No, no thank you. I'm fine."

"Okay," he said, giving her his usual warm smile.

He straightened himself and started for the wheelhouse to check in with the captain, but stopped when he noticed the movement on the beach. He slowly moved toward the starboard railing and crouched down, peering over it. He could see Ransom in the distance, strolling down the beach as if he had no particular purpose in mind. The detective's progress was neither slow nor fast, so it didn't seem as if he were looking for anything or heading for a specific place.

"What the hell are you doing?"

The voice made the young steward leap to his feet with a cry. He found himself face-to-face with David Douglas, who wore an expression of perplexed displeasure.

"I was just looking at that detective."

Douglas followed Hoke's glance and saw the now remote

figure. He turned back to his subordinate. "So what? So he's on the beach."

"It makes me nervous, having the police around."

"That's what happens when some old fool gets herself murdered."

"But that happened on the boat. Why should he go there?"

"Why do you care?" Douglas said, eyeing him suspiciously. "You weren't there."

"No...no, I wasn't."

Douglas sighed and shook his head. "He asked me about paths between the lake and the road. He's probably just gone to check it out."

"But I don't understand—"

"You don't have to understand! Weren't you supposed to be making the rounds? Seeing if anybody needed anything?"

"Yes. Okay."

Hoke walked away toward the entrance to the wheelhouse, and after a single knock went in. Douglas watched him, then headed for the stairs, shaking his head.

RANSOM WAS UNAWARE OF the scrutiny of the two stewards as he made his way down the beach. He was, in fact, not aware of much of anything other than the gentle, quiet rush of the water to the abbreviated shore. His aim had been only to satisfy himself on one minor point, something that he didn't believe mattered one way or the other. The beach was blissfully clear to someone used to the endless debris one finds along the shore of the portion of Lake Michigan that borders Chicago. Here there was little more than some damp, dark green clumps of alga that had worked up onto the sand, and perhaps more driftwood than he would've expected. Walking on the sand made his progress slow going.

On his left were the woods, thickset and not more than fifteen yards from the water. He had gone nearly three-quarters of a mile when he found it: a path that had been worn through the trees by a steady stream of campers as a shortcut from the trails to the beach. He turned into it and went into the woods.

The path was much rougher than the well-maintained trails, and much narrower as well. He was surprised at how dark it was among the trees, despite the brightness of the sun and the lack of clouds.

It was only about a five-minute walk from the beach to the road. When Ransom came out of the woods, he found himself on the opposite side of the road's crest, and farther along than the entrance to trail number one, the trail that Driscoll and company had taken.

So that checks out, he thought with an inward sigh. *Douglas walked down the beach, crossed over here exactly where he would've seen Muriel Langstrom and Jackson Brock. This is a thoroughly aggravating case. The suspects are irritatingly honest.*

He headed up the hill, back toward the parking lot beside Friendly's where he'd left his car. When he topped the rise, he found Driscoll heading for him on the path beside the road. The old man was walking at a leisurely pace, his eyes cast down at the ground. Driscoll's sudden appearance reminded Ransom of something Emily had told him about her first afternoon on the boat, when Driscoll had appeared out of nowhere to wake her. *Oh, well,* he thought, *I might as well follow up her dreams as well.*

It was then that Driscoll looked up and saw the detective. He came to an abrupt halt and half turned as if to retreat, but stopped himself, apparently realizing that it would not look good. He managed a smile.

"Hullo there, Detective."

"Hello, Mr. Driscoll," Ransom replied as he continued down the hill. "Out for a stroll?"

"Yes. Yes, can't stand to be on the boat anymore. At least, not stuck at the dock." He sighed. "Isn't this always the way? If the murder had happened in Sangamore, at least there would've been somewhere decent to eat. But here! Nothing to see and nothing to do! Nothing but nature as far as you can see!''

''Murder tends to be inconvenient,'' the detective said flatly. ''And some people like nature.''

''It's got its limits as a pastime,'' the old man replied, wrinkling his nose.

His florid complexion would've been enough to tell Ransom that he'd been drinking, but the light afternoon breeze carried with it a strong scent of alcohol. ''Tell me, Mr. Driscoll, did you know Claudia Trenton before you came on this trip?''

He was so startled by the question that his eyes widened and his mouth dropped open. The reaction brought to Ransom's mind Foghorn Leghorn.

''Claudia? No, I didn't know Claudia! Why should I? Of course, I knew who she was. I've seen her at church. And you can see she's something to look at. Fine-looking woman. But as to knowing her...'' He shook his head doubtfully. ''I'm not the sort she'd be likely to take up with, whether or not...well, never mind. She's way too snooty. And I'm too...'' He made a pretense of searching for the least demeaning term. ''I'm too...down to earth for her. If she were to take up with anyone, I would think it would be Jackson—if only he wasn't such a sissy—or Stuart, if only he wasn't such an old bag o' bones!''

''Hmm,'' Ransom replied, his narrowed eyes never leaving Driscoll's. ''I wondered, because from what I've heard, you seem to be keeping around her quite a bit.''

''What? Has she complained?''

Ransom flashed the smile that his partner had once observed made him look like an evil elf. ''No, I just thought it was a curious circumstance since, as you say, you're not exactly her type.''

''She could do a helluva lot worse than me, you know! I may not be upper class, but I can dress up and I know how to act in public!''

Do you, now? thought Ransom.

The old man must've read his mind, because he suddenly

began to backpedal, sounding exactly like an elderly school-boy. "I haven't been paying her any more attention than any of the other guys!"

"You were seen having dinner with her."

His already ruddy cheeks flushed more deeply. "That was just a...circumstance! We just got thrown together, that's all! No matter what anyone says!"

Ransom's right eyebrow slid upward, and Driscoll averted his eyes. He couldn't have looked more guilty—of something—if he'd tried.

"Anyway," Driscoll continued, "I'm surprised she came on this trip. To tell you the truth, this isn't her kind of crowd at all, I wouldn't think."

"So I'm told," said Ransom. "I have one other question for you. Ms. Charters told me that she ran into you when you were on your way back to the boat."

"That's right."

"She said that after talking to her, you went back up the path to find Mr. Brock and Ms. Langstrom."

"Yeah? So?"

The rather devilish smile deepened. "It's not long after that that Brock and Langstrom, and David Douglas, came this way. But none of them reported seeing you. That seems rather curious, doesn't it?"

Driscoll shifted from one foot to the other and looked down at the ground. "Well, I didn't...I'm not proud of it, but even though I told Emily I'd go and find them...I didn't want to see them after what happened. So...so I just waited till Emily and her friend were out of sight, then I ducked into the visitor's center for a while. I waited there till after I saw the others pass, then I went back to the boat."

"I see," Ransom said slowly. "Well, thank you, Mr. Driscoll."

He walked briskly away, leaving the old man a lot less happy than when they'd met. He passed the visitor's center, crossed the parking lot, and climbed into his car. He immediately punched in the dashboard lighter and pulled a cigar from the pack in his pocket.

"You really are enjoying making that old man ill at ease far too much," he said to the rearview mirror. "But we'll just chalk that up for Muriel Langstrom."

The lighter popped out and he lit the cigar. As he took his first puff, he thought, *And putting him ill at ease is not without its other benefits, as well.*

THE LAKEVIEW MOTEL WAS two miles south of the dock where the *Genessee* was moored. The name was a misnomer, since the motel was situated in an area where the road had veered nearly half a mile away from the lake, and the dense woods across the road denied the motel's guests even a glimpse of the water.

The motel was a row of detached cabins that put Ransom in mind of oversized outhouses. They were painted bright yellow with chocolate brown shutters and doors. The lone window on each cabin was underlined by a flower box whose contents were withering in the sun.

Ransom steered the car onto the dirt parking lot and pulled up in front of cabin 3, his temporary home. He switched off the ignition, got out of the car, and stuck the keys in his pocket. There were two other cars in the lot, both with Illinois license plates. He went down the walk to the office, an appendage off the first cabin, with windows on two sides instead of one.

A bell jangled loudly as he went through the door, and a woman hurried from the back room in answer to it.

"Hello again, Mrs. Banks."

She was a slender woman it in her forties, with long raven hair and fair skin. Her eyes were bright blue, and her narrow lips were painted pale pink.

"Oh, hello," she replied as she finished wiping her hands on a red plaid towel. "Back already? You haven't decided not to stay, have you?"

"No."

She dropped the towel in a heap on the end of the counter. "Good, 'cause I hate to quibble." She produced a ready smile that said she didn't much care whether or not she amused anyone else as long as she amused herself.

"Quibble?"

"Sure. You've already been in the room. I couldn't give you your money back."

He smiled. "No, it's nothing like that. I intend to stay, at least for the night. No, I have a question for you. I understand you have someone else staying here from Chicago...."

"Really? Just how do you understand that?"

"Someone on the *Genessee* told me."

It had the desired effect. As he suspected, news of the murder had traveled far and wide very quickly. Mrs. Banks's eyes narrowed slightly, and her upper lip tensed into an accordion pleat. "Are you some kind of cop?"

"I'm a detective, yes."

"From Chicago?"

He nodded.

"So, Sheriff Barnes had to call in the big guns, huh? I thought he had the killer in jail."

"I'm just tying up some loose ends," he said amiably. "Now, is there someone from Chicago staying here?"

She nodded. "I got two of them. Well, three, actually. There's a young couple in cabin five, and an older man in seven."

There was a beat before Ransom asked the question that had just occurred to him. "How do you know these people are from Chicago?"

She shrugged. "They paid in cash."

"I beg your pardon?"

"They paid in cash. I don't trust people that pay in cash. I figure, if a credit company doesn't trust them enough to give them a card, why should I trust them?"

"That's a very sound philosophy."

"So after they checked in, I go out and write down their

license plate numbers. I saw they both had Chicago city stickers in their windows."

"Do you know anything about these people?"

"The couple is here to go hiking—"

He raised his right eyebrow. "And they're staying at a motel?"

"Lots of people stay here at night and hike the trails during the day. Least, that's what they say."

"'Say'?" he repeated, recognizing her desire to be purposely provocative. "You think otherwise?"

Mrs. Banks flashed a canny smile. "What do you think a couple of kids would check into a motel for? You were young once."

"Yes, I was," Ransom said coolly.

"They're enjoying themselves. Stopped for the night and stayed on."

"What about the older man?"

"Registered as Percy Faulk."

"Do you have some reason to believe that's not his real name?"

She shook her head. "Only that a cop's asking about him!" Again the smile. "And I don't got any idea what he's doing here."

"Well, thank you for your help." He started for the door.

"Hey, Detective—if you think you're going to have a shoot-out or anything, come get me, would you? I'd like to watch. Nothing much happens around here."

Ransom's lips curled reprovingly, though he was finding it hard not to laugh. "I don't think it will come to that."

He followed the cracked sidewalk to the door of number 7 and knocked. The door was flung open by a tall, lanky man in his midsixties. His hair was white and streaked with bluish gray, and his eyes protruded as if the sockets had begun to shrivel away around them.

"Stuart, where the—" he began as he opened the door. He

stopped suddenly when he saw Ransom. His eyes bugged out even farther. "Who the hell are you?"

"My name is Detective Ransom. I'm here from Chicago—"

"What?" The older man's voice was hollow, and he faded back slightly. For a moment Ransom thought he might slam the door, but instead he held it there with his hand gripping the edge of it.

"Mr. Faulk, isn't it? Right. I'd like to talk to you, if I may."

"What about?"

"About the murder of Marcella Hemsley."

"Oh. I don't know anything about that." He looked unaccountably relieved.

There was a hint of a smile on the detective's lips. "Do you want to discuss this out here in the open, or would you rather do it inside?"

The wariness returned to Faulk's face. "No, you'd better come in."

He stepped aside and Ransom passed through the doorway into a room that was the mirror image of his own: a bed with a green sateen spread and a dilapidated foam rubber love seat. A television was mounted hospital style in the upper left-hand corner of the room, and was switched on to the local news. A small ladder-back chair was placed beside a dresser that looked as though it had been purchased at a garage sale. On top of the dresser an incongruously expensive leather valise lay open, exposing silk boxer shorts and a handful of balled-up socks.

The heavy brown curtains were drawn across the window, leaving the room in a gloomy haze. Faulk clumsily worked the drawstring, pulling them halfway open so that they'd have some light, and turned the sound down on the television.

"Have a...why don't you sit there?" he said, gesturing toward the love seat.

"Thank you."

Ransom took a seat and Faulk sat on the foot of the bed facing him.

"Forgive me for staring," said the detective, "but you look familiar to me. Have we met somewhere before?"

"No, I don't believe so," Faulk said brusquely. "I'd remember that."

"Yes...well, never mind. I'm here checking up on the whereabouts of all of the passengers of the *Genessee* yesterday morning, as a matter of form."

The old man stared at him for a moment. "Oh...well...how would I know anything about that?"

Ransom allowed his brow to furrow quizzically. "Didn't Stuart Holmes spend the morning with you?"

There was another pause. "Oh. Did he tell you that?"

"Yes?"

"Well, then, I guess it's all right."

When he didn't go on, Ransom said, "So he was with you?"

"No—I mean, that is to say, yes, he was."

"All morning?"

"Well...yes. From the time I met him onward...until the time we...parted."

"When did you meet him?"

Faulk absently glanced at his watch as if he could read the past in its face. Ransom noted that it was a Rolex. "Um...I don't know...it was sometime after ten...um...it was later than I thought it was going to be...but...not long after ten."

"And he was with you until?..."

"Oh, now, let me see...it was until...till well after noon."

"You're sure."

The old man brought his eyes up to the detective's. "Yes."

Ransom shifted in his seat and crossed his legs. "You and Mr. Holmes are friends, I take it?"

"Oh, yes, I've known Stuart for a hundred years! We go very far back."

"And he's also your attorney?"

A jolt went through his body as if he'd received a mild electric shock. "Why, yes, he is...that is to say, he was. He used to be. At one time."

"He's not anymore?'

Faulk shook his head. "He's retired."

"Really?" Ransom replied with mild surprise. "Holmes gave me to believe that he was doing some work for you now."

"What? Oh, he told you that? Well, yes, he does to the odd bit of…now and then, you understand, because we go so far back. And he probably likes to…well, no, I'm sure he likes to keep his hand in. People in his profession do, you know."

"Yes…," Ransom said slowly. "Very peculiar, though, isn't it?"

"What is?"

"That you're both from Chicago, and that you would come all this way to consult with him."

There was another startled pause. "Well…I suppose…yes, I guess it could seem strange…but we all need a vacation now and then, don't we? There's nothing wrong with having a little getaway now and then, is there?"

"No, there isn't," Ransom replied without inflection. Faulk looked so relieved to have successfully answered the question that Ransom didn't have the heart to point out that it was hardly a vacation if the point of doing it was to work.

"So, you and Mr. Holmes spent yesterday morning discussing business."

He nodded eagerly. "Uh-huh, that's just it."

"May I ask what kind of business that would be?"

Faulk blustered indignantly. "Well, really, Detective! I mean, that's a personal matter! After all, it's…well, I assure you it doesn't have anything to do with this case you're working on. I mean, really! Client-attorney privilege, and all that, right?"

"I'm so sorry," Ransom replied smoothly. "Sometimes I get overly curious."

The colorless way he'd said this caught Faulk's attention. Faulk's lips flattened into a sullen line and his eyes seemed to recede a fraction of an inch. He looked not unlike a guilty child who was unsure as to whether or not he'd been found out.

"That's all right," he muttered.

Ransom rose rather carefully from the love seat, not for fear of startling the old man again but because the lack of support from the worn foam cushions made maneuvering somewhat difficult. He paused at the door. "I think that's all I need. How long were you planning to be in town?"

"Huh? Me? Well, I thought…I would've left today, but I was waiting to talk to Stuart again. I guess…I suppose till tomorrow." There was a second of hesitation, then he added anxiously, "Is there a problem with that?"

"I don't think so." Ransom exited the cabin, a satisfied smile on his face, closing the door after him. He stood for a moment considering what to do next. Having arrived at a temporary pause in the investigation, the weariness of his overnight race to Emily's aid and the subsequent investigation caught up with him. He decided to go his room and lie down for a while.

THE STAFF OF the *Genessee* began serving dinner at six o'clock that evening. Unlike lunch, the evening meal was a proper sit-down affair. The passengers were given a choice between two entrees, a variety of salads and dressings, vegetables, and desserts. The food was served by David and Hoke, with Samantha Farraday filling her role as hostess.

But Mrs. Farraday's usual brightness couldn't elevate the atmosphere of the dining room that evening. The tension was evident in the relative silence with which the meal was eaten, the dwindling number of guests a grim reminder of their situation. In addition to Miss Hemsley and her niece, Lynn had taken a sandwich to her room, not wanting to face the stress of a meal with a roomful of suspects, of whom one must be the cause of Rebecca's plight, and Claudia Trenton was absent again.

"Is Miss Trenton not joining us?" Emily asked Hoke as he placed a salad plate before her.

"No, ma'am. She says she's not hungry. Mrs. Farraday brought her some food down, though." He bent closer to her ear and whispered. "She says she does not like to do that— cater to people, I mean...bring food to their room—because then they come to expect it. But she did it for Miss Trenton. I think she's very worried about her health."

"Yes. Yes, I see."

Hoke hurried away from the table and back toward the kitchen.

Emily was seated at a table once again with Lily DuPree, and the others were arranged around the room. Jackson Brock and Muriel Langstrom shared a table with Stuart Holmes; the Millers were together at another; and Bertram Driscoll was alone at a table near the portside door. The arrangement wasn't, as Emily had hoped, conducive for her to learn much more.

"Do you think the police will let us go soon?" Lily said with a sort of apprehensive wonder in her eyes. Emily couldn't quite tell if she was worried that they would be detained or that the excitement would soon be over.

"I expect they will," said Emily. "I don't think they really have any reason to keep us here."

"That young man who came up from Chicago—that detective—he was very imposing!"

"Was he?" Emily smiled inwardly. She knew her friend would appreciate the description.

"He didn't really talk to me, but from what little I saw of him...and what I've heard today from the others...they say he gives the impression that he thinks Rebecca Bremmer didn't kill poor dear Marcella."

"I think he's just being thorough. But of course, he should've spoken with you, since you were on the deck all the while."

"Yes...," Lily replied, sounding rather disappointed. "But I was facing away from the plank, you know...that thing you walk up to get onto the boat. And I kept drifting off to sleep. I didn't really see that much."

"Yes, that is a shame," Emily said. Lily didn't notice, but her companion's eyes had become more incisive. Emily leaned forward slightly and adopted a very confidential attitude. "They say that young man, Hoke, was the last one to leave the boat."

"When?"

"Just before the murder. And you know what that means!"

"What?"

Emily made a pretense of glancing over her shoulder to make sure the man in question was not nearby. "The last one off the boat just possibly could have killed Marcella before leaving." She didn't complicate matters by reminding Lily of the fact that the body hadn't been there when Rebecca first looked in the cabin. It was something she didn't understand herself.

"Oh!" Lily replied, her eyes widening. She sat back in her chair, doubt clouding her face. "Oh."

Emily waited for her to elaborate, but Lily continued to sit quite still with her brow furrowed.

"Oh, that's right!" Emily said, taking the impetus herself. "I seem to remember you saying that he wasn't the last to leave."

"What?" Lily said distractedly. Then she shook her head. "I was so tired after the upset of the night before. He probably was the one who left last. You see, while I was still awake, I looked over when someone passed. But I was so tired...I kept hearing...I kept hearing footsteps. People coming and going...it's just a jumble."

Emily nodded thoughtfully. "Yes. I quite agree."

RANSOM PROBABLY could've slept away the evening and entire night, but he was awoken at six-thirty by the chirping of his cell phone, which he'd placed on the nightstand. It was Lynn calling to ask if he would mind picking her up and driving her to the sheriff's station. He assented and laid the phone down. He lay there for several moments in a hazy state, not quite sure if there had really been a call or if he'd been dreaming.

Like Emily and her overheard conversation, he thought, lying there with his eyes closed.

When he finally realized he was awake, he opened his eyes and had that vague sense of disorientation one often gets when waking in a strange place, but it quickly passed.

The nap hadn't helped much. When he sat up and swung his feet to the floor, he found that his body had the heavy, drugged feeling of someone who had slept too fast and woken too soon. He thought with a rueful smile that it would've been better if he'd never lain down at all. Needing to shake off this lassitude, he undressed and took a quick shower. The Lakeview wasn't much for amenities, but at least the plumbing was vigorous and the water very hot. After standing in the steaming spray for some time, allowing the warmth to bathe and relax his muscles, he adjusted the temperature so that the water became cool and invigorating.

Afterward he stood in the center of a threadbare, minuscule bathmat as he toweled himself off, and was none too happy with what he saw in the mirror above the sink. The fluorescent light over the mirror seemed to set aglow the silver hairs that spread among the dark blond like encroaching crabgrass, and the overnight drive and abbreviated sleep had left dark crescents under each eye.

"Jesus Christ, you look old," he said to his reflection.

Once he had dressed again, he went to his car, switched on the engine, and drove back to the dock. Lynn was waiting for him in the parking lot beside the general store. She placed the two large suitcases in the trunk, then climbed into the passenger seat.

"Did you eat?" Ransom asked as he steered the car back out onto the road.

"I had something," she replied.

They said little more during the short drive.

There were a handful of deputies gathered outside the sheriff's station enjoying a smoke and shooting the breeze. Ransom gave them a nod as he and Lynn went past them into the station.

A different deputy was seated behind the main desk. This

one had black hair, very pale skin, and a small crescent-shaped scar that gave his face a rakish look.

"Is the sheriff still here?" Ransom asked.

"You must be the detective from Chicago," the deputy replied.

"Yes."

"Yeah, Joe is still here. Go on in."

"This is Miss Francis, she's here to see Miss Bremmer," he said before moving.

"Yeah, I was told you'd be back. You'll have to leave those things here."

"All right," Lynn said in a flat tone that meant she was not going to argue despite what she thought of the demand.

As Lynn was shown back to the cells, Ransom went to the door to Barnes's office, gave it a double knock, then went in. The sheriff was seated behind the old wooden desk, his feet up, thumbing through a copy of *Newsweek*.

"You keep late hours," said Ransom.

"Actually, I was waiting for these." He laid the magazine aside and tapped a manila envelope that was lying on top of his desk.

"The pictures?"

Barnes grinned. "Uh-huh. It's the pictures, all right. And it's easy to see why the Millers didn't want you to have them." He swung his feet to the ground and with two fingers slid the packet across to him. "Since we were interested in seeing something that was likely to be in the background, I had Nagel, our photographer, print them up eight by ten."

Ransom opened the envelope and extracted the sheaf of photos. He looked at them one by one, not scrutinizing them but getting an overview. The first few were shots of formations of dead trees and driftwood. Though the Millers had an eye for what would make a good picture, their expertise fell short of the mark. In each photo, they had found an interesting formation and attempted to capture it, but the center of the formation would be slightly off; a little to the left or right, higher or lower, than center, making the photos look a bit askew.

In the next batch of shots the Millers took turns photographing each other on the beach facing north, with the *Genessee* in the background. As the Millers had warned, they were quite a distance from the boat. He made a mental note to come back to these after he'd finished looking through the rest.

"The good ones are coming up," Barnes said.

Ransom glanced at him over the top of the photos, then flipped to the next one.

Barnes couldn't help laughing at the frozen expression on the detective's face.

"This is really why you decided to wait, isn't it?" he said.

"No, really, Nagel just now got them to me."

The photo was much like the earlier ones: a tangle of dead, twisted limbs and branches that put one in mind of a Celtic knot design. But at its center was the broadly smiling Martin Miller, only in this picture he was stark naked.

"Oh, dear," Ransom said, sounding very much like Emily, as he leafed through the rest of the shots in which Miller and his wife had taken turns posing *au naturel.*

"No wonder they didn't want you to take the film!" Barnes laughed.

There were thirty-six photos in all. Ransom took out the few that included the boat and laid the rest of them facedown on the desk. He then looked more closely at the boat pictures.

"They were telling the truth about one thing," Ransom observed. "They were a fair distance from the boat when they took these."

"And farther away when they took the rest."

When Ransom got to the third picture, in which a clothed Martin Miller grinned at the camera, his left palm shielding his eyes from the sun, the detective noted something in the background. He squinted at it, but was unable to make it out, which brought another pang to his vanity.

Without lifting his eyes from the photo, he said, "You wouldn't happen to have a magnifying glass, would you?"

"Matter of fact, I do," Barnes said as he opened the center drawer of his desk. He extracted a rectangle of glass surrounded by a frame of black plastic with a matching handle. He handed it to Ransom. "What is it?"

"It's hard to tell. I think—way in the background—there's a man on the dock. It looks like…David Douglas." He bent the magnifying glass to the photo and peered through it. "Hmm."

"What?"

"I'm not sure…wait a minute. It's not a man at all. Unless I'm very much mistaken, that's Claudia Trenton."

He handed the photo and magnifying glass to the sheriff, and was heartened when the younger man had to use the glass to look at it.

"Where?" Barnes asked.

"Just to the right of Miller's shoulder."

Barnes brought the photo close. "Oh, yeah! I see. That is Trenton." He looked up at Ransom. "She's walking toward the boat."

He nodded. "Yes. That means she went back to the boat. She didn't tell me that. Did she tell you?"

"No, but I didn't ask her that directly. I didn't see any reason to."

"Neither did I," said Ransom.

Barnes looked back down at the photo. "I can't see that it makes any difference, though. This is one of the early pictures. The Millers took over twenty pictures after this. It must've been while the crew was still there doing their thing. She's walking right there out in the open, not trying to sneak back. If the crew was still there, she couldn't really have hidden on the boat until everybody left and then did the old lady in. She probably just went back for something she forgot."

"Yes, I'm sure you're right," Ransom conceded. "It's odd, though."

"What is?"

"That nobody else mentioned seeing Claudia Trenton return. If she went back right after leaving, as you say the whole crew would've been there, and the stewards would have been doing the cabins." He spent a minute pondering this, his jaw firmly set and his eyes narrowed. "I think I'll have a word with Miss Trenton."

Barnes started to get up, though he did it reluctantly. "I'll go with you."

"Um, it might be better if you didn't, if you don't mind."

"I should be there."

"I know, but Miss Trenton was very upset when I spoke to her before, and I think that having you there would make it worse." Barnes started to say something, but Ransom held up a hand. "I realize you're the law here, but my unofficial capacity—with the help of Miss Charters—might make it easier to get Miss Trenton to open up."

"Miss Charters?" the sheriff said with a quizzical grin.

Ransom nodded. "Some things are better left to Emily."

"THEY WOULDN'T LET ME bring your things back here," Lynn said as she took a seat on the bench outside Rebecca's cell. "They're keeping them out there."

"That's all right," Rebecca replied colorlessly. "Thank you for getting them."

There was a long silence. Lynn was finding it difficult to make conversation: discussing the situation seemed futile, and making small talk seemed brutally inappropriate under the circumstances. In the silence she fought with the turmoil of her feelings for Rebecca, another topic that she didn't deem proper at the moment. But the feelings existed, and Lynn had to hold back the overwhelming urge to declare them.

Rebecca was staring at a spot on the cement floor. Without looking up, she quietly asked, "Has...has Detective Ransom found out anything?"

Heat rushed into Lynn's chest. It was a simple question, but it was also the first indication that Rebecca might actually maintain a kernel of hope. It made sense, since the shock of what had happened must be starting to wear off, and she was probably becoming more aware of her position. Lynn only wished her answer could be more positive.

"Yes, he has," she said, inwardly warning herself against fostering any false hope. "Well, not anything tangible—but I know he agrees with Emily, that things don't seem right on that boat." She paused, then added, "He really will solve this."

Rebecca raised her head and revealed a smile. Lynn couldn't remember whether or not she'd seen her smile before. It wasn't broad, and was definitely halfhearted, but it was there.

"You make him sound like The Saint."

Lynn returned the smile. "Nothing like that. Ransom is far from that. But his results are the same."

Rebecca unexpectedly laughed, albeit lightly. But what little there had been of a smile soon vanished. "Lynn, I really can't—I don't know…how to thank you for what you've been doing…."

"You don't have to."

"And I really do appreciate you going to the trouble of packing up my things…and Aunt Marci's."

"It wasn't any trouble."

"I don't know why, but it makes me feel better knowing that everything's here."

"It was no prob—" She broke off and grimaced. "Oh, damn!"

"What is it?"

She sighed. "I didn't bring everything. I just remembered, I forgot something."

"What?"

"That package. Didn't you tell me your aunt had some package that you found when you were unpacking for her?"

"Oh, yeah."

"I'm sorry, I forgot to look for it."

"It's nothing. Given the...the state of her mind, it was probably a box of spoons or something."

"I don't remember seeing it. Do you know where she put it?"

"She slipped it under the bed."

"I'll bring it in the morning."

They fell silent for a time. Lynn thought, not without an inner warmth, that it was as companionable a silence as two people could experience with bars separating them.

DINNER HAD long since concluded by the time Ransom made it back to the *Genessee,* and most of the passengers had gone up to the white deck to relax. When he came up the gangplank he spotted Emily sitting on a chair with its back to the wheelhouse, where she had a full view of her fellow passengers. Her hands were folded in her lap, and her eyes glazed over. She resembled an elderly Buddha pondering the riddles of the universe within herself. When she saw Ransom, her eyes livened.

His appearance had a different effect on the rest of the passengers. Having settled into a postmeal torpor, the sight of the detective caused an immediate crackle in the atmosphere, as if everyone on board had tensed at once.

With his eyes on his elderly friend, he gave a very slight nod in the direction of the staircase, then went to it and descended to the red deck. He glanced into the dining room and found that everything had been cleared, and nobody was around. Emily followed shortly thereafter and they held a brief council by the railing.

"I'm so glad you've come back," she began rather breathlessly. "There's something I want to tell you."

"You've discovered something?"

She hesitated. "No, not exactly that. But I am convinced now that Rebecca did not murder her aunt."

"I thought you were convinced of that before."

"I believed it before, partly because of the bizarre circumstances surrounding the death, and from having observed her on this trip, I didn't think she was capable of the murder. But now I'm convinced of it.''

"Why?''

"I was able to talk to Lily DuPree again at dinner, to try to get her to remember for certain whether or not Joaquin was last to leave the boat. Once the idea was introduced, she became very confused." She paused and clucked her tongue. "Poor thing, I'm afraid she's very easily addled and terribly unreliable.''

"Emily…''

"Oh, yes, I'm sorry. Anyway, Lily said she couldn't be sure because she heard so many footsteps while she was drifting in and out of sleep. She said the whole thing was a jumble. That's why I'm convinced Rebecca couldn't have done it.''

"I'm not following you," he said when Emily failed to elaborate.

"'So many footsteps,' you see. So many people coming and going. The murderer would've been taking an awful chance had he or she *planned* to commit the murder here. Too much of a chance.''

"Yes. That's what you thought from the beginning, and it's the very thing that's bothered Barnes about it. He wondered why Rebecca didn't simply kill her aunt in the woods, then claim she'd lost track of her. It would've looked as if some stranger had come upon her and killed her.''

"Exactly," Emily replied, sounding rather excited. "I don't think the murder could've been planned, and that rules out Rebecca. Why would she have suddenly killed her aunt? That wouldn't make any sense.''

Ransom nodded. "Well, you'll be pleased to know that there's some credence to the idea that someone—even a stranger watching the boat—could've come onto it unobserved." He smiled. "Just like in Buckingham Palace.''

"Really?" the old woman replied, her head tilting slightly.

"Yes. Your friend Claudia Trenton managed it.''

"Claudia?''

He nodded. "She was caught on one of the Millers' photos coming back to the boat."

"Claudia...," Emily said again, looking thoroughly mystified.

"Yes. But I don't think it means she had anything to do with the murder. It's one of their earlier pictures. She must've come right back to the boat, and as Barnes pointed out, she couldn't very well have hidden for the next hour with the stewards doing the rooms, and then killed Marcella for whatever reason, and escaped the boat."

"No, she couldn't," said Emily. "But you know, she didn't come up to dinner this evening. Mrs. Farraday is quite worried about her. It occurs to me, Jeremy, that as distressed as she is over what happened, perhaps she saw something when she came back...or heard something...that has caused her distress. Only..." Her voice trailed off and her expression adopted the vacant quality it had when she was mulling over something that didn't quite make sense.

"Only what?" Ransom said with some impatience.

"Only...*why?*"

He waited, then said, "You'll have to give me more than that."

"Why be so distressed, and keep to herself? She wasn't just distressed, she was afraid. If she didn't have anything to do with the murder....if she only thinks she knows something about it...why not tell you or the sheriff? Surely that is the way to ensure her safety."

"We'll never know until we ask her."

Ransom led Emily down the second flight of stairs and soon they were at Claudia's door. He knocked, and a voice from inside said, "Come in."

Emily preceded Ransom into the room. They found Claudia sitting up on her bed. The tray that the captain's wife had provided her sat on the bedside table untouched. Although her complexion was still very pale, she had brushed her hair and dressed herself in a lavender suit, as if she were planning a dinner out or a shopping expedition.

"What do you want?" she asked without expression.

"Claudia, you haven't eaten anything," Emily said. "That's not good. You must keep up your strength."

"I wasn't hungry."

"You remember Detective Ransom?"

Claudia nodded but didn't look at him.

"Miss Trenton," said Ransom, "I'm afraid there are one or two more questions I need to ask you."

"Yes?"

"You told us, and you told the sheriff, that yesterday you left the boat and went to the visitor's center with the others, then went off on your own to trail three. Is that correct?"

"Yes."

"You didn't do anything else?"

She turned her eyes toward him. The area just above her nose was pinched. "No."

After a beat, he said, "Are you sure about that? You didn't, by chance, come back to the boat for some reason?"

"No!" she said quickly. She attempted her former haughtiness, but it didn't work.

"What if I were to tell you that you were caught on film?"

"What?"

"The Millers were taking pictures, as you might remember. Although they were far away from the boat, I'm afraid they did catch you on film coming back to it."

Tears brimmed in her eyes, and she trembled as if the strain were about to break her apart. "I...I...yes, I did. But I didn't—" She broke off and buried her face in her hands.

"Claudia," Emily said gently, "no one believes you had anything to do with the murder."

Ransom raised an eyebrow at his elderly partner, and she responded with a cautionary glance.

"I didn't!" Claudia exclaimed, looking up at her. "But I've been so afraid!"

"Afraid because you saw something?"

Claudia looked down at the floor and shook her head.

"Because you thought someone might've seen you?"

There was a long pause before Claudia responded. She pulled herself together somewhat, raised her head and wiped the tears away. "Does anyone have a tissue?"

Emily reached into her pocket and withdrew a small pack of tissues, which she handed to her.

Claudia took them without a thank-you, dabbed at her eyes and then blew her nose. She seemed to regain some of her old manner. "Excuse me. I realize I've been idiotic. I thought—" She broke off and turned to Ransom. "There really isn't anything about my coming back. I didn't say anything because I was…frightened to. That was foolish, I know. And…and cowardly. But in my whole life I've never been mixed up in anything like this. Can you understand that?"

She said this last part with an earnestness that surprised her audience.

"I suppose I can," said Emily. "In the past few years I've become rather inured to murder."

Claudia gave her a curious glance, then turned back to Ransom. "As I told you, I wanted to be on my own. Away from anyone on the tour. I picked up one of the brochures and then started out…and then…then I realized I'd forgotten my glasses, and I went back to get them."

Emily said gently, "Claudia, I seem to remember you wearing those large sunglasses of yours."

The sudden, unmistakable tinge of fear returned to the other woman's eyes, then slacked after a moment. "Those weren't prescription. I needed my regular glasses if…if I was going to read anything."

"I see," said Ransom. "When you came back, you didn't run into anyone? A member of the crew?"

She shook her head sadly. "No, but I heard them cleaning the cabins, so I…I just got my glasses and left."

"After getting your glasses."

"Yes…of course."

"And how long were you onboard?"

"Just a…not more than a couple of minutes."

"THAT WAS a very unsatisfying interview," Ransom said quietly once he and Emily had gone back to Emily's cabin. He was seated on the chair that matched the one in Claudia's room, and Emily was seated on the edge of the bed.

"It is very perplexing. I suppose it's possible that she simply came back for her glasses, but…" She shook her head slowly. "There is clearly something wrong. I can't get past the idea that her distress exceeds what one would expect, even under these circumstances. If it was a very sensitive person, or someone who was very timid, I could understand it, but Claudia is neither of those things. She is quite strong. It seems most out of character for her to fall apart because of the death of someone she hardly knew, even if it did happen nearby, or that she would be that upset at the idea of having been seen coming back to the boat."

"Yes," said Ransom. "Her choice of words was very interesting. I mean, when she said 'I've never been mixed up in something like this.'"

"Yes…it's as if her reserve is cracking, and bits of truth were seeping out. It isn't surprising given that she hasn't been sleeping."

"Hmm. And when you offered the possibility that she was afraid that someone might've seen her return to the boat—"

Emily was nodding. "She snatched at it…or at least, she seemed relieved…." Her thin brows knit together. "That's the word for it. Relieved. The puzzling thing is that she seemed more relieved to explain her fear than she was to explain her return to the boat."

Ransom sighed. "But I'm damned if I know what that woman could have to do with the murder!"

RANSOM HAD LEFT the boat long before Lynn returned, dropped off by one of the deputies at the request of Sheriff Barnes, who himself had gone home after showing Ransom the photos. Lynn's footsteps rang hollow on the wooden path alongside the general store. She rounded the corner onto the dock and came to a stop, struck by the grim picturesqueness of the scene. The *Genessee* was moored in place, its patriotic stripes blackened in the darkness. A dim light in the wheelhouse revealed the captain and his wife sitting side by side, her head resting against his shoulder. Diffused light from the portholes on the starboard bow of the red deck indicated that someone might be in the bar, and on the blue deck light shone from only one porthole.

The *Genessee* was set against an inky blue overcast night sky with a thin streak of magenta that formed a false horizon. To Lynn the scene looked like a romanticized painting of a harbor in decay. She shook her head and made her way down the dock.

The weariness didn't hit her until she set foot on the gangplank. As she ascended, she felt as if the skin was sagging from her body, pulled by an irresistibly strengthened force of gravity. She would, she thought, be very glad to get to bed.

But before going to her cabin she went to Marcella Hemsley's. She switched on the overhead light and the room sprang into relief. Lynn gave an involuntary shudder. Viewing the room from the doorway brought vividly back to her the sight of the elderly woman sprawled hideously across the bed, as she was when she and Emily had found her. The bed now empty, the memory somehow seemed unreal, as if it was something she'd imagined or dreamed.

I must be losing my mind, she thought. *It didn't bother me at all to be in here alone this afternoon.*

She marshaled herself and went into the room. Getting down on her hands and knees, she lowered her face near the floor and peered under the bed, but there was nothing there.

"What are you doing?" asked a voice out of the blue.

"Jesus!" Lynn exclaimed, instantly righting herself.

David Douglas was standing in the doorway, his hands resting on either side of it. "Sorry, I didn't mean to scare you."

"It's all right," she replied, her manner becoming rigid when she saw who it was. "I didn't realize until you spoke how quiet it was."

"Yeah." There was a hint of a smile. Lynn suspected he was pleased that he'd startled her. "Um...what are you doing?"

"I was asked to pack up Rebecca's things, and her aunt's," she said.

"Yeah, I heard. You already did that, didn't you?"

"Yes, I did," she said as she started to get up from the floor. Perhaps it was a reaction to his overt curiosity, but somehow she didn't like the idea of giving him specific information.

Douglas came into the room and placed a firm hand on her elbow to help her up. She jerked it free and rose with no effort.

"So if you already did it, what are you doing here now?"

"Being thorough," she replied with a hard smile. "I just wanted to double-check and make sure I got everything."

"Oh. Do you want some help?"

"Thank you, no."

He shrugged easily. "Okey-doke."

Douglas went away, then Lynn closed the door. She turned around and looked at the room, absently running the fingers of her right hand through her hair. Her hand came to rest on the nape of her neck, which she rubbed for a moment. Then with a sigh, she went to work searching the room. It didn't take long to cover the small confines of the cabin, and Lynn was left even more puzzled when she found nothing. She sat down on the bed and pondered where an addled elderly woman might hide a parcel, and after a while decided that the prospects might not be limited to her own room. Someone on the outskirts of Alzheimer's disease might very well have taken it into her head to hide it in the boat's pantry, or a storage cupboard somewhere, or under someone else's bed.

Lynn sighed again, got up, and crossed to the door. She

switched off the light and went to her own cabin. She didn't undress but rather lay on the bed, her hands cupped behind her head, staring up at the faint rippling circle on the ceiling, reflecting off the water though the porthole.

Something about the package was nagging at her mind—not the fact that she couldn't find it but something else: only she couldn't remember what it was.

NINE

RANSOM WAS JUST ABOUT to leave his motel room the next morning when a call came on his cell phone from his partner, Gerald White. After the customary greetings, Ransom said, "Did you get anything?"

"None of the names you gave me has a record attached to it," he said, "except for David Douglas."

"You surprise me."

"For possession. Two years ago. It was a first offense. He got probation."

"I see. Nothing else?"

"Nope—"

"Good. I want you to do one other thing for me. Stuart Holmes was a lawyer. I want you to find out exactly what kind of law he practiced, if you can."

"Sure thing. Uh, Jer, I may have a complication for you."

"What?"

"I had to tell Newman what I was doing—"

Ransom raised his right eyebrow. "Am I in danger of being called up in front of the principal?"

Unseen by his partner, Gerald smirked into the receiver at area headquarters in Chicago. "No. I told him about it because a case came in very early this morning that may be connected."

"To this?" Ransom said with genuine surprise.

"Yeah. A murder. Jackson and Franklin are on it, and told me a little about it when I checked in this morning. It's a young man, about twenty-five, shot twice in the head after being beaten up. The thing is, according to his driver's license, the kid's last name was the same as someone on your list. Turns out, apparently it's his next of kin.''

"Yes?"

"His grandmother is Claudia Trenton."

"Aha," Ransom said slowly.

"His name is Johnny Trenton."

"Can you get me a picture?"

"I can when they get up here. We need her to identify him. Does your friend the sheriff have a fax machine?"

Ransom smiled. "This is only a geographical backwater, Gerald. They do have the proper equipment. I'm supposed to meet him soon over at the boat. I'll give you his number. Call him and get the fax number, and send the photo as soon as you can."

He gave Gerald the number, then hung up and stuck the phone back in his pocket. It was, he thought, an interesting new wrinkle, and for the sake of his own investigation he hoped it would not turn out to be another simple coincidence.

EMILY WAS just finishing doing up the tiny light blue buttons of her favorite navy dress when she heard a tapping at her door.

"Emily? Are you up?" Lynn's voice asked quietly.

"Yes, dear, come in."

The door opened and the young woman entered, closing it behind her. Her face was noticeably drawn, and her tawny hair wasn't quite brushed properly.

"Lynn!" Emily exclaimed, "What's the matter?"

"I haven't slept. I couldn't get to sleep. I was trying to remember something, but I couldn't. I didn't fall asleep until about four o'clock this morning, and then when I woke up, suddenly there it was."

She explained herself to Emily, whose expression grew very grave. When she'd finished, Emily said, "This may be very significant...but then again, it may not. The events of that night may appear exactly as they seem, and as you say, with Marcella's mind deteriorating, she may have hidden the package anywhere at all. I have known others with Alzheimer's disease, and they are capable of the most extraordinary things. But I think we'd do well to tell Jeremy about this right away.''

"I'll phone him from the general store."

When the two ladies left the blue deck they found the rest of the passengers assembling for breakfast. At the bottom of the steps leading up to the top deck, Lynn happened to glance down the dock.

"Wait! There he is," she said to Emily, who was just about to enter the dining room.

The old woman came over to the railing and looked. Ransom was nearing the gangplank, accompanied by Sheriff Barnes.

"I'll go up with you," Emily said.

Ransom had arrived in the parking lot at the same time as the sheriff. Unfortunately, Barnes had left the station before receiving Gerald's call about the fax. When he heard the news of the death in Chicago, he radioed back to the station to make sure one of his deputies would be watching for the photo.

"It might not have anything to do with what's going on here, you know," Barnes said to Ransom. "People get killed in Chicago all the time, so I'm told."

The detective smiled. "Yes, I know. But if it's a coincidence, it's a very poorly timed one."

"I was planning to tell the captain they could leave this morning," Barnes said as they walked out onto the dock, "but it looks like they may be here awhile longer. Should we tell your friends, Miss Charters and Miss Francis?"

"Not yet," said Ransom. "We should wait until we are absolutely sure we have a positive ID."

Emily and Lynn reached the top deck just slightly ahead of the two representatives of the law. They came together by the railing halfway across the deck.

"I've discovered something," said Lynn. "I mean...I think..."

"It's something that may be important," said Emily. "Something is missing."

"What?" asked Barnes

"It's a small package," Lynn explained. "Well, smallish, I think."

"You think?"

"I've never seen it."

"As you know," said Emily, "Rebecca asked Lynn to pack up their things, which you kindly allowed."

"Uh-huh?"

"And I did," said Lynn. "But there was one thing missing. A package. From what Rebecca told me, it's a little smaller than a shoe box, wrapped in brown paper—soiled brown paper—and tied with twine. It's missing."

"What is it?"

"I don't know. Rebecca didn't know. It was something her aunt apparently packed on the sly. But the thing is—"

Barnes was nodding. "It's gone, I understand. But anything could've happened to it."

"There's more, Sheriff," Emily said firmly.

Ransom smiled.

"The other night," said Lynn, "the night before the murder…the night Rebecca's aunt screamed and woke everybody up, something strange happened, and I only just remembered it this morning because of the package being missing."

"Yeah?"

"I couldn't sleep. I came up on deck and found Rebecca at the point of the boat…the front…whatever you call it. She couldn't sleep either. We got to talking, and she was telling me about how worried she was about her aunt, and the crazy things she'd been doing…and she told me about the package. Right after that, we heard footsteps rushing away from us…well, it seems to me now that they were rushing. I looked around the side of the wheelhouse, but it was too dark. I couldn't see anybody."

"Uh-huh?"

"But you see, it was right after that that it happened."

Barnes shot a glance at Ransom to see if his urban counterpart was as confused as he felt.

"It was right after that that Marcella Hemsley screamed and claimed someone had come into her room," Lynn explained. "You see, I was so surprised by the sudden noise that I didn't connect the two things."

"So what you're saying is, you think someone heard Miss Bremmer say that her aunt had this box in her luggage, and went straight down to her cabin to find it?"

"Yes!" Lynn couldn't keep the edge out of her voice, particularly since she felt the idea sounded quite foolish when he put it so plainly. "And remember, Marcella Hemsley said that it was David Douglas who was in her room."

The sheriff sucked in his lips for a second. "Yeah, but that doesn't make sense, ma'am. He wouldn't have to go into her room to steal something while she was in it. He could wait till the next day, when she was off the boat. There was no hurry."

"I quite agree, Sheriff," said Emily. "However, there are two facts to deal with here. Miss Hemsley is dead and the package is gone."

"But like I said, anything could've happened to it. It could've been taken since. Or she could've done something with it herself."

"Yeah, I did think of that," Lynn said reluctantly.

"Did you search the boat after the murder?" Ransom asked.

"We had a look 'round," Barnes replied. "But there wasn't any reason to do a full search. We knew where the woman was killed."

"Hmm," Ransom said, staring unblinkingly at Barnes. "Well, one way or another, one of Miss Hemsley's possessions has disappeared. Would it hurt to search it now?"

Barnes returned his gaze, pulled his radio from his belt. "I told you from the start this whole thing didn't set right with me. I'll get a couple of my deputies over here to help."

"Thank you, Sheriff," Emily said, eyeing him approvingly.

WHEN THE DEPUTIES arrived, Barnes assigned them the task of
searching the white and red decks, which held far less in the
way of hiding places than the cabins. He then went to the
dining room where the passengers and crew were assembled
and made a general announcement to the effect that nobody
was to return to the blue deck until he'd given the all-clear.

Ransom and Barnes decided to begin at the beginning, with
cabin 1, and to that end enlisted Emily's aid in extricating
Claudia Trenton, the one passenger who had not been in the
dining room. It was apparent that Claudia had finally managed
to get some rest the previous night and had regained some of
her poise, though the deepened lines on her face evidenced the
strain of the past few days. Given her state since the murder,
Ransom had expected her to bridle when she learned that her
cabin would be searched. But much to his surprise, she accepted the news with complacency and allowed Emily to usher
her to the dining room for breakfast.

"I thought there would be hysterics," Ransom said once the
two women were gone.

"She hasn't been taking this well, has she?" said Barnes.
"I don't know what it's going to do to her when she hears
about her grandson."

The closet contained three suits, neatly spaced out to prevent
wrinkles. Ransom noted that her wardrobe was a cut above
tasteful and a step below elegant, but definitely out of class
with this particular mode of transportation. She had left her
purse on the bed: a medium-sized black bag with a long shoulder strap. Ransom picked it up and glanced inside.

"What we're looking for's too big to be in there, isn't it?"
said Barnes.

"The box, perhaps, but we don't know what was inside the
box. The contents might've been taken out and hidden anywhere."

He found nothing out of the ordinary in the bag; merely a
variety of cosmetic items, a red leather wallet, and a cell phone.

This last item caused the detective's brow to furrow. He examined it, and found it set to vibrate rather than ring.

"Find something?" Barnes asked, noticing the change of expression.

"Just a cell phone."

"Everybody's got those things, nowadays."

"Yes, I know." He replaced the phone, snapped the bag shut and laid it on the bed.

They went through the rest of the passengers' cabins in turn, including Lynn's and Emily's, assuming that someone could very well have hidden the package in one of their cabins.

"Hard part of it is," said Barnes as they finished Muriel Langstrom's room, the last of the passenger cabins, "we'll probably find the darn thing, open it and find out it's just a bunch of brushes, or a blow-dryer, or something."

"Keep a good thought, Sheriff," Ransom said wryly.

They moved on to the crew's quarters. The first on the left was the one unused space on the boat, and they found nothing there. Then they moved on to Joaquin's cabin, which was rather unkempt. Apparently the effort he put into keeping the passengers' cabins and the rest of the boat immaculate left him little time or inclination to tend to his own. White socks were strewn about the floor and the bed was unmade. The bedside chest was coated with a thick layer of dust, made all the more obvious by the clean circle that had been left when the compass lamp had been pushed out of position. The sheriff dropped down to his knees and looked under the bed, finding only an empty Pepsi can. When he righted himself, he found Ransom staring down at the lamp.

"What is it?" asked Barnes.

"Hmm? Nothing. I was just thinking that as neat and clean as Joaquin is himself, this room is awfully sloppy."

"Yeah, well, the package isn't in here."

They next went to Douglas's cabin, which they found perfectly in order. The bed was made, the blanket stretched so smoothly it looked as if you could bounce a coin on it. The table and lamp were beautifully polished, and there wasn't a speck on the carpet. The closet was in the same condition, the few garments that Douglas had brought with him looking so crisp on the hangers they might have been new.

"They're exactly the opposite, aren't they," Ransom said.

"What do you mean?"

"Somehow I would've expected Douglas to be the sloppy one."

Barnes smiled. "If you ask me, this looks compulsive."

"Hmm."

"Say, what's wrong with you, Detective? Something on your mind?"

"Yes, as a matter of fact," Ransom replied with a sigh, "only I'm damned if I know what it is."

The corners of Barnes's mouth turned down slightly. Unlike Gerald White, the sheriff wasn't inclined to be tolerant of artfulness or conundrums. "What do you mean?"

"I don't know myself. It's something just on the edge of my brain. It's something to do with…" The lines across his forehead deepened, then he relaxed and shrugged.

"It'll come to you the minute you stop worrying it," said Barnes helpfully.

Next was the captain's quarters. The Farradays' cabin spanned the aft of the boat and was over three times the size of the others, with a decor that was far homier. The bed was covered with a wedding-ring quilt, and a small maple dresser sat beside the double-length closet. A shelf above the dresser held an array of well-thumbed paperback books, the kind that Ransom classified as nearly-best-sellers.

When he and Barnes had given the cabin a thorough going-over and come up empty, Barnes sighed. "Nothing!"

"Hmm," Ransom replied, his arms folded as he held his chin between his thumb and forefinger.

"She probably never had any box."

"You forget, Rebecca Bremmer actually saw it. It isn't something Marcella Hemsley made up."

"She probably did something with it herself, then. She could've just chucked it over the side of the boat or something."

"Perhaps."

Barnes sighed again. "Turning out the passengers' rooms like this, I'm going to look like a big fool if we don't find something."

"I don't think so."

"Really? How do you figure that?"

Ransom dropped his hands to his side. "Far from looking foolish, it will be very interesting if we don't find that package."

Barnes pursed his lips, unable to see the importance. "Well, I'll go see how my men are doing with the other decks, and I'll tell the passengers they can have their cabins back."

While Barnes went to the red deck, Ransom continued his way up to the top. Emily and Lynn were there, occupying the two deck chairs closest to the boarding plank.

"Did you find anything?" Emily asked.

"Not in any of the cabins, no."

"I see," she replied with interest. "If it isn't in any of the cabins, I don't think it will be found anywhere else. It seems to me it would be too risky to hide it anywhere else on board. There would be too much of a chance of it being discovered." She paused for a moment, then a new idea came to her. "Unless…"

"Unless what?" Lynn asked.

Emily shook her head slowly. "I've been extremely slow-witted in this matter. I suppose I can chalk that up to being on the water. I said before that it has a soporific effect…."

She stopped, her pale lips set in a slight frown, and her eyes staring straight ahead. She looked exactly as if she were silently scolding herself for her mental truancy.

"Emily, you didn't answer my question."

"What?"

"You said you didn't think the package would be found if it wasn't in anyone's cabin unless..."

"Oh, yes! I was forgetting that Marcella's mental state was well known to everyone. I was looking at it backwards. It would make much more sense to hide the thing anywhere else on the boat. That way, the person who took it—if anyone, indeed, did take it and Marcella didn't do something with it herself—wouldn't be in danger if the package was found. Everyone would believe it was just another one of Marcella's lapses."

"But—" Lynn began to protest, but Ransom cut her off.

"I know you want to believe that you and Rebecca were overheard on the deck and that led to the incident of someone supposedly being in Marcella's room, but Lynn, you have to look at it reasonably. The sheriff was right about that: even if someone did overhear you, there was no reason to go for the package while Marcella was in her room. But more than that, why go for it at all? There was no indication that there was anything valuable in it. You didn't say what was in the package, did you?"

"No," Lynn said, reluctantly accepting that he was right. "Rebecca didn't know what was in it."

They fell silent for a time. Ransom rested his palms on the railing and looked down at the small strip of water between the dock and the boat. Then movement to the left caught his eye and he looked up. One of Barnes's deputies was approaching the boarding plank, a sheet of paper in his right hand.

"Are you Detective Ransom?" the deputy asked when he'd reached them.

"Yes," Ransom replied, shaking the younger man's outstretched hand.

"I'm Deputy Mitchell. This here's for you."

He handed Ransom the sheet, and the detective looked down at it. It was a photo of a young man with tousled brown hair. There were bruises and smudges of dirt on his face, but the head had been turned judiciously so only the barest edge of a bullet hole could be seen.

Lynn had helped Emily to her feet. "What is it?" the old woman asked.

"Gerald called me this morning," Ransom explained. "There was a murder sometime last night, and it appears that the young man was the grandson of Claudia Trenton."

"Oh, dear," Emily said, drawing back slightly. "This will be a terrible blow to Claudia."

"Yes, I know. Gerald sent a copy of one of the pictures up for positive identification." He handed it to Emily.

Emily's eyes widened, and she looked up at Ransom. "But Jeremy, I know him!"

"You do?"

"Oh, no, I don't mean I *know* him, but I've seen him before. He was on Navy Pier the day we sailed."

Ransom shrugged. "It's perfectly natural that he'd be there to see his grandmother off."

"But that's just it—he wasn't seeing her off. He was hovering very furtively in the background, in the shadows inside the building. Claudia was sitting off to the side. He made no attempt to make himself known to her."

"That is…curious."

"Good heavens!" Emily exclaimed.

"What is it?" Lynn asked, slightly alarmed.

"When I first saw that young man on the pier, he was carrying a package—one wrapped in brown paper. But when we set sail, I saw him walking and he no longer had it."

The group was momentarily struck dumb by this announcement. Lynn was the first to speak.

"But…but that doesn't make sense. Why would Claudia's grandson have something that belonged to Marcella Hemsley? I mean, if you're thinking that he put it in her suitcase—"

"Remember, Lynn, we all left our suitcases on the pier lined up in a row as those young men were helping us onto the boat."

"You mean he put it in the wrong suitcase?"

"You said it yourself," Emily reminded her, "'I've never seen so much Samsonite in one place.'"

"But Miss Hemsley said the box was hers!"

Emily arched her thin brows.

"Oh, God!" said Lynn as the realization hit her.

Emily nodded. "Her mental state, you know. She probably *believed* it was hers. The real question is why on earth Claudia and her grandson were playing this elaborate sleight of hand in the first place."

"Assuming she knew about it," said Ransom. "The best thing to do is ask her."

They all turned around as Barnes emerged at the top of the staircase. He came onto the deck and crossed to them. "Hey, Mitch," he said to his subordinate.

The deputy returned the greeting.

"This is the picture that I was expecting," Ransom said, handing it to the sheriff. "And we have a little more information." He explained what Emily had seen on the pier.

By the time Ransom finished, Barnes had cocked a curious eye at Emily. "You're a sharp old thing, aren't you?" he said with admiration.

Though crudely put, Emily's cheeks turned pink nonetheless. "Thank you."

He turned to Ransom. "I just talked to my men. They did this deck and they're just about finished with the second one. They haven't found hide nor hair of the package. It still could be that Marcella Hemsley, whether or not it belonged to her, just threw it overboard."

"It could also be that she got in the way of the person who wanted to get it back," said Ransom.

"Uh-huh. Yeah, well, I guess that kind of changes things as far as Miss Hemsley's murder goes, and Miss Bremmer's situation...though the timing is still pretty hard to deal with."

Emily heard Lynn sigh with evident relief. Apparently Barnes noticed it, too. "I'm not saying that Miss Bremmer is innocent yet, but this other thing here doesn't look right." He turned back to Ransom. "This also means I have to take up the investigation."

"Yes. I understand that," Ransom said judiciously. "However, it may be related to the murder that took place in Chicago, so I'd appreciate it if you'd let me sit in when you talk to Claudia Trenton."

The right side of Barnes's mustache elevated a fraction of an inch. "No, I'll sit in with you for the time being. After all, you're the one that needs to have the picture ID'd."

"Thank you," Ransom said with a wry curl to his lip. It was obvious that the sheriff didn't relish the idea of breaking the news to Claudia.

"Well, I'm going to go to the station and let Rebecca know the good news," Lynn said. "At least I can let her know there's some hope. Do you think one of your deputies could drive me?"

"What?" Ransom said suddenly, peering at her with narrowed eyes.

"I meant the sheriff," she said, confused by his reaction.

"Whatever is the matter?" Emily asked.

"Lynn, when you called me yesterday, I'd been asleep," said Ransom.

She gave a perplexed shrug. "Sorry."

He shook his head. "That's not what I mean. You see, I wasn't fully awake. After you hung up, for a short time I had the strange feeling that I'd dreamed it." He turned to Emily. "I just realized what it was that was nagging at the back of my mind after Barnes and I searched Claudia Trenton's cabin: she had a cell phone. The conversation you heard the first day out, when you were half-asleep…you said you couldn't make out what the other person was saying. Could it be that you couldn't hear the other person because there wasn't one!"

"Oh, of course!" Emily said as the understanding came to her. "She was on a cell phone! It was because Mr. Driscoll came on the scene at the time that I'd thought she might've been talking to him. Oh, I've been very stupid.''

''Why do you say that?'' Lynn asked.

''Because I should've realized that if it had been a furtive conversation between the two of them, they wouldn't have had it knowing I was there on the deck with them. They couldn't have been sure I was asleep.''

''I wouldn't think she would've made a call with you there, either.''

''Yes, but she might not have made it, she might just have taken it.''

''The phone was set to vibrate, so it wouldn't ring,'' Ransom said.

''Either way, she would've *known* that her end of the conversation wouldn't mean anything to anyone''—her expression suddenly became vague—''or might have been too upset to care.''

''Well, we won't find out until we talk to her,'' said Barnes.

Lynn left for the sheriff's station with Deputy Mitchell, and Emily accompanied Ransom and Barnes down the stairs. They were about to descend the second flight when a glance through the dining room window stopped Emily.

''Jeremy—'' she said.

Ransom and Barnes stopped and looked in the window. Claudia Trenton was sitting on the far side of the dining room staring languidly out the port window, the hazy sunlight making her look like a faded silhouette. The three sleuths entered quietly through the starboard door. Claudia was alone in the room, the other passengers apparently eager to check their cabins after the search. The tables had all been cleared except for the lone coffee mug on the table beside the seated woman.

Ransom advanced toward her, followed by his two companions. Emily was rather alarmed by her appearance: Claudia's stylish beige suit seemed to hang on her as if it had been hastily tossed onto a mannequin three sizes too small.

It's as if she's shrinking away, thought Emily.

Claudia didn't look up when the three of them reached her. She said listlessly, "Did you find anything?"

"No, Miss Trenton," said the detective. "We didn't find the parcel."

The mention of the item caused her to look up sharply, her mouth set in a grim line.

"Miss Trenton, may we sit down?"

"As you please." She sighed after a long pause.

Ransom sat on the chair to her right, Emily took the seat on the left, assisted in the most gentlemanly fashion by Barnes, who then sat across from Claudia.

"We've had some news today from Chicago," Ransom said with surprising gentleness. "About your grandson."

A tremor passed through the old woman's frame. "Johnny?"

"Yes."

"Is he—he's dead, isn't he?"

"I'm afraid he is. I have a photo. Could you identify him for me, just to be sure?"

He held it out to her. She didn't take it, but looked down at it. Her face remained immobile, except for the lower lip, through which ripples were passing. After several seconds, tears overflowed and ran down her cheeks. But she made no sound, nor did she attempt to wipe the tears away.

"I suppose it's all over now," she said, her voice sounding as if were carried on the wind through a graveyard. "I suppose they killed him."

"Who did, Miss Trenton?"

"His...his 'friends.' The people he was involved with." She was silent for a time. "They were no friends."

Ransom's eyes had narrowed. "Do you know who killed your grandson?"

She slowly shook her head. "He has been involved with drugs. He...I did what I could. I paid for his rehabilitation. Twice, I did. It was—" She suddenly broke down and buried her face in her hands, her elbows resting on the table.

"It was what I had to do to keep him out of jail. It was the only way. I tried to be a good grandmother to him, ever since his parents died. I was the one who had to take care of him. I gave him everything that he wanted, but it wasn't enough. He got mixed up with the very people..." Her voice hardened. "And *they* got him involved with drugs! He never would've done it on his own."

"The rehabilitation didn't take?" Ransom asked.

"They don't know what they're doing, those doctors! They released him, they said he was fine. But he went right back to using drugs, so he couldn't have been well, could he? The doctors couldn't have done their jobs! If they had, he would've been cured!"

"But he always had you to help him out," Ransom said evenly, the scenario familiar and one of which he greatly disapproved.

She nodded somewhat proudly. "It was what you do for your family. More than once...more than once I've had to pay off a debt to those...those people...when they threatened to do him harm if he didn't pay. But you have to understand, Johnny...my poor Johnny couldn't help himself."

Not with you helping him, thought Ransom. "But you don't know who they are?"

She looked up. Her face was pale and blotchy, her cheeks streaked with tears. "No, I— No, I don't."

"Claudia," Emily said, "the day we sailed, I saw your grandson on Navy Pier."

"You did?" She had tried to sound surprised, but it rang hollow and there was fear in her eyes.

"Yes. He made no attempt to get your attention. You were in plain view while we waited on the dock, and he didn't come over and make his presence known to you, although you were less than a hundred feet away from him."

"That's...that's very odd."

"What's even more odd is that he was carrying a package wrapped in brown paper. I saw him leaving the pier as we set sail, and he no longer had it. I suspect that the package found its way into Marcella Hemsley's suitcase by mistake.''

Barnes was sitting back in his chair, his mouth hanging slightly open. As with many before him, he found Emily's directness rather impressive.

Claudia seemed to be deflating even more inside her suit. Her eyes were wide and dull. ''I...I don't...''

''It would appear,'' Emily continued, ''that Johnny meant to put the package in your suitcase, but accidentally put it in Marcella's instead. Despite the fact that you say it was odd that he was there, I suspect that you were expecting him to put the package in your suitcase.''

There was a quick intake of breath. ''How could you know—think that?''

''Because I overheard your end of a phone conversation not long after we sailed. Now, the first question that comes to mind is why would you engage in such a bizarre means of receiving a package?''

''I don't know what you're talking about,'' the other woman replied weakly.

''Come now, Claudia,'' Emily said with a sympathetic *tut*.

Ransom had been happy to hand over the questioning to Emily for the time being, confident as he was in her abilities and given the help she'd already been in handling the woman. But now he felt he should take up the reins. ''Miss Trenton, we have two problems here. The death of your grandson, and the death of Marcella Hemsley. And the things that connect them are a brown paper parcel...and you.''

Barnes's eyebrows went up at what the detective was suggesting, but he was even more surprised by the woman's reaction. He'd expected Claudia to be horrified, or furious, or frightened. Instead she looked resigned.

''Johnny is dead. I suppose it doesn't matter what happens to me now.''

''To you?'' Emily asked with surprise.

Claudia nodded. She looked down at her hands, which were

now folded and resting on the table. "Johnny was in trouble again. Using drugs. It had been building up for some time. And…I was tired. I decided to go on this trip, just to get away for a few days."

"Ah," Emily said quietly.

There was a long pause, then Claudia sighed wearily. "He was always in trouble. He came to me for help, as he always did. But…this time he didn't want money. He said his…associates wanted me to do something for them." She turned to Emily pleadingly. I *know* what his friends were. I never would've done anything to help *them,* you must understand."

"Of course," said Emily.

"All they wanted me to do was deliver a package for them."

"What was in it?" asked Ransom.

Claudia stiffened. "I don't know. They didn't tell me, and since I never ended up having it, I didn't look…I don't think I would've, anyway."

"But you must have had some idea," said Emily.

"No. No, I didn't," the other woman said emphatically.

Emily made a noise under her breath. "I'm sorry, Claudia, but you must have—otherwise your grandson's mode of delivery was completely incomprehensible. You never wanted to touch the package, did you?"

"All right, I didn't want to touch it!" Claudia burst out. Then she was silent for a very long time. At last, she said, "You're right. I didn't know, but I know what those friends of Johnny's were like. So I didn't have to guess what would be in it."

"Why did you agree to do it, then?"

Tears welled in her eyes again. "Because…because Johnny said that they would kill him if I didn't. And I knew they would, because they'd hurt him before! I just…had to. But I couldn't face Johnny, not after he'd gotten me into this position. I told him I didn't want to see him again. I told him I didn't want to handle the package. I told him he would have to put the thing in my suitcase himself...at the pier...that I would leave it there, so that he could do it.''

So that, thought Emily, *was why you walked so purposefully away from your suitcase.*

"The only trouble was," Emily said to Ransom and Barnes, "that the steward gathered the luggage together—suitcases that were not all that dissimilar to begin with—and most likely Johnny was still...under the influence. So his mind was confused enough on its own."

Barnes had been sitting quietly in his chair, his arms folded, stroking his thick mustache with the thumb and forefinger of his right hand. Now he shifted in his seat and sat forward. "Yeah. Excuse me, Detective, Miss Charters, but it seems to me that this is where it becomes my case. Miss Trenton, you say you were supposed to deliver the thing...where? Here?''

She nodded. "I received a call the day before we left. All the person said was that I was to deliver the thing to someone at a place called Lookout Point at this stop. After the steward put the case in my cabin, I went down and looked in it. There was nothing there! No package! And I thought...I thought that maybe Johnny was finally coming to himself, and he decided not involve me.''

"But then he called you?" Emily asked.

Tears flooded her eyes again. "To say he was sorry. That was when I found out that something had gone terrible wrong. But I wasn't sure...He'd lied to me so many times before. I didn't know what to do...I was beside myself. I couldn't sleep, so I went up to the deck that first night out, sometime in the middle of the night.''

"So it was you who overheard Lynn and Rebecca."

She nodded. "I knew at once what had happened. That foolish old woman! I didn't mean to scare her. I...I should have waited to look in her cabin, waited until the next day. But I was frantic! I was supposed to meet those dreadful people the next day, and I had to have it!''

"So you left the boat with us the next day, then came back to try to get the package from Marcella Hemsley's room."

She nodded. "Yes. But I couldn't, they were doing the cabins—the stewards—and all the doors were open. They would've seen me...and I couldn't wait any longer, because I was supposed to be there at eleven o'clock. So...I had to go."

"Without the package?" Barnes said, a faint note of admiration in his voice.

"I thought it would be more dangerous for Johnny if I didn't show up at all."

"And were they there?"

She gave a shudder. "Yes. I was so afraid...there were two of them. Very young. A girl with dirty, stringy hair, and a young man with brown hair...He had hard, mean eyes. Tiny eyes..."

"The hikers," said Emily.

"I told them what had happened, and they didn't believe me. At least, not at first. The man accused me of lying. He said Johnny had stolen the...the 'catch,' I think he called it, to sell for himself. And that...well, I was terrified."

"Because you feared it might be true," said Emily.

Claudia nodded reluctantly. "But Johnny had been adamant about having put it in my suitcase on the phone. And I finally convinced—at least I think I did—those two people that it was onboard the boat, even that I knew what had happened to it."

"Do you mean you told them who it was you thought had it?" Ransom asked.

She averted her eyes. "I told them that I could get it for them as soon as I could, and bring it to them." She sputtered and broke down, holding the back of her right hand to her trembling lips. "They said if I didn't find it, they would kill me and then kill Johnny."

Barnes waited awhile before asking his next question. "So you did come back to the boat a second time."

She looked up. "Yes, of course. But—" Her jaw dropped open and her eyes grew wide. "No! I don't mean that! I didn't come back right away. After they left me, I sat there for quite some time and...I just didn't know what to do. I couldn't believe what Johnny had gotten me involved in. By the time I got back to the boat, the hue and cry had already begun. Marcella had been discovered dead...and...and..."

Emily was gazing at her shrewdly. "And you thought that the young couple had come to the boat looking for their package and murdered her."

Claudia nodded briskly. "I've never been so frightened in my life! She was murdered, and once everything was...over... once everyone was gone, and Rebecca had been taken away, while everyone was at dinner I searched Marcella's room. The package was gone! And the sheriff's people hadn't said anything about finding it when they searched the room. Don't you see? That couple had taken it!"

"Yes, I do see," Ransom said flatly

Claudia looked over at Barnes. "Please...please, I'm so tired. Could I go now? I need to lie down."

"Yes, I think that's all for now," Barnes said after a beat. "We'll need a full description of the couple, but that can wait awhile."

"Thank you," she said. Without a word or glance at Ransom and Emily, Claudia got up shakily and left the dining room.

"You seem angry," Emily said to Ransom.

"I am—at the thought that that woman, knowing what she did, would let an innocent woman go to jail rather than risk herself or that strung-out grandson of hers."

"I daresay you're right," Emily said with a sigh. "But familial devotion can be very strong—and very misguided. Particularly if it is for one's only living relation."

"I also have very little patience for stupidity," Ransom said. "Especially when a seemingly intelligent woman can't see what her grandson's friends are really trying to do."

"She knew there were drugs in that package, all right," said Barnes, "even if she won't admit it."

"I don't mean that. These people were trying to get her on

the hook. They must've known where the grandson was getting the money to pay them off. They thought if they could just get her to do this one little thing, they could bleed her of all her money. They could hold over her head that she'd been involved in drug trafficking, or something of that sort. I doubt if she would've tried to fight them.''

Emily clucked her tongue.

Ransom continued. ''I would be even angrier if it weren't for one thing—I don't think that couple did the murder.''

''What?!'' Barnes exclaimed.

Emily's brows had risen to points. ''Really?''

''We already know one or both of them could've sneaked onto the boat unseen,'' said Barnes. ''Claudia Trenton did it.''

''Not entirely unseen,'' Emily reminded him.

''They could've gotten on the boat,'' Barnes said, ''and then when they were in her cabin, she could've come back unexpectedly and found them, and they killed her. Makes perfect sense to me.''

''It would to me as well if it weren't for one thing,'' said Ransom, the right corner of his mouth turned upward. ''Unless I miss my guess, that young couple is currently staying at my motel.''

''Well, that's great! Then we don't have to look for them!''

''Yes, but that's just the point.''

''Oh, I see…yes…,'' said Emily.

''You want to tell me?'' Barnes said.

''You see, it's easy to believe that they would stay here if they were waiting for Claudia Trenton to come up with the package. It's much harder to believe they'd stay after committing murder and getting what they wanted.''

After a moment, Barnes sat back in his chair dejectedly. ''I see what you mean.''

''Although…,'' Emily began, her gaze becoming somewhat distant, as if she were picturing something written in the air, ''although they might have stayed if they committed the murder, but hadn't been able to find the package, knowing that Claudia had ample incentive to find it for them.''

"Whatever's in that thing, it would have to be awfully valuable.''

"I'm sure it is," Ransom said darkly.

"So we just go over there and talk to them," Barnes said impatiently.

"No. In the first place, I don't *know* it's the same couple. Secondly, we don't have any evidence that they had anything to do with the murder. There were no strange fingerprints in the cabin, remember?''

Barnes huffed irritably. "We just sit on our hands?''

He hadn't noticed Emily's cunning smile. "There is one way we could get evidence, at least of one crime.''

"How's that?''

Her eyes twinkled. "Would you happen to have a shoe box we might use?''

TEN

IT HAD TAKEN Barnes nearly an hour to come up with a box of the right size, wrap it in brown paper, tie it with twine, and get back to the boat. He appeared on the deck carrying the box concealed in a black plastic bag, just in case the boat was being watched.

"How are we supposed to contact those people?" Barnes asked.

"They must have given Claudia a way to do that," said Emily. "Remember, we were supposed to sail the morning after she saw them. There was no guarantee we'd still be in Macaw when she was able to get the box, so she'd have needed some way to let them know she'd found it and where she was."

"If the boat was going to sail," Barnes said, "I don't know why they would be hanging around here."

Ransom supplied the answer. "If they've gone out of their room at all, they know the boat's still here. Everyone within a twenty-mile radius knows about the murder, and they'd know the boat was being held. I've never been anywhere that news travels as quickly as it does here."

"You don't get out of Chicago much, do you?" Barnes said with a sly smile.

"No, thank God," the detective murmured.

The trio found Claudia sitting on the bed in her cabin. As Emily had predicted, the couple had given her a number to call when she'd found the package, presumably for another cell phone.

"We want you to call them," Ransom explained, "and let them know that you've found the box."

"Oh...oh, I couldn't," said Claudia, her eyes wide with fear. "They're killers! I couldn't..."

Ransom crouched in front of her so he could look her in the eye. "I know it's difficult, but I believe you can do it, Miss Trenton. Tell them you'll bring the thing to Lookout Point. Tell them it has to be today, because the boat is definitely going to sail in the morning."

Tears coursed down the old woman's face. "I really, I can't."

Emily sat down on the bed beside her and laid a stabilizing hand on her leg. "Yes, you can," she said firmly. "You have always been a very strong woman—you've already faced much more than most any other woman I know could bear—and I know that you can gather the courage to see this through. I also know how much you must have loved your grandson, and this may very well lead the police to the people who so callously used him, and killed him."

She had chosen her words judiciously, and they had the desired effect. Claudia's back straightened as she listened to Emily, and the tears stopped. She gave a final sniff, then said, "All right."

The tragedy of her grandson's death, the stress she'd already been under, and the genuine fear she felt at dealing with the people who were involved in the murder, gave Claudia's telephone demeanor the exact note of distress it needed to convince the young man who answered the phone that she was in earnest. He told her to be at Lookout Point in an hour, then abruptly hung up.

"Well done, Claudia," said Emily once the call had been completed. Then she went into the hallway with Ransom and Barnes, closing the door after them.

"She made the call," said Barnes, "but I don't think she's going to be able to do the rest of it."

Ransom sighed. "Perhaps not."

TRAIL NUMBER SIX was much like the other paths at its start: wide enough to be comfortably walked, with occasional plaques describing the local flora and fauna. The old woman wended her way carefully along the path, clutching the parcel in both hands. The woods smelled musty and dank. The path was deserted except for the lone figure in the floppy sunhat, its string tied beneath her chin.

Half a mile into the woods the land to the left of the path began to fall away, forming a ridge along which the path continued, protected by an old fence of dark brown wood.

Lookout Point was a semicircular natural balcony on the edge of the ravine. From its bench, one could look down through the trees below and see the dried bare outline of the stream that had created the anomaly.

The old woman sat down, laid the package to one side, and waited with her hands neatly folded in her lap. The scene was silent except for bird calls and an occasional rustling in the woods behind her. Under normal circumstances, she would have found the peacefulness a welcome change, but at the moment she was far too concerned with the matter at hand. Her back was straight and stiff, her ears pricked up, listening for the stealthy approach of the man she was supposed to meet.

She needn't have bothered to strain her ears. After an interval of about a quarter of an hour, a loud voice cut through the tranquility with a booming, singsong air: "'Heigh-ho, heigh-ho, It's through the woods we go.'"

It was a male voice, not too far off and approaching at a steady pace. It sounded unnaturally—almost menacingly—carefree as it sang the same lines over and over again.

The old woman listened as not one but two sets of footsteps sounded on the wooden floor of the lookout.

"Hey, old lady," the man's voice demanded, "where's my stuff?"

The woman turned around and looked up from under the hat. There were the two of them: a young man with stiff brown hair and pale skin. His nose was slightly bent in the middle as if it had been broken and hadn't set properly. His cheeks were sunken, and his chin came to a narrow nub. His eyes were exactly as Claudia had described them: small and cruel. With him was the young woman with long, stringy blond hair. She was severely emaciated and had dull, vacant blue eyes. She wore a formfitting shiny pink knit top and a pair of skintight blue jeans.

"Hey! You ain't old lady Trenton!" said the young man.

"No, I'm not," Emily Charters replied, manufacturing an excessively timid manner. "I'm just acting as...her agent. Miss Trenton was not well enough to come, so she asked me to do it for her."

"Well, you better've brought my stuff. I don't care who you are, you ain't got it and you're gonna get hurt!"

"I wouldn't...I wouldn't...what is the phrase for it? The one they use in the movies? Oh, yes—double-cross! I wouldn't double-cross you," Emily fluttered. "Neither would poor, dear Claudia. She told me what the...consequences would be!" She widened her eyes. "She told me about her grandson!"

"Too damn bad about him!" the young man sneered contemptuously. "But my pals thought he'd 'double-crossed' us." He broke off and laughed, amused by the mocking way he'd said it. "We thought he'd stolen the stuff to sell it! But it taught his granny not to screw with us, didn't it?"

"Yeah," the young woman said limply.

"Well...I have the box right here," Emily said fussily. The box had been blocked from their view. Emily now turned to the side and picked it up, then handed it to the young man.

"It don't feel right!" He frowned, shaking it. "It don't feel heavy enough! Not for what was in it! That Trenton kid must've taken some out!"

"What was in it?" Emily asked breathily.

"Heroin!" he spat back. "Real pure, and real simple!"

"Heroin," the girl echoed lazily.

The young man leaned in toward Emily, towering over her. "You been delivering heroin—you and old lady Trenton. Tell her that. Tell her we got it on her now—she's been delivering heroin!''

A slight flutter in the foliage was the only noise that preceded the appearance of Barnes, Ransom, and a pair of deputies from the woods onto the platform.

Barnes's rich baritone called out calmly but firmly, "All right, you two, don't move.''

Presumably it was the couple's familiarity with similar situations that caused them to freeze the moment they heard him. The young man continued to glare down at Emily as one of the deputies searched him, turning up both a gun and very nasty-looking knife, while Barnes read them their rights. Suddenly the young man's face relaxed, and still staring at Emily he began to laugh—lightly at first, building to something unnervingly out of control. His girlfriend giggled helplessly at his side, her eyes shifted back and forth as if she were trying to figure out what was so funny.

RANSOM WAS ALLOWED to sit in on the interrogation of the pair, whose names proved to be Denny and Janet. Whatever amusement Denny had found in their situation in the woods had disappeared the minute he was at the sheriff's station. Barnes assured them that they were "going down"—a phrase that, to Ransom, sounded hopelessly anachronistic coming from his rural counterpart—as he put it, on drug charges and complicity in the murder of Johnny Trenton, but the surly youths were unimpressed, particularly when pressed about the matter of Marcella Hemsley.

When Barnes asked them what they had done after they left Claudia Trenton at Lookout Point, Denny replied churlishly, "We just went back to that fleabag dump and *partied*." He childishly emphasized the last word, as if he intended for it to encompass a multitude of sins that would shock his listeners.

"What I think you did," said Barnes, "was go to the boat, the *Genessee*, and tried to find that package yourself. And you got caught. And you panicked and killed a woman.''

"Yeah, prove that!" Denny replied with the curt confidence of someone who knows an accusation can't be proved.

It went on like that for some time, and Ransom finally left. Emily had waited in the outer office, and rose when Ransom came out.

"Is it over?" she asked.

"Not by a long shot. The drug charge is certain, and probably their part in Johnny Trenton's death. But they're not going to admit anything, and they insist they never went to the boat."

As they walked out to Ransom's car, Emily said, "It makes my blood run cold to see young people like that. So lost at such an early age. And no comprehension of the value of life. They must've called their confederates and told them to take care of Johnny."

"That much we can assume from what they said to you."

Ransom opened the passenger door and helped her in. Once she was buckled into her seat, he closed the door, went around to the other side, and climbed in behind the steering wheel. But before he started the car, his phone rang. He pulled it out, flipped it open, and said hello.

"Jer, it's me," Gerald White's voice crackled across the not-too-clear connection. "I got an answer on Stuart Holmes. He was a divorce lawyer. He was supposed to be a really good one—wealthy clients, that kind of thing."

"Ah," his partner said, grinning into the phone.

"You planning to get a divorce?" Gerald said, amusement in his tone. "'Cause I should tell you, you have to get married, first."

"Then I'll have to find another lawyer. Holmes is in his seventies. By the time I get married, he'll probably be dead."

Gerald laughed. "You making any progress up there?"

He told Gerald about the arrest of the young couple and the Chicago connection.

"So you have a couple of names to go on now," he concluded.

"Great. Does this mean you'll be back soon?"

Ransom paused. "I'll tell you tomorrow." He disconnected, snapped the phone shut, and stuck it back in his pocket.

"What was that about Stuart Holmes?" Emily asked.

"Holmes was a high-powered divorce lawyer. Rich clients." He stopped for a second, knitting his brow. Then he smiled. "Oh, yes! That's where I've seen Percy Faulk—his client—before. In the newspapers. I can't remember in what context, but he's got money."

"So Mr. Holmes really was seeing a client, just as he told you, completely unconnected to this case. There really was nothing shady about it."

"I wouldn't say that. The surreptitious way they were going about it leads me to believe that Faulk must not have wanted anyone to know he was consulting Holmes. If he was simply getting a divorce, it would be natural for him to see the proper attorney. So I would suspect that there's something more to it…perhaps not quite legal….Perhaps he's interested in hiding assets? Anyone with Holmes's experience would know how to do that."

"But it didn't have anything to do with Marcella's murder. It was exactly as Mr. Holmes said. Oh, dear!" Emily's brow furrowed so deeply that she almost looked cross. "I really have been very, very stupid!"

"What is it?"

She didn't appear to have heard him. "Weaving mysteries out of things that have perfectly logical explanations."

"Emily, what is it?"

She turned to face him, leveling her crystal blue eyes at his. "Jeremy, suppose *everything* is exactly as it seemed?"

"I don't follow."

She took a deep breath. "Well, Holmes was telling the truth; the reason for the Millers' anxiety over their pictures had a perfectly natural reason…."

"I think you mean *au naturel* reasons," Ransom said wryly.

She ignored this. "We now also know that what I overheard that first day on the deck was Claudia talking on her cell phone, so Mr. Driscoll's arrival on the scene was just coincidence. So I think we can also assume that there was nothing really suspicious about Mr. Driscoll and Claudia having dinner together at the pub in Sangamore. It was just as he explained. Propinquity.'' She stopped abruptly. Her eyes widened and her mouth dropped open slightly. ''Propinquity. Oh, dear, dear, dear! It's exactly as I thought from the beginning!''

''Emily, what is it?'' Ransom asked with concern.

''There is one other thing I think we can assume was exactly as it appeared to be. If we do that, it's the answer to everything.'' She told him what it was.

He pondered this for a long moment. ''But *can* we assume that?''

''I think we have good reason to,'' she said with finality. ''Now, Jeremy, you must go back in there and talk to the sheriff. He has to tell Captain Farraday that we can sail tomorrow morning.''

ELEVEN

THE PALL THAT HAD been deepening over the *Genessee* and its passengers had lifted somewhat at the news that they would be allowed to leave the following morning, despite the fact that the delay meant they would have to sail directly back to Chicago rather than continuing the trip. Not that any of them wanted to. The atmosphere at dinner that evening was one of reserved jubilation.

Their number had further diminished: Claudia Trenton would be having to stay on for a day or so in Macaw, and had removed to the Lakeview Motel, made safe now that her tormentors had been taken into custody. Her absence allowed the mood aboard the boat to lift a bit more.

After dinner, the passengers spent the evening on the white deck chatting and watching the sky grow dark. Now that they were going to be loosed from the town to which they'd been unwillingly moored for the past few days, some of the charm returned to it, and they spoke of leaving in surprisingly wistful terms.

At a little after ten the passengers began to retire to their cabins one by one, disappearing from the white deck like stars quietly going out.

Midnight found Emily sitting up very straight in her room in the chair beside the chest. She had changed into a robe of pearl gray silk, which she wore over a powder blue nightgown. The compass lamp was turned on, and she was reading, though she found it difficult to concentrate: every snap and thump of the boat snatched at her attention.

The white deck was deserted and shrouded in darkness, the lone worklight having been switched off. The wheelhouse was empty, lit only by the dim light reflected from a quarter moon.

It was nearly 12:45 when a thin ray of light appeared around the corner of the general store: its source was a penlight, thin and weak enough that it didn't provide much illumination, just enough to be sure of one's footing.

The light proceeded down the dock and snapped off as it reached the foot of the gangplank. Catlike footsteps quietly padded up the plank, across the deck, and down the two flights of stairs. The figure then turned left, went into the short hallway, and with great care to ensure silence, very slowly turned the handle to the cabin door.

Once the door was opened, the sound of a hand groping for the wall switch could be heard, followed by a sudden flood of light.

Detective Jeremy Ransom was seated on the chair, which he had drawn up in front of the table so that he wouldn't be trapped in the corner.

"Good evening, Mr. Douglas," he said airily.

The steward stood in the doorway, a soiled parcel tucked under his left arm. His eyes bulged with surprise and fear, and he made a sudden move as if to bolt, but found his way blocked by Sheriff Barnes and Deputy Mitchell, who had silently stolen up behind him.

"Damn that woman anyway," Douglas said bitterly.

Ransom wondered which one he meant.

"How DID YOU finally figure it out?" asked Lynn as she folded Emily's dress. She'd already packed the linens and was now in the process of adding the items from the closet. Emily was seated on the corner of the bed while Ransom leaned against the door.

"It was simple, really, once one put aside the little sidelights that had nothing directly to do with the murder," Emily replied.

"I'd hardly call Claudia Trenton's dilemma a 'little side-light,'" said Ransom.

"True, but the only thing it actually had to do with Marcella's murder was that it was responsible for bringing the parcel into the matter. It was as I'd said at the outset. Marcella was killed because she happened to walk in on someone." She paused and sighed, not very pleased with herself. "I suppose I can console myself with the fact that there really was something terribly wrong on this tour, but I was utterly mistaken as to what it was. It wasn't until Jeremy had discovered that the secretive meetings between Stuart Holmes and the stranger didn't have a sinister connotation, and that what I overheard on deck had a logical explanation, that I realized my error." She paused again and clucked her tongue. "I daresay I'm becoming a fanciful old woman, seeing plots all around me."

"Nonsense," said Ransom. "You sensed something was wrong here, and there was. And it was something very dangerous. That fact is what made you suspicious of the other things. All you said was that if Rebecca hadn't killed her aunt, then these little things might have significance. In a normal murder investigation, those are exactly the kinds of things we would've had to follow up."

She bestowed a benignant smile on him.

"But how did you figure it out?" Lynn asked again.

"Well, realizing those two things, I thought perhaps we should take *everything* at face value."

"And that meant Lily DuPree's statement as well," said Ransom.

"Exactly. You see, Lily had said she'd seen Joaquin leave the boat before David Douglas. Well, everyone else said that David left first, so we chalked the discrepancy up to the fact that Lily had been dozing, and so wasn't clear about what she'd seen. It wasn't until I pressed her about which one had left first that she became vague about it—much in the way some people do when you challenge something they really believe to be true.

If we took Lily's original statement at face value, it meant that Douglas had left last, and that he'd lied about the fact.''

"But what about the people who verified it?" asked Lynn.

Emily shrugged slightly. "Well, you see, Mrs. O'Malley had been told by David himself that he was leaving, and Joaquin thought he had left because he looked for him and didn't find him onboard. But Douglas had secreted himself somewhere."

"In the captain's cabin," Ransom chimed in.

"How do you know that?" asked Lynn.

"Because like most clever people with healthy egos, once Douglas knew he was caught, he got very chatty. He wanted us to know how clever he'd been. He hid in the captain's cabin because he knew Joaquin wouldn't look there."

Emily nodded. "Of course. So Joaquin looked for him, then left, and Douglas had a free hand."

"To do what? Search the cabin?"

"No, he didn't need to do that. He'd already found the package while cleaning the cabin…and he took it."

"But…but wait. That doesn't make sense. If he took it while he and Joaquin were cleaning the rooms, then how could Marcella have caught him at it? She didn't get back to the boat until they…well, at least Joaquin…had left."

"Ah, but you see, she didn't catch him at that."

Lynn wrinkled her nose attractively and sat down beside her. "Now you've completely lost me. He had to have killed her in that ten or fifteen minutes between when Rebecca came back to us from the boat after looking for her aunt, and when we found the body."

Emily shook her head. "When Rebecca looked through the boat, her aunt was already dead."

"That's impossible! Are you saying…are you saying that Rebecca lied about her aunt's body not being there?"

"Not at all, my dear," Emily replied, giving the young woman's leg a gentle pat. "Her aunt's body wasn't there because that is not where she was killed."

"What!"

"Douglas told us what happened," said Ransom, "or most of what happened, once we got him to the station. When he found the package, he thought it might be valuable—partly because of that middle-of-the-night scene Marcella Hemsley had caused. So he took it to his cabin, looked inside, and recognized the contents. Then he hid it there, planning to wait until the coast was clear, take it off the boat, and hide it somewhere safer."

"Why would he do that?" Lynn asked.

"Because he's a very crafty young man," Emily explained. "He fully expected that a fuss would be made when Marcella discovered the loss, and that the boat would be searched. When nothing was turned up it would naturally be assumed that it was just poor, dotty old Marcella, at it again."

"But Rebecca—"

Emily was already nodding. "I know. Rebecca had seen the package. But what would everyone think? Just what Sheriff Barnes did, that Marcella had simply done something with it herself, and that the package was lost. After that, Mr. Douglas could safely retrieve it and keep it somewhere. Perhaps even in his own cabin."

"He carried it off the boat lengthwise, at his right side—it was, after all, smaller than a shoebox," said Ransom. "So that if Lily DuPree happened to be awake she wouldn't notice it."

"That was really a risk!" Lynn exclaimed.

"Not really," Emily said. "Remember that Lily was facing the opposite direction. Even if she was awake, it wasn't that likely that she would completely turn around. When I first talked to her about the murder, Jeremy asked where everyone was—do you remember the difficulty she had in trying to look over her shoulder at the deck?" Ransom nodded. "Mr. Douglas was just taking the precaution that if she did try to look around, she wouldn't see the box. And it worked. She did happen to look as he went past, and she didn't see it. She just noticed what rigid posture he had." Emily smiled at herself. "Something else that I missed at the time. When she told me she'd seen Douglas leave the boat she remarked on his posture. I thought it was just one of her little incongruities, but as it turned out, it was significant.''

Ransom continued the story. ''He then went south on the beach, holding the box in front of him, and hid it in the woods just off the path leading from the lake to the road. Then he continued down the road so that if anyone saw him it would look as if he was returning from the south, distancing himself from the murder. And it was just his luck that he came upon Brock and Langstrom, who thought just that.''

''I still don't understand,'' said Lynn. ''If all that's true, then how was Marcella killed? And what did she walk in on?''

''Absolutely nothing!'' said Emily.

Lynn curled her lips. ''Emily, I'm beginning to think you're pulling my leg.''

''Not at all,'' Emily replied. ''She found absolutely nothing. And that was the problem.'' She shifted in her seat as she began her explanation. ''Of course, we can only conjecture about the first part of it, but we do know the outcome. You see, Marcella got back to the boat after Joaquin had left and before Douglas could get off. She went to her cabin, and in a fit of…'' Emily paused, searching for the right word. ''I don't know what you'd call it—a whim, or whatever—decided to look in the package…or at it…we shall never know. But when she looked under the bed where she'd put it, it wasn't there. So what did she think? She remembers that someone came into her room the night before—someone she believed to be David Douglas.''

''That was Claudia Trenton,'' said Lynn.

''Yes, but you and I saw Marcella when it happened. She was *convinced* it was Douglas. Who can say why? Because she had a fleeting glimpse of light-colored hair, and a flash of blue. Douglas was wearing blue pajamas, and Claudia a blue robe. As I've said, I've known people with Alzheimer's disease. Once they get something into their heads, it's impossible to get it out, even if you have the chance.''

Ransom said, "What we do know is that Douglas claims she came barging into his cabin and found him there with the package. He says she was like a madwoman, but whether or not that's exactly true, he was startled and afraid because he'd been caught red-handed. And he knew that Mrs. O'Malley and Miss DuPree were still on the boat, and while they couldn't hear much normal noise a deck or two away and on the other end of the boat, they were bound to hear Miss Hemsley if she started screaming again. So he grabbed up his lamp and struck her with it. He said he wasn't sure whether or not he'd killed her then, but at that point he was desperate, and knew that if she came to, she would accuse him…and though her mind might've been foggy, she would have the gash in her head to prove that something had happened. So he strangled her with her belt."

"And Rebecca?" Lynn asked.

Emily was the one to answer. "Ah, Rebecca! While David was trying to decide what to do with the body, what does he hear but Rebecca calling for her aunt!"

"He watched through the part in the curtains as she went into her aunt's cabin and her own," said Ransom, "then he waited until she'd gone away, dragged Marcella's body to her own cabin, and arranged the lamp by the body, smearing some blood on it to make it look as if it had been the weapon, knowing that this would confuse the matter. He surmised—as it turned out, rightly—that with things the way he'd arranged them in Marcella's room, and given the fact that Rebecca had been to the boat around the time of the murder, that there would be no reason for the authorities to look elsewhere on the boat. So he had all the time in the world to polish his own lamp and make sure there were no traces of the murder in his cabin."

"Carrying the package off the boat like that was a very bold thing to do," said Emily, "but it was the best he could do on the spur of the moment, and he hadn't much time."

"I don't get it," said Lynn with a frustrated sigh. "Didn't Lily DuPree tell you that Douglas left the boat *before* Rebecca came back to it?"

"Yes, but it was after Joaquin left that she really started to doze. That was the time about which she was most confused—when I questioned her about it, she said it was difficult to tell with so many people coming and going, so many footsteps. Well, there were really only two she should've heard: Marcella returning, and then Rebecca, and Rebecca leaving again. But it was during that hazy period that she saw Douglas. The one thing she was sure about, until I foolishly pushed her, was that Joaquin left first."

"What exactly was in that package, anyway?" Lynn asked Ransom.

"Two bricks of heroin. They have a very, very high street value."

"Good God! And those two idiots trusted it to Claudia Trenton? I'm surprised they would let it out of their sight!"

He nodded. "Valuable, yes. But they couldn't fill the box with something else and take a chance that she'd get curious and open it and find out it wasn't drugs after all—they wanted her good and securely hooked, so they could bleed her of her money. And they probably wanted the drugs here anyway. My guess is they planned to continue on to the Upper Peninsula and sell it there."

Lynn slowly shook her head in amazement. "And to think that Marcella Hemsley was killed and Becky almost went to prison for good because of that little box!"

"Rebecca might have gone to prison," Emily said, "were it not for Jeremy."

"Huh!" Ransom said shortly. "Now I think you're trying to pull my leg. You know I've been completely at sea up here on this case, with nothing to go on and no authority whatsoever. You, at least, had your brain working."

"Overtime, so it would seem," Emily said ruefully.

SHERIFF BARNES WAS waiting on the white deck as Emily, Lynn, and Ransom came up the stairs, the latter carrying the ladies' suitcases. He put them down when Barnes extended his hand.

"I want to thank you. I don't know what would've happened without you."

"Don't you?" Lynn said under her breath.

If he heard this, he chose to ignore it. "But like I said, we don't get cases like this up here."

Ransom flexed his hand after it was released from the firm grip of the sheriff. "You're welcome, but Emily's the one you should really thank."

"You're damn right about that!" He looked down at her, a broad smile pushing up the ends of his mustache. "Miss Charters, I said it before and I'll say it again. You're one sharp old lady. And I hope you don't take any offense to that."

"Not at all," Emily said modestly. "Thank you very much."

"I'll take these to the car," Lynn interrupted impatiently. She picked up the suitcases and left them.

Emily exchanged knowledgeable smiles with Ransom: Rebecca had chosen to wait for them at the sheriff's station. Despite having been exonerated, now that she herself was out of danger, the loss of her beloved aunt had hit her full force. She'd chosen to ride home with Lynn and her friends, and Lynn was anxious for their journey to begin. In more ways than one, Emily suspected.

"Well, I'm off now—got to go check the campgrounds," said Barnes. "Thanks again, Detective, Miss Charters. I hope to see you again sometime."

"Under different circumstances," said Emily.

He laughed. "You said it!" He started to walk away, but stopped and said quietly to Ransom, "By the way, I gave the Millers back their negatives. I told them after we'd printed the first few, we'd found what we wanted, so didn't do the rest. Thought I'd save them some embarrassment."

"Were they relieved?" asked the detective.

Barnes smiled. "Damned if they didn't look disappointed!" He left them.

Ransom and Emily headed for the gangplank, but before they reached it Joaquin Vasquez came up to them, a bright smile on his face. "I want to say goodbye. It has been very, very nice meeting you, and traveling with you. I hope you come back again."

"I shall remember you," Emily said kindly.

He beamed at her, gave an awkward salute, and went his way. Captain Farraday and his wife were waiting for them at the plank. They thanked Ransom and Emily for their help.

"Who would've thought it!" Samantha Farraday exclaimed. An attractive smile lit her features, as if despite the circumstances she was rather charmed by the surprise.

"I suppose we should have checked his references," the captain said.

"I don't know what good it would've done," Ransom replied. "There's very little in one's work history to indicate homicidal tendencies. Usually."

Farraday's lips pursed for barely a second, all the time he gave to consider this. "Still, we'll make sure to do it in the future. Matter of form."

Samantha Farraday laughed, then reached up and tousled his hair. "Come on, Neil, we've got to get ready to sail!"

He shot her a disapproving glance, belied by the amusement in his eyes. They said their goodbyes, and then went to the wheelhouse arm in arm.

"Shall we go?" Ransom asked.

"Just a moment," said his companion, who had noticed the approach of Lily DuPree.

The slightly hunched, frail little woman wore her usual befuddled smile. "I wanted to say goodbye, Emily. It's been most exciting, hasn't it? To think that that young man was a murderer! I always knew there was something not quite right about him."

"Did you?" Emily said.

"Oh, yes! He was so nice and so pleasant. He was simply too good to be true, wasn't he?"

"As a matter of fact, he was," she replied thoughtfully.

"I think you're very, very clever to have figured it out."

"Oh, no, Lily. You were the one who held the key."

Lily's eyes widened with delight. "Really?"

"Of course! It was your astute observations that gave us the solution."

"Really!" Lily beamed. Then she extended a hand to Emily. "I'll miss you on the way home."

"That's very nice of you to say, thank you. I will most likely see you in church."

The little woman shook her hand, said a warm goodbye to Ransom, then hobbled away.

"Astute observations?" Ransom said, his right eyebrow arched.

Emily smiled. "After all, Jeremy, she did hold the key."

"She'll be dining out on this story for the rest of her life," he replied with a curled lip.

They took one last look across the deck. The paltry remainder of the ship's complement was scattered across it. Martin and Laura Miller were seated on the port side, chatting excitedly. A few chairs down from them, Stuart Holmes sat poring over a newspaper. Bertram Driscoll was alone on the starboard side, sleeping in his chair. Along the aft railing, looking out over the water, were Jackson Brock and Muriel Langstrom, their hands clasped together, suspended dreamily between the chairs.

Emily smiled. "It looks as if Lynn isn't the only one who found a new friend." She slipped her hand through Ransom's arm, and they started down the gangplank.

"By the way, Emily, I really must say you've surprised me."

"Why is that?"

"You got all the way through this case without once citing

the bard. I'm amazed that you couldn't find a Shakespearean correlation in this situation.''

"Oh, there was one for the situation, but it didn't have any bearing on the murder,'' she replied, a twinkle in her eye.

"And what was the correlation?''

"*A Midsummer Night's Dream,* of course!''

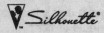

HARLEQUIN®
INTRIGUE®
WE'LL LEAVE YOU BREATHLESS!

If you've been looking for thrilling tales of
contemporary passion and sensuous love stories
with taut, edge-of-the-seat suspense—then
you'll love Harlequin Intrigue!

Every month, you'll meet six new heroes
who are guaranteed to make your spine tingle
and your pulse pound. With them you'll enter
into the exciting world of Harlequin Intrigue—
where your life is on the line
and so is your heart!

THAT'S INTRIGUE—
ROMANTIC SUSPENSE
AT ITS BEST!

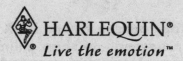

HARLEQUIN®
® *Live the emotion*™